9/16/70

Image of America

In testimony of my gratitude,
I dedicate this book to C.D. Jackson,
Andrew Heiskell, Peter F. Drucker, Denver Lindley,
and to the American Dominicans,
who have aided me in every way to such an extent that
this work is as much theirs as mine.

By the same author

The Seven Miracles of Gubbio
The Stork and the Jewels
One Sky to Share
Mary Magdalene

Image
of America

R. L. BRUCKBERGER

translated from the French by

C. G. Paulding and Virgilia Peterson

NEW YORK

The Viking Press · 1959

Contents

Foreword to the American Edition

By Peter F. Drucker

The author of this book, Father Bruckberger, Dominican, priest, artist, theologian, and intellectual, does not attempt to portray America. He attempts to understand it. His theme is not "America as a civilization" but "America as a reality." Father Bruckberger writes primarily for the European, and especially the French reader. And though he has lived among us for quite a few years he sees, thinks, feels, and writes as a Frenchman. But this should make his book all the more important to the American reader.

Father Bruckberger does not talk of any of the things we know and put first in our own attempt to understand our own country: its size and sweep and beauty; the yearning and the labor, the faith and the promises that built this nation; the ghosts that haunt our history from meeting house and cotton plantation, from Mormon Trail and from the wilderness; the Federalist Papers and the frontier; the completely secular state and the religious society it presupposes and nurtures; the moments of greatness and the decades of complacency. He talks neither about our purposeful optimism nor about the brooding sense of the tragic that informs every enduring American work of fiction. Even less does he talk about American education or American technology.

Father Bruckberger knows all these things. Not only has he lived among us, he has traveled the length and breadth of the country. And solid years of research preceded the writing of this work. What distinguishes this book from a book an American might have written is not its knowledge but its purpose. Precisely because it was written by a Frenchman, the knowledge that is meaningful to us is pushed aside in the book. Father Bruckberger knows—as far too few Americans know—that Europeans do not lack information about America; in fact works about America, by American and European authors alike, flood Europe. What most Europeans lack is understanding; and the more books they read that portray America, the less, apparently, do most understand. Hence Father Bruckberger's question: What must I, what must a European know to understand America?

The answer, the essence of America, Father Bruckberger says, is the primacy of the person, the live, real, three-dimensional man. This theme is developed like a fugue in three parts reflecting respectively on our political principles and institutions, on our economic beliefs, and on our economic and social achievements. And contrapuntally this is contrasted with the heresy of Europe: the subordination of Man to abstraction—to rhetorical phrase parading as intellectual system, and to the suicidal pride of man-made absolutes. And because the person is real, it is America that is "scientific"; what the European intellectual calls "scientific" is pure demonology and superstition—no more "science" than was the superstition of Molière's doctors.

Obvious, an American might say (especially if he misreads "primacy of the person" to mean either "individualism" or "pragmatism"). But it is important, however obvious. For what follows therefrom is by no means obvious and cannot be taken for granted—in respect to what we are, should be, and should do; in respect to what we stand for and portray; in respect to what we see in ourselves and what we talk about to ourselves and others. This is a book of a warm friend and sincere (once in a while even uncritical) admirer of America. But no American can read it, I believe, without asking himself disturbing questions: Are we true to our best self today? Are we ourselves seeing the essential thing and do we even try to help others see it when they look at us?

But this book can tell the American reader perhaps even more about Europe. In raising the question, "What does Europe need to learn from America?" Father Bruckberger has had to think as much about Europe as he did about the United States. The unique quality of this book, at least to me, is its superb and masterly grasp of basic European habits of mind and action, and the success with which these are conveyed. This is something very few of us in America understand—despite the flood of books about Europe, despite the thousands of Americans who visit Europe every year, look at its museums and churches, and read its authors. And this is something we in America need to understand. It was not Father Bruckberger's intention to write a book that will make Americans understand Europe; but I know of no book that does the job as well and as effectively as *Image of America*.

I am afraid I make this book sound like an erudite Germanic "handbook," or, worse still, like a "Whither are we bound?" book on "problems." But Father Bruckberger is above all a writer. This is a very serious book but also a very witty, in places even a very funny one. It is the work of a scholar but written in a prose without jargon, a prose of simplicity, controlled strength and power, an eminently readable prose. It is the work of a trained and disciplined mind; but it is above all a labor of love. Few American readers will wholeheartedly agree with everything in the book—its interpretation of our early history for instance, or of our industrial society. But the American reader will not only learn a great deal from this book. He should, above all, enjoy it.

Author's Note

This book, in its original French version, was published in October 1958 by Gallimard in Paris under the title *La République américaine*.

In addition to the altered title, the American edition contains one important change: the last two chapters of the French version have been replaced by a final chapter entitled "A Letter to Americans," written especially for this edition.

The reason for this change is a simple one. The last eighty pages of the French version deal with the present situation in the United States in the economic, social, and political spheres. In those pages I had a good deal to say about matters largely unknown to the French public but quite familiar to Americans. A writer's first duty is to protect his reader against boredom.

Aside from this and a few omissions in over-lengthy discussions, the American edition conforms strictly to the French original.

It is impossible to write a book such as this without precious assistance from numerous persons. I should like to mention here the intelligent and inexhaustible aid I have received from Mr. Herbert H. Hewitt, librarian of the Public Library in Chicago, Mr. Charles Moore, vice president of the Ford Motor Company, Mr. Arthur Page, director of the American Telephone and Telegraph Company. I take particular pleasure in thanking the various secretaries I have encountered in my task who never counted the time and trouble they devoted to the service of my book. Finally, I retain the most agreeable memory of the hospitality I received during two years in the offices of Time, Incorporated, in Chicago and the extreme courtesy of Edward King, vice president of the company, and of the whole staff.

—R.L.B.

PART I

The Political Revolution

1

Montaigne
and the Cannibals

Montaigne, who wrote something about everything, had his say, too, about the Americas and Americans. The title of his essay, "Of Cannibals," is highly uncomplimentary. Yet the essay itself contains much that is favorable. It is interesting to observe how the very discovery of the new world plunged the old world into an argument about civilization; how this argument has gone on ever since, and how relatively little its terms have changed; how it always revolves around the same questions; and how, from the start, it has abounded in misconceptions. The fact that the Americans Montaigne wrote about were Indians, living in what was later to become Brazil, makes no difference. As I embark on my book about the United States of North America, those "Americans," and Montaigne, help me clarify my intent.

"I had with me for a long time," wrote Montaigne, "a man that had lived ten or twelve years in that other world which has been discovered in our century. . . . This discovery of so vast a country seems worthy of consideration. . . . This man that I had was a plain ignorant fellow, which is a condition fit to bear true witness; for your sharp sort of men are much more curious in their observations and notice a great deal more, but they gloss them, and to give greater weight to their interpretation and make it convincing, they cannot forbear to alter the story a little. . . . We should have a man either of irreproachable veracity, or so simple that he has not wherewithal to contrive and to give a color of truth to false tales, and who has not espoused any cause. Mine was such a one. . . ." Such a one I propose to be in this book.

When Georges Bernanos spoke to delegates from all over intellectual Europe, at Geneva, in September 1946, he said, or rather he cried out in a voice distorted by anguish, "The truth is that European civilization is crumbling and we are putting nothing in its place." This the delegates received in silence; it was news to none. Bernanos was only echoing what the most penetrating observers have known and proclaimed for more than thirty years. But they stop short with the diagnosis. They publicly declare that Europe must succumb to the dissolution of old age, and, according to their temperaments, they accept it with either gloomy resignation or bitter sarcasm.

But what if they should be wrong? What if, after all, it were still possible to begin anew—to salvage, if not everything, at least the essential? What if it were not too late, even now, to give new life to European society and European man?

If Europe could still be saved, should we not do our utmost to save it?

By the time Byzantium, the ancient stronghold of Christianity and Western civilization, was crumbling—more from internal disruption than from the onslaught of the Turks— men were founding a society along the shores of the Atlantic in France and in England upon the same ancient heritage, and in founding it they were founding Europe. Had the Byzantines only recognized this, Byzantium would have been saved. But Byzantium chose to despise the boorishness of the Franks, and to hate Rome, rather than to survive.

For more than three centuries now, while Europe has been slowly disintegrating, a society has been in the making in

America, based on the same religious, political, and cultural principles that built Europe. And now, once again, these principles are being put to the test. It goes without saying that America is not Europe, yet the face it shows the world has a European cast. From afar this portrait may seem as garish as a picture postcard, as oversimplified as Charlemagne's Empire doubtless looked to the ambassadors from Byzantium when they came to Aix-la-Chapelle in 812 to confer upon him the title of Basileus. Nevertheless, the portrait is authentically European; no essential feature of European civilization has been left out. If, God forbid, Europe were now to vanish as Byzantium vanished, its tradition, fundamentally unchanged, would live on in America. Noah's Ark was built to save, not all the living, but life itself.

Far be it from me to invoke another deluge. Nor do I suggest that Europe should try to ape America. But I feel compelled to say, and say clearly, that the vital springs from which Europe once drew to create its civilization are not dried up; that those same springs can nourish Europe afresh, since they have given life to a new society beyond the Atlantic—a society, to be sure, with a style all its own, but in the prime of health and vigor. To take notice of its existence, even to give it some thought, might not be amiss. "The discovery of so vast a country," as Montaigne observed, "seems worthy of consideration." More today, perhaps, than at the time he was writing.

"Now to return to my subject," Montaigne wrote, in another pertinent reflection, "I find that there is nothing barbarous and savage in this nation according to what I have been told, except that everyone gives the title of barbarism to everything that is not according to his usage; as, indeed, we have no other criterion of truth than the example and pattern of the opinions and customs wherein we live. There, is always the perfect religion; there, the perfect government; there, the perfect and accomplished usage in all things."

Though America has never broken with its European heritage, it is still not Europe, and its difference proves again the
extraordinary fertility of that heritage. France is not England;
nor, long ago, were England and France Byzantium. I admit
that it requires a great effort to understand the difference. It
is far easier, as Montaigne said, to call every difference a barbarism and let it go at that.

I am not an American citizen; I shall never become one.
Nor am I, to use another of Montaigne's expressions, "wedded" to America. There is no such thing as unqualified admiration for any country. One can fervently admire the painters of the Paris school, and yet have well-founded objections
to the teaching at the Sorbonne or to the obsolete system of
food distribution in the Paris market.

But I am not wedded, either, to the slanderous clichés
about America circulating throughout the world today. It is
now the fashion in Europe to think and say the worst about
America. So far as fashion is concerned, I stand as much in
awe of it—in its proper place—as did Baudelaire, who looked
upon it as a "sign of the primitive nobility of the human
soul." But we should be able, after all, to distinguish between
one set of values and another, and I see no reason why social
and political philosophy need borrow their methods from
dress designers. Fashion belongs to the realm of art; philosophy is concerned with truth. Toward the end of his life Einstein sadly observed, with the childlike astonishment common
to all great scientists in the face of human stupidity, "I can
never quite understand why fashion, particularly in periods
of change and uncertainty, plays almost as significant a role
in science as in women's clothing. In everything, man is indeed an all too suggestible animal."

At the end of his chapter on the "cannibals," Montaigne
warned against the folly of judging a society by the way it
dresses. He foresaw that this was exactly how people would
judge his own observations on America. As if discouraged in

advance, he summed up their attitude: "This is all very well, but—they don't wear breeches."

"I confess that I saw, in America, more than America," wrote Tocqueville in the introduction to his great book, more than a hundred years ago. Today, in this mid-twentieth century, when all our certainties must be weighed again, how can anyone living in America, and scrutinizing it deeply, fail to see more in America than America? In its history, in its traditions, in its many races, America is obviously more than America.

"I have not studied America merely to satisfy however justifiable a curiosity," Tocqueville went on to say. "I wanted to learn from it lessons from which we might profit."

This is precisely my own aim and intent. Either America is the hope of the world or it is nothing. There are those who have begun to despair of the West. It is for them that I am writing.

Like the fascist systems, Communism is not the cause but a symptom of Europe's disintegration. It is just one more way of turning one's back on the problems that confront the European conscience. But to some of the problems that most torment Europe's conscience, America, I am convinced, has found answers, and found them with no disavowal of the European heritage. America brings to this Western heritage something concrete of its own, its own seminal otherness, as in former times England, France, and Spain brought something of their own, their own otherness. But the otherness of America, like that of France, England, or Spain in the past, stems from the fact that it is alive. If one fails at first to understand how its contribution can be blended with the common heritage, this is simply for lack of having tried.

2

Tabula Rasa

and Utopia

It is extremely difficult to realize at this distance how the discovery of the American continent fired the imagination of the Old World and kindled men's hopes to the point of frenzy. But this is what great discoveries of any kind have always done. The invention of the printing press, at about the same time, excited a wave of enthusiasm which surely must have served the Reformation. If the Protestants gave such great importance to the Bible as the sole vessel of God's Word—excluding the Catholic concept of tradition and authority—one reason for that emphasis was the fact that printing, for the first time, made the Bible available to everyone. In the nineteenth century, developments in biological research gave rise in certain quarters to the hope, only now beginning to cool down, that man would one day discover how to create life and conquer death. In the early part of this century, Freud's discovery set in motion another wave of enthusiasm. And now, today, the release of the atom, first manifested in the terror of ruined cities, has launched still another hope—the hope of man's limitless mastery over matter. Thus humanity, as in classic tragedy, caroms onward, from hope to terror, from terror to hope.

Before Christopher Columbus, other explorers, most probably Vikings, may well have reached the shores of the American continent. Either the news of their discovery never reached Europe or, if it did, it made no impact upon the Europeans of that day. Columbus was important not just because of his actual discovery but because of the hope to which this discovery was an answer and a miraculous substantiation. Columbus came at a time when Europe, stirred by a confused and restless longing that it could not name, awaited, longed for, and needed the discovery of America.

With the fall of Constantinople, vast territories were closed to the spread of the Faith, and Christendom was barred from the routes which linked its trade and culture with the East. It had become imperative to find a western route. So when the explorers first sighted land, they thought they had reached, not a new continent, but the East Indies they were seeking.

For centuries the Crusades had sustained Europe's spirit of adventure. Now they were abandoned. Perforce, the adventurous turned elsewhere.

In most of Europe the mounting surge toward political freedom that marked the peak of the Middle Ages had been thrown back. Everywhere the emergence of absolutist monarchies and of nationalism, together with the spread of both national and religious wars, were creating minorities that had to choose between their faith, their political aspirations, and exile. It had become hard to breathe in Europe. The peasant and the artisan found it impossible to live, let alone to live in dignity. The feudal aristocracy, forgetful of its responsibilities and obligations, had forfeited much of its usefulness, yet continued to cling to its privileges. Social inferiority had gradually come to mean enslavement to wealth and power.

For the missionary, as for the adventurer; for political refugees and religious outcasts; for the poor without hope of daily bread; for the serf whose bondage to his liege lord's fields would not end with his son or his son's son; for all plain folk, sickened of wars and theological hair-splitting; for the criminal in fear of the law and for the lawless who had contempt for it—the discovery of America burst like a shell breaching prison walls. At last the imprisoned could escape; at last a corner of the world had been found where they could breathe easily and live as they pleased.

Before long, of course, the New World's gold whetted the appetites of kings and merchants. The existence of countless human beings to whom Christianity was unknown roused the ardor of the missionary. Strange and explosive was the fusion of the theological virtues of faith, hope, and charity with the ferocity of human greed; of the humblest hopes for bed and board with the most grandiose dreams; of the love of glory with the taste for seclusion; of the vision of gold-freighted rivers with the irresistible call of virgin lands "where one may enjoy the freedom of being an honest man." Of this fusion America was made.

Many factors—geographical, economic, racial, religious, political, and linguistic—determine the character of nations. Needless to say, all these factors played their part in the founding of the first English-speaking colonies on the Atlantic coast between what are now Florida and Canada. But what emerges most strikingly from a study of the origins and development of America is the dominant importance of geography. From the very first, the settlers assigned an almost mystical value and meaning to this geographical factor. They made it the symbol of the freedom they had won, the ineradicable mark of what they were.

To start with there was distance, the distance of a whole ocean to cross in fragile vessels. An appalling number of ships foundered with all hands on the way. Now distance has lost its meaning, and when one thinks today of a one-way journey, it is only in terms of people who vanish behind the absurd, arbitrary curtains that certain nations have drawn down. But in the sixteenth and seventeenth centuries those who crossed the ocean seldom returned. Between them and the land they left behind lay the multitudinous, empty, terrifying seas.

The first regular passenger service between England and its colonies was not established until 1755, only twenty-one years before the Declaration of Independence. In 1775 Edmund Burke, speaking on reconciliation with the colonies, could still tell the English, "Three thousand miles lie between you and them. No contrivance can prevent the effect of this distance in weakening government. Seas roll and the months pass between the order and the execution, and the want of a speedy explanation of a single point is enough to defeat a whole system." But the settlers, far from lamenting this distance, always congratulated themselves that it was there. They lived as though on another planet, and this was their dearest wish.

What did these settlers find in America that so captivated them? Their delight lay in finding nothing. They had to start afresh, on a continent they could not measure, among primitive, nomadic tribes against whom they would soon have to fight. The land they came to was stern, rockbound, thick with forests that added to its strangeness; the climate was extreme in heat and cold. They had to clear the forest, plow and plant the soil, stand continual guard to protect their crops and their families against the Indians. Suddenly these men from the Old World were rediscovering the call for that elementary, simple heroism which had marked the dawn of civilization. In that solitude, in that hostile wilderness, every man stood alone facing God, facing a cruel nature that had to be mastered, facing the daily need for subsistence and security. No man could depend on anything but his own hands. The settlers had to begin anew, as though they stood at the threshold of history. They had to be priests, soldiers, and producers for the society they were building on virgin soil.

The extraordinary thing about these settlers, indeed the true measure of the disillusion which had driven them from

Europe, is that from the start this land, this life they led, seemed a paradise. They spoke of it with the fervor and love of the Hebrews for the Promised Land, "flowing with milk and honey." Their journey across the ocean was to them like that of Moses through the Red Sea waters and over the desert. They so longed to escape from Europe that any land would have become a Promised Land. They came to believe that the land they found had awaited them from the beginning of time and that they were as much its chosen people as it was the land of their choice. When they looked back on the Europe they had left behind, they spoke of it with the bitter scorn of the Hebrews for Egypt or for the bondage in Babylon. "There never was a generation," wrote Increase Mather in 1677, "that did so perfectly shake off the dust of Babylon, both as to ecclesiastical and civil constitution, as the first generation of Christians that came into this land for the Gospel's sake." And William Penn exclaimed, "Oh, how sweet is the quiet of these parts, freed from the troubles and perplexities of woeful Europe."

It would be absurd, of course, to suppose that all the settlers were conscious of a Messianic mission, but the New England Puritans were peculiarly imbued with it, and this mere handful of men shaped history when they formulated the main principles of what was to become the great American republic. Narrow, confined, and mediocre as was their political and social experiment at the start, to them, as to the Jews of the Old Testament, it encompassed the vastness of a Promise which would one day be fulfilled on earth as in heaven. To use the memorable image of an English Utopian of that time, James Harrington, they did not propose to plant a frail hothouse flower in a small pot, but rather a great wind-blown tree, with "the Earth for her Root, and Heaven for her Branches."

Western historians have always emphasized the importance of the Reformation, the French Revolution, and Cartesian philosophy, and rightly so, for they indeed formed the world we know. Yet the historians may have been somewhat parochial; they may have failed, as Europeans, to realize the full import of the American experiment. Perhaps at first it was not particularly impressive. It was slow in developing. It did not spring full-blown from the head of Jove. But a closer look reveals with startling clarity how much there was in common between the American adventure in politics and the Cartesian adventure in philosophy.

Descartes was no sport of history; he belonged very much to his time. For me that time deserves to be called the Age of Utopia even more than of Reason and Enlightenment. Though Thomas More did not actually invent Utopia, he immortalized it in his vision of a far-away island on which men lived in political and social perfection. But that island was remote, nonexistent, allowing its creator to give full rein to an imagination liberated from the harsh confines of reality. That far-away island on which the imagination could build from scratch is nothing else but the *tabula rasa,* the clean slate, of Descartes. No Utopia is conceivable unless there is a clean slate upon which it can be inscribed. Once a Utopia becomes flesh and blood, it means either a Reformation or a Revolution.

It is this radicalism of the *tabula rasa,* this prerequisite of Utopia, which seems to me essential to the modern world. It underlies all the great achievements of our history. Descartes did not invent it. It was the mainspring of the Reformation. It colored the dreams of Thomas More; of Cervantes; perhaps those of Molière in *The Misanthrope,* and surely those of Swift in *Gulliver's Travels.* It reappears in Rousseau and in the French Jacobins, and later in the anarchists and even Lenin. It gave Descartes the excuse to simplify everything and make philosophy itself Utopia. After his *tabula rasa* the idealists denied objective reality, a procedure that greatly facilitated matters for the philosopher. Thomas More, Cervantes, Molière, and Swift were content to remain in the realm of creative writing; and this is what gives their work the disillusion, or cynicism, or hidden despair of their respective temperaments. Revolutionary Utopians such as the Jacobins and Lenin, finding no available *tabula rasa,* and not to be satisfied by a far-off, imaginary island, used Terror to create a clean slate all around them. Intolerant by nature, the Utopian can build his Promised Land only on the ruins of a Babylon. Literary Utopians are well aware that their intolerance has a comic side, as Cervantes and Molière made plain; but political Utopians, revolutionaries, never laugh. Saint-Just solemnly called a sorry king, Louis XVI, a Tyrant, and had his head chopped off. Marx and the Communists have been no more playful in their treatment of the bourgeoisie. Nor were the Puritans joking when they said that Europe was Babylon.

For the philosopher to create a clean slate, it is enough to sit by a stove, to be a genius, and to write. But to find or create a *tabula rasa* in politics is not so simple. In the sixteenth and seventeenth centuries neither Europe, nor Asia, nor even what was then known of Africa was a *tabula rasa.* America provided the political and social radicals of New England with an undreamed of, God-given clean slate, a country where there was nothing, where they could conduct as they pleased a human experiment as pure as behooved Utopians who deliberately called themselves Puritans. As they set foot upon those wild, abandoned shores, they first carefully shook from their feet the dust of the ancient European Babylon, then kneeled to bestow a pious kiss upon the Promised Land, the *tabula rasa* of their Utopia.

All over the world, colonies have been founded simply because of accidents of navigation or the ambition of navigators. On this subject Swift is bitterly eloquent. Colonies have also been founded out of mere lust for conquest and greed for land, without superfluous expenditure of a political imagination, only to repeat in a new world the known pattern of the old. For many, America was the land of gold and tobacco, of spices and furs, of opportunity to make a fortune quickly or to become viceroy of a new Spain or of a trans-Atlantic France. But the New England Pilgrims were very different; their ambitions were on another plane. Between them and those opportunistic colonists there is the same difference as between Descartes, who remolded philosophy itself, and all the scholastic professors of his time who philosophized and are now forgotten. The Puritans were determined not only to establish a colony but to conduct a political experiment and carry it through to the end.

With due admiration, Tocqueville quotes the social contract agreed upon and signed by the first Puritan pilgrims.

> We, whose names are underwritten . . . having undertaken for the Glory of God, and advancement of the Christian faith, and the honour of our . . . country, a voyage to plant the first colony, do by these presents solemnly and mutually, in the presence of God . . . covenant and combine ourselves together in a civil Body politick, for our better ordering and preservation, and furtherance of the ends aforesaid; and by virtue hereof do enact, constitute, and frame such just and equal laws, ordinances, acts, constitutions, and offices . . . as shall be thought most meet and convenient . . . unto which we promise due submission and obedience.

If revolution consists in transmuting Utopia into reality, the American Revolution began in the seventeenth century with the landing of the Pilgrims at Plymouth. What the Pilgrims accomplished is what, a century and a half later, the French Jacobins might have succeeded in doing if they had journeyed to some desert island to found the society they wanted instead of making their Revolution in France by creating a *tabula rasa* through Terror. Only the Puritans had the privilege of finding a *tabula rasa* ready-made, and of being able to transmute their Utopia into reality without destroying irreplaceable values. It is highly debatable whether, without the special geographical attributes of America, the Pilgrims could have succeeded.

Unless one sees the ocean and the forest, the *tabula rasa*, and Utopia as the myths they became, I doubt if it is possible to understand such inexplicable manifestations of the American character as, for instance, isolationism; the work of William Faulkner, in which the forest has a mythical life of its own; H. L. Mencken's iconoclasm; or the seeming anomaly of Henry Ford, who was not even able to separate his Model T from a sense of personal mission. That a lord mayor of London would enter Paradise without his wig is inconceivable. But Americans, always ready to start again from scratch, long ago consigned their wigs and traditions to an ocean grave.

I am certain that one cannot do full justice to the American Revolution without recognizing its place in the history of that Utopian radicalism which, throughout the modern era, has inspired revolutions of all kinds and one masterpiece after another. There are a thousand possible Utopias, but this does not mean that every Utopia is desirable. One must understand the kind of Utopia one is looking at before pronouncing judgment. What was the Utopia of the New England Puritans?

3

Magna Charta and
the Word of God

At the end of the sixteenth century European politics were dominated by the hostility between two great nations and two great rulers, Catholic Spain under Philip II and schismatic England under Elizabeth. Both laid claim to rule the world, and because the same ambition consumed them conflict was inevitable. Each side found every conceivable justification for the conflict. Each saw the other in unqualified terms of black and white, in the mystical absolutes of villain and hero. To the English, Spain, Philip II, and the Pope were fiends, risen straight from hell. To the Spanish, England was an infernal many-headed monster and Elizabeth the Great Prostitute of the Apocalypse. England proscribed Catholicism, not merely as abominable superstition, but as treason against the security of the State. Spain proscribed Protestantism for the same reasons. In such a climate of tension, if the time comes when a hero believes himself strong enough to destroy a villain, he feels justified in seizing the opportunity. This is called "preventive war," and it is the story of the "Invincible Armada." Spain, like its national hero Don Quixote, expended all its strength and treasure in battling the winds.

England was victorious, and every Englishman took on he-

roic stature in his own eyes, happily convinced that God Himself was English and that it was His wish that the world
He had created should be English too. Had England been
defeated, political freedom would surely have been arrested
for some time, and the American experiment would have as-
sumed a different shape.

During the early Middle Ages, England and France had
evolved politically along much the same lines, toward a growing autonomy for communes, guilds, and universities, and
therefore toward some degree of participation by the people
in their government. In France, however, from Philip the
Fair on, the monarchy opposed this advance; Richelieu and
Louis XIV crushed it altogether. But in England the evolution toward political freedom, while certainly a long and
painful process, often interrupted and sometimes even forced
back, was never actually brought to a halt. The English thirst
for political freedom was first voiced in the Magna Charta
and much later reasserted in the victory of Parliament over
the Crown.

In proclaiming the right to private interpretation in religion, the Reformation enormously stimulated men's aspirations for political freedom. No limits can be put to a principle
of this kind; once proclaimed, it is bound to spread from
one realm to another. Many Protestants were quick to recognize that the principle of private interpretation applied also
to politics.

In England, paradoxically enough, the Reformation acquired a different hue. Neither Henry VIII nor Elizabeth
was notably enthusiastic about private interpretation in religion, still less in politics. They were concerned not so much
with "reforming" religion as with making the English Church
into a national church, rescuing it from the Pope but submitting it to their own power. The schism in England was by no
means a movement of liberal reform either in religion or in

politics, but simply a determination to give the State complete power over the ecclesiastical body.

The great Elizabeth's successor, James I, took a clear enough stand when, in answer to the Puritans' petition for something more radical in the way of religious reform than mere separation from Rome, he said that, if the Puritans wanted the kind of Protestantism prevalent in Scotland, "it agreeth as well with a monarchy as God with the Devil." And he added, "No bishop, no king. If this be all your party has to say, I will make them conform themselves or harry them out of the land." Rather than "conform," the Puritans dissented from the dissenters, gathered up their worldly goods, and journeyed to Holland from where they sailed on to America.

The Puritans insisted upon the right to private interpretation in politics as well as in religion. They were anti-Catholic, and violently so, because to them Rome meant the principle of ecclesiastical enslavement. Soon they became anti-Anglican too, because they saw that the Established Church, far from renouncing the principle of ecclesiastical enslavement when England broke away from Rome, had on the contrary further entrenched it. They were accused of being republicans, and they were indeed against the divine right of kings. They believed that no king could be invested with sacred and inviolable rights. For them a king was no more than a partner, a steward accountable to them, but to whom they need not account.

The Puritans did not study the Bible as scholars do, as a text about which to argue. They lived the Bible. They found in the Bible their very simple certainties. God created man. He created him in His own image and likeness. He created him free and gave him dominion over nature. Furthermore, God had given men a Law, and that Law was Holy Writ. But God had also given man, first and foremost, the Natural Law, written in his heart and mind, from which it could never be effaced. Man owed obedience to God rather than to other men.

These Biblical certainties were, to the Puritans, both mystical and practical truths, so explicit that they needed neither interpretation nor explanation. They had to be taken literally, just as they were, and acted upon. In this lay the genius of the Puritans. They made no distinction whatever between metaphysical and political freedom. If God created man free, it was a scandal and a sacrilege, an offense against God, to deny man his freedom in any domain, not excepting the political. This concept of political freedom, which was at the same time mystical and practical, constituted the discovery and the glory of the Puritans. That was the real foundation of their Utopia, the great, original idea which they brought into the world and upon which America still stands today. That was the basic principle of the Puritan revolution—a revolution as radical, as original as that of Descartes in philosophy, but undertaken in an infinitely more practicable field.

The Puritans were anything but anarchists. To them the Law was ironclad. But they were unwilling to be deprived of their say in the making of the laws they were to live by, since they were convinced that in them was vested Divine Authority to decide upon questions of a political order. The Law, their Law, was the very Word of God which they had spelled out for their guidance. At the same time the Law ensured their freedom, inasmuch as it stemmed from their own free will. They were, in fact, the exact opposite of anarchists. As Nietzsche was to write, "Great despisers make great zealots." They carried political nonconformism to its extreme limit. Like Descartes with his nonconformist philosophy, they created a *tabula rasa* not because they had no concept of an ideal society, or because their ideal was to destroy society altogether, but rather because they cherished an ideal of society so lofty that it was actually religious. Theirs was a Biblical Utopia, a "Bible Commonwealth."

Of marriage it is written that whom God has joined let no man put asunder. To the Puritans political society was just as sacred. Yet marriage, however high and holy an estate, is sacred only because those who enter it give their consent. Puritan society, like marriage, was the result of a contract freely entered into by its members; it too acquired, once established, a sacred character. It bore the seal of God, and woe to him who tampered with it.

The Puritans were as acutely conscious of the legitimacy of their free society as are certain primitive peoples for whom marriage is so inviolable that the adulteress is burned alive. They entered political society as one enters the religious life, and it was in God that they found the sanction for the contract they made. Their covenant was based on free consent, without which there can be no covenant. A political system imposed from above, merely by royal decree for instance, would have seemed to the Puritans as outlandish and as contrary to divine and natural laws as, nowadays, a marriage of convenience, arranged by parents without free consent of husband and wife, might seem to us. In short, they recognized rule by divine right for the prodigious fraud it was. In the context of that time, their Utopia was admirable.

Good and evil are inextricably mingled in human affairs, and the words we use to describe them often meet with an ironic fate. The word "Puritanism" is an example. It does not at once evoke for us the best of the Puritan heritage, but rather the worst, a Manichaeism that poisons the most normal human relationships. But what concerns me here is the political Utopia of the first American Puritans, an experiment all the more invaluable for their having succeeded in translating it from an imaginary, disembodied world into reality. They left no great book, no *City of God,* no *Social Contract;* they were not literary Utopians. But they directly in-

fluenced the Declaration of Independence and the American
Revolution. On virgin soil they founded a modern Christendom, a society based upon the Bible. They were revolutionary Utopians.

While the English, beset by problems of organizing and
administering a great empire and distracted by increasing
wealth and power, had temporarily turned away from their
own tradition of political freedom, this same tradition, put
to the test again, was developing and thriving under the Puritans who had been unwilling and unable to "conform" in
England. The Puritan experiment was far more radical than
anything heretofore attempted, even in England. Yet it was
from England that the American English were to obtain the
philosophical support they needed. They found the mystical
wellspring of their political evolution in the Bible; their intellectual armature was provided by an English writer, John
Locke. He gave the American revolutionaries their political
handbook. What Marx would one day be for Lenin, Locke
was for the Puritans.

From time to time a book far surpasses the author's original intent. This is what happened to Locke's book, *Two
Treatises of Government,* published in 1690. Locke was not
thinking of the future, as Marx was when he wrote *Das Kapital.* Locke's sole purpose was to justify the revolution which
Parliament had just completed by its victory over the Crown
in 1688. In order to strengthen his argument, he laid down
certain principles and, as happens with principles, they were
found to have not only a specific but a general application.
Thus the American English, using the principles that Locke
had expounded to justify what had been won in England,
went on to use them as justification for their own opposition
to the encroachments not alone of the King, but of Parliament. The Puritans placed Parliament in the always embar-
rassing position of refusing others rights it claimed for itself.

For it is one thing to resist power, and quite another to exercise it. With power, the perspective changes. Locke denounced this change of perspective, and the Americans fired back his ideas at Parliament, hitting the bull's eye every time.

Perhaps the most significant thing about Locke's book, however, is not so much the work itself as the fact that, out of all the English books available, this was the one the American English chose. Here again is an enormous difference between Marxist revolutions and the one in America. *Das Kapital* is a prerequisite of any Marxist revolution. The whole point of a Marxist revolution is to organize the kind of society Marx prescribed. Locke's work, on the contrary, was chosen by the American English as the handbook of their revolution only because it happened to fit their own political ideas and could be used to support their cause.

If Locke had never written, the American English would still have known what they wanted; all Locke did was formulate what they already believed and thus give them a tactical advantage over Parliament.

Locke's political doctrine was not particularly original, as the American English were well aware. He maintained that man, who existed before society, has an inalienable dignity which society has no right to violate but must always respect and foster. Before societies existed, man was in what is called a "natural state"; he enjoyed complete social and political freedom. The land he chose to cultivate was his own. The family he founded was his to rule. The only law he had to obey was the natural law, written in his heart by the Creator to guide him. The fact that men later organized themselves into societies could in no way affect this natural law or the primordial rights men had always enjoyed. If men ultimately entered into social contracts, they did so of their own free will. It was therefore up to them to keep so tight a rein on government that it could never encroach upon their natural rights and their duty to their Creator. When government encroaches, it is tyranny; to resist tyranny is not merely a right, but an obligation.

It must be repeated that all this is not exactly original; it may even be somewhat obvious. An abyss divides so simple a philosophy from the philosophical ramifications of a Hegel or a Marx. However, it is in this very simplicity that we find the essential honesty of the American Utopia. It is precisely the fact that it can be understood by everyone that constitutes its strength. One cannot help suspecting of sophistry political doctrines which only doctors of philosophy can appreciate and understand. Let me reiterate, what is so remarkable about the American Utopia is its simplicity, its availability to everyone. Without need of long and complex instruction or systematic indoctrination, it could be transmuted from men's minds into reality. It became a reality because it was profoundly Christian, because the simple, Gospel-reading Christians of America understood it completely and believed in it passionately, with a faith that was not only religious but social and revolutionary. Of all the texts one could quote to express this faith, I have chosen the justly famous words of Alexander Hamilton: "The Sacred Rights of Mankind are not to be rummaged for among old parchments or musty records. They are written, as with a sunbeam, in the whole volume of nature, by the Hand of Divinity itself, and can never be erased or obscured by mortal power."

To the end, to the moment of final victory, the American Revolution, promulgated as it was by preachers who cited John Locke from the pulpit as readily and with almost as much reverence as they cited the Bible, never lost its religious character. The deep-rooted connection between Christianity and civil liberty, so firmly established by the American Puritans, was definitively described, at the very time of its creation, by Burke:

The People are Protestants; and of that kind which are most averse to all implicit submission of mind and opinion. This is a persuasion not only favourable to liberty, but built upon it. I do not think, Sir, that the reason of this averseness in the dissenting churches, from all that looks like absolute government, is so much to be sought in their religious tenets, as in their history. Everyone knows that the Roman Catholic religion is at least coeval with most of the governments where it prevails; that it had generally gone hand in hand with them, and received great favour and every kind of support from authority. The Church of England too was formed from her cradle under the nursing care of regular government. But the dissenting interests have sprung up in direct opposition to all the ordinary powers of the world; and could justify opposition only on a strong claim to natural liberty. Their very existence depended on the powerful and unremitted assertion of that claim. All Protestantism, even the most cold and passive, is a sort of dissent. But the religion most prevalent in our northern colonies is a refinement of the principles of resistance; it is the dissidence of dissent, and the Protestantism of the Protestant religion.

4

The Pride of Being

English

Time passed, the grievances of exile were forgotten, and the Americans began to realize that though England might well be Babylon it was still the land of the Magna Charta. More and more they thought of themselves as Englishmen, free Englishmen. In 1700 Cotton Mather told the Massachusetts Assembly, "It is not a Little Blessing of God, that we are a part of the English Nation."

The American colonies had been founded long before the final victory of Parliament over the Crown. For the American English, watching the struggle from afar, Parliament's victorious stand against the power of the throne was sacrosanct. But when, on the heels of this victory, Parliament arrogated to itself the same absolute power against which it had fought —just as, later, the Convention and the Committee of Public Safety were to do during the French Revolution—the American English saw no reason to yield and give up their liberties to an Assembly any more than they had given them up to the Crown. As Englishmen, and precisely because they were English, they kept up the struggle against absolute power, fighting Parliament as they had fought the King.

Now that we have enough perspective upon events to judge them, there can be no doubt that it was the Americans who

were right; that it was the Americans who, without betrayal
or compromise, vigorously upheld the English tradition that
Parliament repudiated.

Their conflict with the mother country was therefore of a
very special nature. The most convincing evidence of the
right of the American colonies to independence was that they
had attained a degree of political development and of actual
political maturity unequaled at the time, even in England.
But perhaps the clearest proof that they were ready for independence is that they were not even seeking it. Independence
was actually thrust upon them.

The conflict that divided the English English from the
American English was primarily over principles and traditions. What made it all the more serious was that these
principles and traditions were common to Englishmen everywhere, in America as in England. This gave it the character and the dignity of a schism. When the Arabs in Algeria
rise up against France, it is essentially because they know
they are different from the French and therefore reject community with the French; they do not claim to be more French
than the French. The American English, on the other hand,
refused to admit that they were different, nor had they any
desire to be different from the English English. Most important of all, they did not reject the English tradition or
their community with England's Empire. Rather, they
claimed exactly the same rights as the English English and
very soon concluded that the English English were yielding
too many of these rights to Parliament. They wanted to re-
store to all Englishmen the full measure of their rights and
rid the colonies, and eventually perhaps even the mother
country itself, of what they considered an intolerable devia-
tion from the authentic line of English political tradition.
What they were saying—with Corneille—was that "Rome is
no longer in Rome; where I am, all Rome is too."

This concept is no mere flight of fancy. A man as cool-headed and judicious as Benjamin Franklin wrote, in 1760, to Lord Kames, "I have long been of the opinion that the *foundations of the future grandeur and stability of the British Empire lie in America;* and though, like other foundations, they are low and little now, they are, nevertheless, broad and strong enough to support the greatest political structure that human wisdom ever yet erected."

The moment came when, to preserve the unity of its Empire, England would have had to accept the American interpretation of its own tradition. Perhaps this is just what England eventually did accept when it organized the flexible commonwealth system of our times. But in that day, England was far from being disposed to admit its mistakes and take lessons from its colonies. This is the great debate on political orthodoxy that underlay America's War of Independence. On the political level, America did to England just what the Church of England had done to Rome on the religious level. The Church of England, its separation won, claimed to be more Catholic than the Pope. In the same way, English America, revolting against England, claimed to be more English than England itself. Such internecine quarrels can almost never be reconciled. They lead to mutual excommunication, followed, if one side is strong enough, by a crusade to bring back the dissenters into the fold. But a crusade rarely succeeds in recreating unity. The misfortune is to reach this stage.

As in all crusades, it goes without saying that orthodoxy was not the only controversial issue. Historians have made the economic and constitutional causes of this particular conflict abundantly clear. And the historians are right. Those causes existed. But they were conditioned by the underlying debate on orthodoxy. Indeed, they sprang from it.

With the growth of Empire the English conscience had a new problem to face. Empire meant responsibility, but, even more, it meant a terrible temptation. The problem was one of choice: whether to consider the colonies as an extension of English civilization and the English political system beyond the seas, and grant them basic equality of status, or to exploit the riches and markets of Empire for the exclusive benefit of the mother country. From the start, the American English insisted on equality of status. But the English English decided on that form of exploitation known as "mercantilism." The English English maintained that their political system had been evolved on their own island, for their sole use, and was not for export. They alone were worthy of some degree of political freedom. As for those others so far away, those English who yet were not English—they could be forced to labor and pay taxes at will. Policy for the colonies was one thing, policy at home quite another.

Inevitably the American English refused to play the role assigned them. Once again, Edmund Burke understood:

> The temper and character which prevail in our colonies are, I am afraid, unalterable by human art. We cannot, I fear, falsify the pedigree of this fierce people, and persuade them that they are not sprung from a nation in whose veins the blood of freedom circulates. The language in which they would hear you tell them this tale would detect the imposition; your speech would betray you. An Englishman is the unfittest person on earth to argue another Englishman into slavery.

The American colonists resented the refusal of political equality even more bitterly than the curbs imposed on their commerce and industry and the pettifogging of officials. But they also found the curbs and the pettifogging unendurable. They felt no call to enrich the mother country by impoverishing themselves. At first they found a way out by smuggling, a practice which soon became quasi-official in New England. Then, when they saw that smuggling no longer sufficed to insure their commercial autonomy, they openly resisted the London government. They were so extraordinarily ingenious at inventing financial ways and means to bring the English governors to heel that some officials, rather than engage in endless bickering, came to terms at the outset of their administration and let themselves be bought. They set their price; the Americans paid it, and were left free to do what they wanted, in the way they wanted to do it.

The manner in which the colonists thus established a link between political rights and taxes was typically English. No taxation without representation. Since they were never granted representation in Parliament, they paid almost no direct taxes. The right to "self-determination" became the right to "self-taxation." At first glance it might seem as though the colonists were lacking in dignity when they reduced the whole concept of political rights to a mere question of taxation. Yet that is undoubtedly the most effective way to protect such rights and assure their recognition. The American colonists were not trying to buy their right to political representation, since they considered it their natural and inalienable right, even while it was denied them. They had simply grasped certain elementary truths. No government in power voluntarily grants the governed all their rights; it must somehow be forced to do so. Every government, well-meaning or not, needs money. Without money, slight difficulties become serious, and serious difficulties become utterly insoluble. Since, in the last analysis, every government depends entirely on the money of the governed, the most effective way for the governed to obtain their rights— a more effective way than violence and certainly more effective than oratorical recrimination—is to refuse to pay taxes until their rights are won.

Governments are cynical. They do not mind at all when people call them tyrants. What they cannot stand is to go six months with empty coffers. This humble rule of politics is not romantic, but it has the advantage of being practical. The American colonists remembered that rule when they pressed their claims. It is striking how little violence there was in the feverish period before the American War of Independence. It is striking that the very leaders of the revolt against England apologized for, and disowned, every outburst. Actually, almost all Americans were horrified by the occasional spontaneous acts of violence and even more by anything that could be called organized terror. This was no indication of weakness, but rather a proof that they knew where to concentrate their strength.

Those who pay taxes have the right to a voice in the decisions of their government. On the basis of this most English of principles, the American English stubbornly demanded representation in Parliament. Just as stubbornly, representation was refused them. From the English viewpoint, there were weighty reasons for refusing. If, in a fast-growing empire, the English were to acknowledge that the right of representation applied everywhere, eventually they would become a minority in their own Parliament, and England, instead of being a mother country for the colonies to serve, would be no more than a province in a vast, decentralized empire. Stripped of power, it would be forced to submit to laws enacted by its own colonies. At that time no one thought of federation. The English English could not endure the idea of one day having to submit to laws they had not themselves created; the American English could not endure the idea of submitting indefinitely to laws in the creating of which they had had no voice at all. The quarrel was therefore between brother and brother.

Though the political reasons for the quarrel were the same, and sprang from authentic English tradition, on both sides the arguments became envenomed by that personal and derisive kind of comment which, when exchanged between members of the same family, is impossible to forgive. Once again, the fatal absolutes of hero and villain poisoned the already troubled atmosphere on both sides of the sea. The English made up their minds that the Americans were socially inferior. The Americans made up their minds that the English were thoroughly corrupt. To the English the Americans were "the scum and off-scouring of all nations"; "a hodge-podge medley of foreign, enthusiastic madmen"; "little more than a set of slaves, at work for us, one degree only above the Negroes that we carry for them." To grant such people the right of representation in Parliament would be to suppose "that a body of adventurers could carry the Legislative Powers of Great Britain along with them." In 1768, an Englishman declared, "I think we might now, with equal propriety, seek a representative from among the French or the Spaniards, as from Boston, for neither of these countries have, as yet, outdone the Bostonians in malicious combinations against our existence."

Patient as they tried to be, though they were not any too patient, the Americans soon had enough. Samuel Curwen wrote, "It picques my pride, I confess, to hear us called 'our colonies, our plantations' in such terms and with such airs as if our properties and persons were absolutely theirs, like the *villains* and their cottages in the old feudal system." And here is what Benjamin Franklin had to say: "When I consider the extreme corruption prevalent among all Order of Men in this rotten old State, and the glorious publick Virtue so predominant in our rising country, I cannot but apprehend more mischief than benefit from a closer union." By now the Magna Charta and even John Locke were forgotten, and if the American Puritans still quoted the Bible it was only because it provided references to Babylon. In the colonies and in England, the mystical absolutes of hero and villain had taken hold completely. This is the familiar stepping stone to war.

Not everyone went into the war lightheartedly. Now, nearly

two centuries later, it is easy for us to see how America has benefited by independence. But for those who had to make the choice it was not easy, American merchant adventurers and sea captains, in whose hands lay so much of the wealth of the colonies, sided against the English administration—but only up to a certain point, to the exact point where their interests were hurt by tariffs, and restrictions to navigation, and trade. Beyond that point their local patriotism cooled down, for they knew by experience the many advantages of being part of the Empire and under the protection of the English fleet. They were undoubtedly not as quick to react to the price of honor as to the price of cotton and tobacco, a reaction both normal and universal in the world of commerce. Remarkably enough, however, once war was declared, the great majority of them remained loyal to the American side. It was of course the side of the future, even the future of their trade. But they deserve some credit for recognizing the fact, in the context of their time.

For America the blessing of blessings was that, in this critical hour, it had produced an elite, a group of superior men who not only sympathized entirely with the popular feeling but were also able to channel it. Inevitably, as in all revolutions, there were demagogues and fanatics aplenty, but it was not these who had the final say, who actually determined their country's fate. Rather, the responsibility was taken by this small number of essentially intellectual Americans, whose minds had been shaped by the European disciplines, who were steeped in the English tradition, but who were at the same time sharply aware of the peculiar needs and the personality of America. Though these men were the political heirs of the New England Puritans, they had rid themselves of prejudice and fanaticism. They were revolutionaries rather than Utopians.

Two centuries had inscribed a history upon the *tabula rasa* of the new continent and transformed it into an incomparable native land, already as deserving of respect as of love. The question was no longer, as it had been for the first Pilgrims, how to conduct a political experiment on virgin soil; now there was a country to defend as one protects a young, vulnerable, but sturdy plant.

The American elite had extraordinary political insight. These men were keenly conscious of the need for compromise in all human affairs, but they were also unfailingly conscious of those moral limits to compromise by which honor is defined. If England proved incapable of reaching an agreement with such minds as theirs, it was because there was no possibility whatever of agreement. Honor, English honor, required rebellion against England. Speaking ideologically—and it was primarily ideological questions that set off the American War of Independence—this was a civil war, the most ineluctable, the most justifiable of wars. An ideal was common to both sides; each fought the other in the name of that ideal. Few, very few, colonial wars of independence can claim such dignity.

5

The War

This war, like so many others, was set off by a misunderstanding. In 1773, Boston was having another dispute with the English government over the tax on tea. One night a group of some fifty Bostonians, disguised as Indians, boarded three English tea ships at anchor in the harbor and dumped their cargoes into the sea. The incident, childish as it undoubtedly was, roused general indignation throughout the Colonies. Boston itself was preparing to apologize and make amends to the Crown, but Parliament, in its hasty reaction, brought on disaster. To punish one instance of sabotage it passed the so-called "Intolerable Acts," which closed Boston harbor. It sent Lieutenant General Gage with five thousand men to see that the Acts were enforced. This was a serious miscalculation. One of the most deeply rooted and tenacious characteristics of Americans is to rush to the defense of the underdog. The Colonies which, on the very eve of this move, had still been deploring and disclaiming the drastic action of the sham Indians, hastened to the rescue of Boston now that the mother country was attempting to starve it.

The Colonies did something still more astonishing. All of them, except Georgia, elected delegates to send to a Congress

in Philadelphia in 1774. This was the First Continental Congress, and it met before independence was declared. In the
words of Samuel Adams, they agreed that "this is the time
when *all* should be united in this opposition to the violation
of the liberties of us all." Only Boston had been struck, but
for the first time a tyrannical act against a single colony created, in the face of the English government and in opposition
to it, the unity of an American nation; it also endowed this
new political entity with a platform, a tribunal, and a voice.
Moreover, this all took place in the open, above ground as it
were, under the very noses of officialdom and of the English
army; it was the spontaneous outcome of political convictions long since become traditional. Threatened by oppression, the Americans elected a Congress, their own Congress, to represent them, as naturally as an apple tree bears
apples. The stage was set for independence even before the
word itself had been sounded, even before the majority of
Americans had thought of it.

But the English had thought of it. When George III put
his name to the "Intolerable Acts," he said, "The die is cast.
The Colonies must either triumph or submit." But in any
political conflict there is probably no more fatal error than
to demand unconditional surrender. When issues begin to
overtax the nerves, the hope of solving them is abandoned,
and the enemy is forced to choose between total victory or
total defeat. Henceforward everything the English did could
only hasten American independence.

When a situation becomes so inflammable, there is always
a match to set it ablaze. On the morning of April 19, 1775,
General Gage dispatched a column of a thousand men to
destroy a depot of colonial military stores some miles north-
west of Boston, at Concord. On the way, the column found
itself briefly in action against American minutemen—for
these amazing Colonies not only had elected their own Con-

gress but had organized their own militia and supplies, in point of fact the nucleus for a national army. That first skirmish took place at Lexington. Eight Massachusetts minutemen were killed, ten were wounded. The English column proceeded to Concord without further incident and destroyed what military supplies the Americans had not had time to remove. On their way back the English encountered, for the first time, not just the resistance but the wrath of Americans. The whole countryside was up in arms. Its militia attacked the English, drove them back, harried them, and finally turned their retreat into a rout. By the time the column made its way back to Boston, it had lost 273 men. The militia, now 16,000 strong, promptly followed up their advantage and put the city under formal siege. This siege did not end till March 1776, when Washington, who was in command, forced the English to evacuate.

Many years later a young student interviewed an American veteran of the Battle of Concord.

"Captain Preston, why did you go to the Concord fight, the 19th of April, 1775?"

The old man, bowed beneath the weight of years, raised himself upright, and turning to me, said: "Why did I go?"

"Yes," I replied, "my histories tell me that you, men of the Revolution, took up arms against 'intolerable oppression.' "

"What were they, oppressions? I did not feel them!"

"What? Were you not oppressed by the Stamp Act?"

"I never saw one of these stamps, and always understood that Governor Bernard put them all in Castle William. I am certain that I never paid one penny for one of them."

"Well, then what about the tea tax?"

"Tea tax? I never drank a drop of the stuff; the boys threw it all overboard."

"Then I suppose you had been reading Harrington or

Sidney and Locke about the eternal principles of liberty."

"Never heard of 'em. We read only the Bible, the Catechism, Watts' Psalms and Hymns and the Almanack."

"Well then, what was the matter? And what did you mean in going to the fight?"

"Young man, what we meant in going for those red coats was this: we had always governed ourselves, and we always meant to. They didn't mean we should."

To me, what the old Concord soldier said is of the utmost importance. It is conclusive evidence that the Utopia of "self-government," brought so long before to the American continent by a group of Puritan refugees, was no longer a Utopia at all, but had entered into the flesh and the bloodstream of a whole people. Disembodied, it would have come to nothing. That old soldier had not read Locke, he had not cared a rap for the tea, yet he had gone straight to the heart of the debate. This is the way of Americans.

Benjamin Franklin recounts in his *Autobiography* a conversation he had, when the Colonies sent him to London back in 1757, with Granville, then president of the privy council.

"You Americans have wrong ideas about the nature of your constitution; you contend that the king's instructions to his governors are not laws, and think yourselves at liberty to regard or disregard them at your own discretion. But those instructions are not like the pocket instructions given to a minister going abroad, for regulating his conduct in some trifling point of ceremony. They are first drawn up by judges learned in the laws; they are then considered, debated, and perhaps amended in Council, after which they are signed by the king. They are then, so far as they relate to you, the *law of the land,* for the king is the LEGISLATOR OF THE COLONIES." I told his lordship that this was new doctrine to me. I had always understood from our charters that our laws were to be made by our Assemblies, to be presented indeed to the king for his royal assent, but that being once given the king could not repeal or alter them. And as the Assemblies could not make permanent law without his assent, so neither could he make a law for them without theirs. He assured me I was totally mistaken. I did not think so, however. . . .

Thus, almost twenty years before the war, Franklin was already thinking along exactly the same lines as the veteran of Concord. Far more than the English minister could realize, Franklin represented a nation which, while still loyal to its sovereign, had already come of age. The dialogue between Franklin and the president of the privy council was doomed to be fruitless. In fact, one could hardly call it a dialogue; it was two antiphonal monologues, or—to put it still another way—the deaf was speaking to the deaf. Where could this lead, save to Concord?

But if Concord was the inevitable, logical conclusion to a long dialogue between the deaf, it was also the introduction to a long war. To start a war is always relatively easy; the difficulty lies in carrying it through to final victory. It is also easy to find generals who can win battles; but to find generals who can sustain a war from beginning to end and win it is far more difficult. When Washington and his militia drove the English out of Boston, it was a fine feat of arms. But his real stature lies in the fact that he did not stop with Boston. He faced an immensely difficult war. He had almost no trained troops, and the enemy was at the peak of its wealth and power. Even more than genius, the commander of the American forces had to have inflexible tenacity of purpose. Indeed one might say that it was in Washington's inflexible tenacity that his genius lay.

In dwelling upon the character of Washington and searching in my mind for someone with whom to compare him in European history, it is de Gaulle who comes to mind. In June 1940, what de Gaulle needed was not only to foresee all the

possibilities and practicabilities of the war that was just beginning but also an unconquerable faith in his country's
destiny, in order to be able to proclaim that France had lost
merely a battle, and not the war itself. After Boston, where
the English had been thrown a first time into the sea, George
Washington must have been able to envision the full scope of
the task ahead. Far from having won the war, he knew that
America had won no more than a single battle, and that until
the war itself had been won nothing would be achieved. Just
as the world in 1940 was quite unaware of what manner of
man de Gaulle was, so in 1776 London and the rest of the
world did not know what manner of man George Washington was. But the world was soon to learn. Having won the
first battle, Washington went on to win the war.

6

Independence

Americans are a slow people, but they seldom retrace their steps. I do not mean to imply that all Americans are slow. There are some who are only too hasty, but these are exceptions; moreover, they do not go far and are often obliged to repent of their haste. Americans are slow because they are profoundly aware that life is a continuous movement, advancing only through contradictions and becoming fuller and richer only as it succeeds in reconciling as far as possible these contradictions, never when it ignores or silences them. Americans strive heroically and with rare obstinacy to keep extreme opposites on speaking terms and to find a way to reconcile them, even if the reconciliation is merely superficial. They do not give up an extreme position until it becomes more than obvious that it cannot possibly be reconciled with its opposite and merged with the continuous movement. But once they do give it up, they look upon it as an obstacle to be removed forthwith. Americans are a slow people because of two seemingly contradictory elements in their nature: a desire for compromise at almost, though not quite, any price, and an undeniable rigidity wherever their honor and their interest are concerned. But once they have reached a decision—either to compromise or, if compromise proves impossible, to refuse to compromise—they are then as swift and direct in carrying out their decision as they were slow and indirect in coming to it. Observers, however, see only the action itself, the carrying out of the decision. It is this manner of taking action, together with the remarkable tempo of American production, that gives America its reputation for breathtaking speed. Innately, America has the slowest pulse in the world. If Americans seem obsessed by the need for haste, it is because they are always slow to start.

This process might suggest the Hegelian dialectic of thesis, antithesis, and synthesis, but the American dialectic is entirely practical; it cannot really be defined as a dialectic; it is rather a certain style of life and a way of getting things done. It is never a philosophical attitude, still less an exercise of wits. It is the embodiment of a continuing effort toward a goal so remote that it may be impossible to formulate until finally achieved. As an indication of character, it shows a certain authentic modesty: who dares to claim that all the right is on one side and all the wrong on the other? But it also expresses a healthy optimism: when people do their best, things must always come out right in the end. Often, the spectacle of America in action gives the impression that Americans are continually shifting their ground and contradicting themselves. But what they actually do is weigh thesis and antithesis before reaching a synthesis.

The First Continental Congress would undoubtedly have seemed chaotic to an observant witness. Certainly the more radical delegates were already thinking of independence, though they did not dare admit it. Others were pledged to keep the Colonies within the Empire at all costs. But primarily the delegates were determined to maintain colonial unity in the dangerous crisis in which the Colonies found themselves. It was only through unity that the Colonies could survive. Yet nothing was more difficult than to preserve it in the face of the differing needs and attitudes of the various Colonies. On one major point, however, unity did exist, for all agreed that it was absolutely essential to defend the traditional rights of the Colonies against the impingements of the English government. But these rights, in order to be defended, had first to be defined, and that was a further difficulty, since not all the Colonies had the same concept of these rights or of what they encompassed.

The attempt to resolve the contradictions took up all the time and was the subject of all the debates of the delegates to the First Continental Congress. But Americans have a compulsion to get things done. John Adams wrote as follows:

> After a multitude of motions had been made, discussed, negatived, it seemed as if we should never agree upon anything. Mr. John Rutledge of South Carolina, one of the committee, addressing himself to me, was pleased to say: "Adams, we must agree upon something; you appear to me to be as familiar with the subject as any one of us. . . . Come, take the pen and see if you can produce something that will unite us." Some others of the committee seconding Mr. Rutledge, I took a sheet of paper and drew up an article. When it was read, I believe not one of the committee was fully satisfied with it; but they all soon acknowledged that there was no hope of hitting on anything in which we could all agree with more satisfaction. All therefore agreed to this, and upon this depended the union of the colonies.

A close study of the Declaration and Resolves of the First Continental Congress shows that it is just as remarkable for what it does not say or only half says, as for what it says. The repeated appeal to traditional English rights clearly proves that, even after Concord, the Congress and the American people still hoped to remain within the Empire. It is always painful to create a schism in the orthodoxy to which one

belongs. In the Declaration and Resolves the Congress proclaimed:

> That the inhabitants of the English colonies in North
> America, by the immutable laws of nature, the principles of
> the English Constitution, and the several charters or com-
> pacts, have the following RIGHTS:
>
> That they are entitled to life, liberty, and property; and
> they have never ceded to any foreign power whatever a right
> to dispose of either without their consent. . . .
>
> That by such emigration they by no means forfeited, sur-
> rendered, or lost any of those rights, but that they were, and
> their descendants now are, entitled to the exercise and en-
> joyment of all such of them, as their local and other circum-
> stances enable them to exercise and enjoy.
>
> That the foundation of English liberty, and of all free
> government, is a right in the people to participate in their
> legislative council . . . and as the English colonists are not
> represented . . . in the British Parliament, they are entitled
> to a free and exclusive power of legislation in their several
> provincial legislatures, where their right of representation
> can alone be preserved, in all cases of taxation and internal
> polity, subject only to the negative of their sovereign, in such
> manner as has been heretofore used and accustomed.

They are fortunate mother countries whose colonies are
mature enough to draw up, on their own initiative, such a
program as this. Had England accepted it, the federation of
the British Commonwealth would have been founded then
and there. Since, in the determining of taxes and the making
of laws, the right of representation is recognized as the basis
for any political society, the unity of that society must be
forged upon that right, and not in defiance of it.

The rights of the Colonies had been defined; it remained
to reaffirm the other extreme of the contradiction then exist-

ing in Congress. In order to make it perfectly clear that, in spite of everything, the Colonies wished to remain part of the Empire, this Declaration was sent to the King with a highly respectful petition that he graciously take it under consideration.

But in circumstances such as those in which the Colonies now found themselves, the momentum of events is far stronger than the will of men. The decision as to whether or not to remain in the Empire was no longer in the hands of Congress. The momentum of events foiled men's intentions and even belied their words. For after all, when Congress insisted that Americans had never ceded their rights to any "foreign power," what did the words "foreign power" mean? Did they refer to France or to Spain, both of which, during their wars with England, had upon occasion attacked the Colonies? Or did these words refer to England? The whole context of the Declaration implies, even though it may not be explicitly what Congress meant to say, that this "foreign power" was none other than the mother country itself, which must obviously have ceased to be the mother country if it had become a "foreign power."

Moreover, at the very moment when Congress was still protesting its loyalty to the Empire, it was already acting as though it spoke for an independent nation. It was acknowledging a state of war with England and voting a war budget; it was organizing the Continental Army and naming George Washington commander in chief; it was secretly seeking alliances. When a nation is not sovereign, such acts are called treason. This is certainly how the English government looked upon them. The King threw out the petition of rights and grievances, and in the so-called Prohibitory Act of December 22, 1775, decreed that the Colonies were henceforth outside the protection of the Empire and its fleet. Even if the Colonies were not seeking independence, they were being inexorably driven to it.

France too played its part. It had just emerged from a disastrous war with England and was therefore not unnaturally
pleased by London's difficulties with the American Colonies,
since it saw in these difficulties an opportunity for revenge.
To the Colonies, in revolt against the mother country, France
seemed an obvious ally. In fact, the relations the Americans
then had with France were much the same as those of
de Gaulle with Britain in 1940 in London, and later with the
United States. The American colonials wanted to make their
own war; in 1940 de Gaulle wanted to carry on France's
war. Both the Americans at the time of their Revolution, and
de Gaulle at the time of the fall of France, knew very well
that once a war is declared it must be won, but neither was
strong enough to win alone and unaided. However, to enter
into an alliance is the act of a sovereign state. Before the government of Louis XVI would agree to commit France to an
alliance with the Colonies, it stipulated that they must declare their independence. Precisely at this point, the comparison with de Gaulle ceases to hold true. In 1940 Britain,
and later on the United States, sought to confine de Gaulle
to a purely military role, to preserve the fiction of a *de jure*
Vichy government, and to deny the sovereignty of Free
France. On the other hand the King of France refused to enter into the fiction of the *de jure* sovereignty of England over
the American colonies and forced the Americans, as the price
of his alliance, into independence and sovereignty. This is an
illustration of one of the marked differences in character
between the Anglo-Saxons and the French.

As the war went on, the Colonies could not do without
help from France. A nation must have a flourishing commerce to prosecute a war, and if it is a maritime nation there
must be a fleet to protect its commerce. The Americans, no
longer protected by the English fleet, were inevitably compelled to seek the protection of the rival fleet. France did not
give that protection on the seas alone. France sent money and

arms. It also sent Lafayette with troops. The support of these troops, together with the blockade enforced by the French fleet, proved the deciding factor in the battle which won the war for America.

Throughout that first year of war, Congress remained divided and even torn. Yet the delegates saw more and more plainly that the only choice before them was, as the clergyman John Joachim Zubly kept reiterating, either "a reconciliation with Great Britain or the means of carrying on the war." Reconciliation would mean dishonor, the abandoning of the most sacred rights of the Colonies, and this the American people themselves protested more and more loudly that they would never accept. War, and the prosecution of it, would entail independence. Honor called for war. Congress, pressed by public opinion and the need for help, now had no choice. On June 7, 1776, in the name of the Virginia delegation, Richard Henry Lee called upon Congress to vote on three resolutions, the first of which declared that "These United States are, and of right ought to be, free and independent States, that they are absolved from all allegiance to the British Crown, and that all political connection between them and the State of Great Britain is, and ought to be, totally dissolved."

Less than a month later, on the second of July, this motion was carried by the Congress. With the consent of the American people and by the declaration of its representatives, a sovereign America was born. Between the skirmish at Concord and independence, hardly fifteen months had gone by.

7

The National

Vocation

At this point something extraordinary took place. Congress, having solemnly proclaimed independence on July 2, 1776, proceeded two days later, on July 4, to vote a Declaration of Independence. I call it extraordinary because in those two days America, without even perhaps being fully aware of it, moved from war into revolution. The proclamation of independence made official the state of war with England. The independence it proclaimed would be achieved by a treaty with England in 1783, after final victory.

But the Declaration of Independence on the Fourth of July, 1776, belongs to an entirely different sphere from either the war, the victory, or the treaty that crowned the victory and brought the war to an end. This Declaration is in line with the long debate over political orthodoxy that underlay the disputes of the Colonies with the mother country, as it is also in line with the political Utopia of the original founders of the Colonies. It lifts the debate above the immediacy of civil war and national disputes and definitively transforms Utopia into the reality of revolution. Initiating a revolution, it does so on a revolutionary plane far beyond mere territorial claims or political sovereignty or even a change of regime. A revolution worthy of the name is fought for social principles, for the mutual rights and obligations of men and nations. An event of this nature does infinitely more than establish a nation's political independence; it voices a political ideal which must from then on determine the very way the nation lives. Such is the American Revolution. It overflows the boundaries of America itself, in setting an example to all societies. Once begun, theoretically at least, it can have no end or limit whether in space or time.

This Revolution is more original than would appear. Let us compare it with some of those in our own day. When, after a long struggle but nevertheless without a war, India, Egypt, and Tunisia won their independence, they did not look beyond it; they had what they sought; they were satisfied. Now they seek only to make themselves greater, richer, more respected. None of them, upon winning national independence, felt obligated to make a declaration of principles. Actually, of course, national independence always involves revolution, but the word revolution in this context must be taken in its most limited and practical sense as a change of government or of administration. Yet, in gaining independence, none of these other nations sought to make a revolution in the very principles of human society. America did. The Americans knew instinctively that it is at the very moment when a nation is in danger of losing all it has that it must give the most of itself. The founders of the American nation did not consider it enough merely to fight for their own independence. They gave the world a revolution.

On July 2 the Congress had affirmed the inalienable right of the American nation to exist. On July 4 the Congress defined the nation's lasting responsibility and revolutionary vocation. And since there is far greater dignity in accepting responsibility than in claiming rights, America is never so truly America as when it lives up to its full responsibility and its revolutionary vocation. It is therefore not without significance that the Fourth of July, and not the Second, was chosen as the national holiday of the American Republic. For America gives even more weight to its revolutionary vocation than to its national independence, or rather one might say that its national independence finds complete justification only in the faithful fulfillment of its revolutionary vocation.

Naturally enough, a nation that frees itself from foreign dominion celebrates its national holiday on the anniversary of its freedom. This is what all the South American republics have done. Yet it is the revolution that coincided with its freedom, rather than that freedom itself, that North America has chosen to celebrate. It is true that the two great nations of France and Russia have also set revolutionary dates for their national holidays. Russia celebrates the overthrow of a government, the seizure of power by the Bolsheviks in 1917. France celebrates the seizure and demolition of the Bastille. But Russia could have celebrated, instead, the Communist Manifesto; France, the Declaration of the Rights of Man and of the Citizen. They did not. Both chose to celebrate a revolutionary but a violent act. America also celebrates a revolutionary act, but an act that was wholly intellectual, a declaration of principles. In this sense America is more revolutionary than either France or Russia. What America celebrates is not an act belonging only to the past, but an act that transcends time and space, an act that is still —as much for all peoples as for Americans themselves—a responsibility and a hope.

Joan of Arc would have remained an illiterate little peasant girl, unknown and lost in the depths of history, had she not been given a mission, heard a call which lifted her out of her village to plunge her into deeds of greatness and finally into the flames. The never-ending admiration for the destiny of that shepherd girl is born of the call she heard and of her heroic devotion to her mission. The call comes to a fisherman on the Lake of Galilee and transmutes him into a fisher of men; it comes to a little herder of sheep at the edge of the Lorraine forest and transmutes her into a herder of whole armies of men.

This happens with nations, too. They are what they are, they live from day to day, trying to be themselves and persevere in being, wholly bent upon national interest and survival. One after another, many nations have sunk into history without leaving so much as a name. But a few have been given a vocation which imposes upon them a responsibility and a universal mission above mere national interest. It is when nations respond to this call without reservation that they become most truly themselves and that they earn the admiration and gratitude of generations of men. To remember the Israel of Isaiah, the Greece of Plato, the Italy of Leonardo, or the France of Pascal is to know a welling-up of pride in belonging to the world those nations have belonged to and in inheriting from them.

This is the spirit that fired the founders of the American republic to an awareness, not only of a nation and its needs, but even more—of its vocation. On the Fourth of July, 1776, Thomas Jefferson pronounced for them and for us and forever America's national vocation.

8

Thomas Jefferson
and Saint-Just

Immeasurable time, vitality, talent, ink, fervor, and even blood have been vainly expended, lost, lost forever, over the question of what is the best form of government. But the question, put this way, has little meaning. It is infinitely more important to decide which comes first—man or his system of government. After all, a political system is always a creation of the intellect, whereas men exist first, they are there. They are born, mature, perpetuate themselves, and die, in their unpredictable, immutable, and perhaps also ungovernable individuality. That a political system, a creation of the intellect, should take precedence over man, and that men should be made to conform to it, is an attitude which has always had and always will have some support, in every kind of government, whether monarchy, aristocracy, or republic. This is the argument with which tyranny always seeks to justify itself. To put man first, ahead of the political system he lives under, whatever that system may be, means to turn the whole movement of political life completely upside down. It is as drastic a reversal as that which opposes deductive to inductive knowledge, or a theology based on revelation to natural science built entirely upon experimentation, or, to the vindictive theologians, Galileo's answer: "E pur si muove."

And yet, in all truth, man is more important and more valuable than the most perfect creations of his intellect and his most harmoniously conceived political ideologies. This idea, in its own orbit, constitutes as revolutionary a change in thinking as the transition from Aristotelian to Copernican astronomy. Alas, however, it is a revolution in constant jeopardy, a revolution to be fought again and again, since every system of government—monarchy, aristocracy, democracy— instinctively leans toward tyranny. But we tend to forget this, just as in everyday speech we tend to forget that it is not the sun that rises and sets, but the earth that moves round the sun.

I have been led to these reflections by Thomas Jefferson. For in my opinion a Copernican revolution in politics was transformed for the first time, by America, into a concrete fact. "If once people become inattentive to the public affairs," wrote Jefferson, "you and I and Congress and Assemblies, Judges and Governors, shall all become wolves. It seems to be the law of our general nature, in spite of individual exceptions." And again: "Certain forms of government are better calculated than others to protect individuals in the free exercise of their natural rights, and are at the same time better guarded against degeneracy, yet experience hath shown that even under the best forms, those entrusted with power have, in time, and by slow operations, perverted it into tyranny." Jefferson even went so far as to say, "Societies exist under three forms: those without government, as among our Indians; those under governments wherein the will of everyone has a just influence; those under governments of force. It is a problem not clear in my mind that the first condition is not the best."

It would be a mistake to see in these observations the bit-

ter sallies of a totally anarchistic mind or even of the skepti-
cal mind of a Montaigne. On the contrary, they are an
expression of vibrant faith in man, in men made as they are
of flesh and blood, and of candid trust in man's innate ca-
pacity to ensure his earthly salvation. They also express a
fearless honesty in facing the fact that man's freedom is
always vulnerable to the encroachments of power, and that
is why Jefferson felt such deep distrust, distrust on principle,
of any government whatever that interposes itself between
men and the management of their own affairs. For Jefferson
the freedom of the individual is always a possession wrested
from government but unceasingly threatened by it, just as
the land that the people of Holland have wrested and walled
away from the sea never ceases to be threatened by it.

To understand a revolution fully, it is necessary not only
to grasp its principles, but perhaps even more to understand
the character of the men who carried out the revolution.
The American Revolution is best personified by Jefferson.
His ideal, highly revolutionary indeed, was entirely to in-
cline government, institutions, and laws toward a respect for
man. In contrast to Jefferson, it may be illuminating to draw
the portrait of a different kind of revolutionary, the kind who
instinctively, and also, alas, out of a sense of mission, shapes
men by force to the ideal of revolution. Just as Jefferson was
the theoretician and one of the foremost architects of the
American Revolution, so Saint-Just was the incomparable
theoretician and one of the master architects of the French
Jacobin Revolution. Jefferson wrote the Declaration of Independence; he was a legislator and President of the young
American Republic. Saint-Just called on the Assembly to vote
the death of Louis XVI, and became the "Archangel of the
Terror," before he in turn was sent to the scaffold.

Saint-Just and Jefferson might have met. Jefferson was in
Paris at the time of the Convocation of the States-General.

Doubtless, however, their paths never crossed, for the political career of Saint-Just began somewhat later. A conversation between these two would have been remarkable.

To begin with, it is interesting to observe Jefferson's attitude toward the French Revolution at its start. The American Revolution had already taken place when he was ambassador to Paris, and the fact that it had succeeded endowed him with immense prestige in the eyes of the French. Lafayette and his friends, then leaders of the French revolutionary movement, sought Jefferson's advice. In the conflict which had already set the Assembly against the King, the republican Jefferson advised a compromise—in other words, constitutional monarchy. "I most strongly urged," he wrote, "an immediate compromise, to secure what the government was now ready to yield, and trust to future occasions for what might still be wanting." "The King," he also wrote, "was now become a passive machine in the hands of the National Assembly, and had he been left to himself he would willingly have acquiesced in whatever they should devise as best for the nation." In Jefferson's opinion the King should have been left "with powers so large as to enable him to do all the good of his station, and so limited as to restrain him from its abuse."

Perhaps the most significant difference between the Utopian and the revolutionary is that the revolutionary, in all his calculations, counts with the concrete dimension of time, while the Utopian discounts time altogether. Jefferson's French friends were Utopians, more passionately committed to the *tabula rasa* than to the Revolution. By comparison, Jefferson is like a cautious gardener. He watches the tree of liberty grow. The tree must be pruned here and there; it must have temporary props to support it until it grows tall enough and strong enough to stand alone. But the gardener knows that the seasons cannot be hurried; Jefferson knew that it takes time for a nation to set itself free, truly free, through its own maturing and not just by decree. Needless to say, the French Revolutionaries had no use for this horticultural viewpoint and rejected any compromise whatever.

Looking back much later upon past events, Jefferson attributed the suppression of liberty in France and in Europe, and the quick collapse of the French Revolution, precisely to this disregard for the dimension of time and this refusal to compromise. It is to this same disregard and this same refusal that he attributed the long period of political enslavement which Europe endured first under Napoleon and then under the Holy Alliance. Speaking of Lafayette and his friends, Jefferson wrote, "Events have proved their lamentable error." They had not foreseen, he added, "the melancholy sequel of their well-meant perseverance; that their physical force would be usurped by a first tyrant to trample on the independence and even the existence of other nations." Their lamentable error would "afford a fatal example for the atrocious conspiracy of kings against their people; would generate their unholy and homicide alliance to make common cause among themselves, and to crush by the power of the whole the efforts of any part to moderate their abuse and oppressions."

Jefferson's attitude toward the French Revolution is not as surprising as it is instructive. It furnishes us with an opportunity to study and define more closely the American political character and the precise nature of the compromise which seems to me basic to that character. In Péguy's celebrated juxtaposing of mysticism to politics, a passage so certain to arouse youth's enthusiasm, he valiantly defends mysticism. But I am no longer so sure that he was altogether right. A close examination of the great catastrophes, the hideous abortions of history, seems to indicate that those cataclysms which most profoundly affected the destiny of peoples were brought about by the introduction of the laws of mysticism into the political order. What is the first law of mysticism, from which all others stem? Essentially, it is the *todo y nada* of Saint John of the Cross, the law of all-or-nothing. And it is also the law of Utopia.

Mystical life has always been defined as the reciprocity of love between God and his creatures. By its very nature, love already tends to be totalitarian; he who is loved more is more loved than all the rest put together. But with God this totalitarianism is carried to its farthest limit. Since God is not only the Creator of everything that lives but is also in Himself the plenitude of being and of intensity in being, He takes the place of all; to possess Him is to consider all else as nothing. "I am That Which is and thou art that which is not," Christ said to Saint Catherine of Siena. Here is the all and the nothing. The most mystical of the saints possessed this sense of the absolute and of nothingness to the highest degree. But whatever is human, and in general whatever is created, is relative, is comparative, belongs to the vast realm of evaluations, distinctions, and successive grades of importance. Human values are not constant; even in relation to God they tend to increase or decrease in importance. And it is to this human realm that politics belongs.

I do not deny that really great statesmen are also mystics, as, for example, Saint Louis and Abraham Lincoln. I do not deny that all great revolutionary movements are inspired by a mystical purpose, as, for example, "liberty or death." But when great statesmen are working within a political framework they obey the law of politics which is the law of the concretely possible. Their greatness is only that they have a more profound awareness of the possible, or rather that, with their determination and their infallible intuition, they themselves make many things possible which all the others considered impossible. Who, for instance, in 1940, would coldly have estimated that France was one day to play its part in the victory? De Gaulle never doubted it, any more than Joan of Arc

ever doubted that the Dauphin would be crowed at Rheims.
And among revolutions, those which have succeeded are the
ones that have been served by statesmen who, while never
abandoning the mystical ideal of their Revolution, still kept
their sense of the possible. The great, successful revolutions
preserved, transformed, created, even more than they destroyed. Such was the American Revolution, and such was
Jefferson, who served it.

By instinct and reason both, Jefferson detested the all-or-
nothing principle in politics. He was in no sense a Utopian.
He was a clear-sighted and effective revolutionary who sought
to advance the cause of freedom. An abyss lay between him
and the New England Pilgrims, although both he and they
were inspired by the same ideal. But time had indeed passed,
and that ideal was no longer a Utopia; it had entered into the
flesh and the bloodstream of a whole people—symbolized by
that veteran of Concord who had always governed himself.

Jefferson knew that whatever is human must also be temporary, fragile, relative. He knew that his country was no
longer a *tabula rasa* and that when every stick and stone
of an old house is taken away before the new house has been
erected to replace it, those who live there may well find themselves with only the sky for a roof, at the mercy of thieves
and murderers, not to speak of the rain and the cold. He
knew also that the impossibility of achieving immediate perfection in human affairs often creates a void which is then
filled by the greatest follies. Unable to achieve the all, one
creates the nothing, and it is in this nihilism that tyranny
flourishes and men are sacrificed. It is remarkable that, out
of all modern revolutions, the American Revolution is the
only one which has surrendered nothing to this nihilism, to
the insane mysticism of "the Nothing" and "the Infinite." It
is not improbable that, if Jefferson's advice had been heeded,
the French Revolution would have been as successful as the
American. But who was there to heed him? This cautious

gardener, this friend of man and of man's concrete freedoms, was speaking to the French revolutionaries who were, alas, mystics in politics, impassioned devotees of a Utopian republic and even of that *tabula rasa* which was to be called the Terror.

The pronouncements of Saint-Just must be read to be believed. Poor Saint-Just, he too thought he loved liberty, yet he spoke of it as a yoke: "When the factions are crushed, they will be forced to pass beneath the yoke of liberty." Saint-Just thought he loved mankind, yet on a mission to Strasbourg he ordered the mass arrest of all suspects and when it was brought to his attention that he had undoubtedly imprisoned many innocent people among the guilty, he replied, "You may be right about a few of them, but there is grave danger and we do not know where to strike. Now, when a blind man is looking for a pin in a heap of dust, he gathers up the whole heap." But that "dust" was men and women, French, like Saint-Just himself. He was a mystic. "In revolution," he kept repeating, "there can be no half-measures." And there he was, completely enmeshed in the horrible dialectic of all-or-nothing. He loved a liberty that was too perfect to be anything but Utopian. He wanted the French to be so perfect that they could not, and never would, exist except in his own ideal. We are continually told that vice corrupts society, and this is true. But fanatic love of virtue has done more to damage men and destroy societies than all the vices put together. "Laws take the place of God," wrote Saint-Just. "They must make everything conform to morality, including themselves." Again the yoke, always the yoke upon the neck of mankind! It is exceedingly childish to try to convince us that terrorists are vicious; they are usually fanatical addicts of virtue, of a special kind of virtue. Neither Saint-Just nor Lenin was vicious. Even Hitler had his own ideal of virtue—the purity of the Germanic race. Someone heard Saint-Just say, "A nation can regenerate itself only upon mounds of

corpses." He used the word "regeneration" in the same sense
that his compatriot Calvin had used it. Saint-Just was a mystic in politics; and the mounds of corpses were there only as
the inevitable result of regeneration and of virtue triumphant. It was Saint-Just who obtained the death sentence of
the King. "It is impossible to reign innocently," he said. "As
for me, I see no middle ground. That man must either reign
or die." And again, "Someday people will be surprised that
the eighteenth century was less advanced than the time of
Caesar. Then, the tyrant was struck down in full view of the
Senate, with no other formality than twenty-five thrusts of
the dagger and no other law than the liberty of Rome." He
did not see a middle ground; he never saw a middle ground,
any more than St. John of the Cross saw it in the mysticism
of the holocaust. But in the realm of politics these words and
this attitude are horrible.

Saint-Just created as much of a *tabula rasa* as Descartes. He
refused to keep anything of the past. Everything was to start
with him. "Every other art has produced wonders. But the
art of government has produced nothing but monsters." Oh,
how French was this Frenchman. . . . He was a purist in
politics as Racine was a purist in his tragedies; as Mallarmé,
who had a Jacobin forebear, was a purist in defending the
purity of poetry; as Cézanne was a purist in sacrificing everything to the purity of his painting. "What makes a Republic," Saint-Just said, "is the total destruction of whatever
stands in its way." Jefferson's proposal to keep the King on
his throne with limited powers, as a concrete step to further
the liberties of the French people, would have roused the indignation of that purist, Saint-Just, as the poetry of the Par-
nassians was to rouse the indignation of Mallarmé.

Herein lies the error. The artist is master of his material;
indeed he is an artist only to the degree that he masters it. In
this same sense, Cézanne said that what makes painting is the
total elimination of everything that is not color. No one can

deny that France has carried to a pinnacle of excellence all the laws of art. What are these laws of art? They are the laws of absolute purity. It is true that a painter always has too many colors on his palette, a pianist too many notes on his keyboard, a poet too many words in his vocabulary. Saint-Just believed that, to create the masterpiece of a French Republic, there were undoubtedly far too many Frenchmen. Hence the Terror, logical enough in his poetics. "A government has for principle either virtue or Terror. What do they want, who want neither virtue nor Terror?" And again, Saint-Just said, "We know no other way of eliminating evil than that of pitilessly immolating on the tomb of the tyrant all that regrets tyranny, all that might wish to avenge it, and all that would bring it back to life among us." Saint-Just was forever seeking to build his Republic upon virtue in the way Mozart composed his symphonies—by eliminating all false notes. But in the symphony of Saint-Just the false notes were men, and their elimination was accomplished by the blade of the guillotine. From the standpoint of art Saint-Just would have been right. All authentic art is a sacrifice and a choice. The artist is, in the practice of his art, an ascetic continually refining his material, as Saint Jerome continually refined his body by chastising it. Art is made up of auto-da-fé and excommunication; it has its stakes, its scaffolds. In summing up, let us say that the law of all-or-nothing, the *todo y nada,* which holds true in mysticism, also holds true in art, but that in politics it is appalling.

I likened Saint-Just to his compatriot Calvin. I could as well have likened him to Torquemada. Just as much as Utopia and the *tabula rasa,* and for the same reasons, the Inquisition overshadows the modern world. Neither the Communists nor Hitler nor Saint-Just had the same concept of Utopia as Torquemada, and that is the only difference; the purpose never changes—to make a *tabula rasa* on which to build Utopia. "Either Terror or virtue." They did not all have the same ideal of virtue, but all Terrors are strangely alike. In the last analysis, they are all Puritans. "Either virtue or Terror." In the whole history of men and nations, I know of no more perfect epitome of Puritanism than this declaration, and it is a Frenchman whom we have to thank for it. It would have infuriated Jefferson.

By one of those historical paradoxes which it would be impossible to believe if it were not true, France, reputedly the least puritan of nations, was the most puritan of all in its Revolution. America, on the other hand, founded by the Puritans, and still bearing upon its ideas and ways of life the weight of Puritanism, made the most human, the least puritan revolution of all. Perhaps all nations, all, without exception, bear upon their bodies this suppurating wound of puritanism, but their puritanism is not always expressed in the same way. That France is purist in art constitutes its glory; in this, France sets a great example. But that France was so totally puritan in its Revolution is a great misfortune. That America is puritan in its ways and ideas is also no doubt a misfortune. But that America was so little puritan, so human, so wisely human in its Revolution constitutes its glory; this is the example that America has set. And in great part, it is Jefferson whom America has to thank for it.

In my portrait of Saint-Just, I do not think I have let myself be carried away by the temptations of system and analogy. Saint-Just spoke of the Republic as Saint Augustine or Saint Ignatius spoke of the Church Triumphant juxtaposed with Hell. And the role of Saint-Just, as he saw it, was to make sure that the Church triumphed and that Hell was filled. "As for you," he said to the Convention, "destroy the opposition, mold liberty in bronze. Avenge the patriots, victims of intrigue. Make sure that there is no single unfortunate, no single poor man left in the State. Only at this price will you have made a Revolution and a true Republic. Besides, who would thank you for the misfortune of the good and the good fortune of the wicked?" There he was, taking on the responsibility of saving the good and punishing the wicked, like God the Father carved on the portals of a cathedral, separating the sheep from the goats on judgment day. For Saint-Just there were only heroes and villains, the heroes all white, the villains all black, as in a Western. And who would dare claim to be all white in the eyes of such an inquisitor? At the end everyone was black except Saint-Just himself. Speaking directly to God, Saint-Just was to cry out, "God, Protector of innocence and truth, since Thou hast brought me face to face with a few corrupt men, it was no doubt to unmask them." Saint-Just was the chosen, the predestined, charged with the mission to purify the world.

In James Hogg's extraordinary novel about Scotch Puritanism, called *The Private Memoirs and Confessions of a Justified Sinner,* which André Gide so admired, the author introduces us to a hero as like Saint-Just as a brother. The hero is dedicated to God by his tutor, and these are the words the tutor uses: "Lord, I give him into Thy hands, as a captain putteth his sword into the hands of his sovereign, wherewith to lay waste his enemies. May he be a two-edged sword in Thy hand and a spear coming out of Thy mouth to destroy, to overcome, to pass over; and may the enemies of Thy Church fall down before him, and be as dung to fat the land." The hero of the novel is delighted with this strange dedication. "From that moment," he said, "I conceived it decreed, not that I should be a minister of the Gospel, but a champion of it, to cut off the enemies of the Lord from the face of the earth; and I rejoiced in the commission, finding it more congenial to my nature to be cutting sinners off with the sword than to be haranguing them from the pulpit." And it happens that the hero is further confirmed in this marvelous mission by a strange companion who says to him, "Thou art called to a high vocation, to cleanse the sanctuary of thy God in this thy native land by the shedding of blood; go thou then like a ruling energy, a master spirit of desolation in the dwellings of the wicked, and high shall be your reward both here and hereafter."

Why is it again Saint-Just who said, "Nothing so resembles virtue as a great crime?" These words could have been engraved below the title of James Hogg's novel, so perfectly do they sum up the novel's action and spirit. And at the end, the hero discovers, too late to escape, that his faithful companion who so strongly exhorts him in his mission is none other than the Devil. James Hogg never actually calls him the Devil, but he is easily recognized by the fact that he exhorts only to crime while he speaks only of virtue. But then, did Saint-Just himself perhaps also have a companion? And who was this companion of the Archangel of the Terror? The countenance of Antichrist will also be austere and he too will speak the language of virtue.

9

Sparta, Rome, the Land of Cockaigne, or Tartary

In France, as well as in America, all the revolutionaries claimed to have drawn their inspiration from the ideal of political liberty established by the first Roman Republic. Saint-Just wrote, "There has been nothing in the world since the Romans; they live on in our memory and still herald liberty." These are admirable words, but in my opinion they apply far better to the American than to the Jacobin Revolution. Plainly it is America which took up again the tradition of political freedom symbolized by Rome.

There are other symbols besides Rome. Danton despised the political puritanism of Saint-Just. "I dislike that eccentric," Danton is said to have scoffed. "He wants to give us the Republic of Sparta, when what we need is the Republic of Cockaigne." It is not hard to understand what Danton meant, or to see that the Third French Republic was much closer to Danton's concept than to that of Saint-Just. The French Republic is not a Roman Republic; it swings back and forth between the system of Terror and no system at all, between Sparta and Cockaigne.

Saint-Just made another remark of prophetic import: "Revolutionaries must be Romans and not Tartars." Sparta or Cockaigne, Rome or Tartary—these symbolic concepts sum up the political history of the West in the last two centuries. As for the Tartar Revolution, we have seen it with our own eyes. Since October 1917, it has encroached upon a large part of the world; it has made Sparta and the Terror its own; everywhere it threatens Cockaigne; it challenges Rome itself.

Effective as symbols are, however, let us leave them now. The world has just lived through the two most extraordinary centuries in the history of politics. Every conceivable experiment has been made and carried to its ultimate conclusion with the beautiful abstract logic of the parabola.

On the one hand, there is the introduction of the laws of mysticism into politics, the *todo y nada,* which has led straight to the *tabula rasa* and to nihilism. Totalitarian Utopia crushes man to extinction. Saint-Just expressed this historical development of Utopia perfectly when he said, "It is in the nature of things for our economic affairs to become more and more embroiled until the Republic, once established, takes over all operations, all interests, all rights, all obligations, and imposes a common pattern on all parts of the State." Much as he might protest that he was following in the footsteps of Rome, it was for Hegel, Marx, Lenin, Hitler, and Stalin that he paved the way; he was the prophet of Tartary. Sovereignty, to Saint-Just, was no longer in the people and in the free expression of popular will. According to him, all power resided in the laws "which take the place of God," in other words, in an abstract political system to which individuals and peoples are sacrificed.

"When the Republic, once established, takes over all operations, all interests, all rights, all obligations." These words embody a terrible concept; never has the leveling process of totalitarianism been more accurately described. Marx, Lenin, the assiduous dunce who wrote *Mein Kampf,* and Stalin, were to create infinite variations on this same theme, each in his own language and with his own particular pedantry, but without contributing anything essential. It was inside a shapely French head, becurled and powdered, that the perfect modern totalitarian monster was conceived. Henceforth it was no longer to be a question of understanding, respecting, and serving nature and man, but rather of transforming nature, human nature included, and making it conform, if necessary by force, to a Utopia. The monstrousness of this beautiful system lies in the fact that it is a system. With all the dialectical reasoning you please; with all the philosophical, economic, social, nationalist, and internationalist explanations you please; with all the puritanical justifications and all the appeals to virtue you please; with all the aesthetic subtleties you please; with all the scientific integrity you please—we still recognize the ideal of that first Jacobin Republic which was to take over all operations, all interests, all rights, and all obligations; we know it in its final form, we have seen it with our own eyes. It is the concentration-camp society with its crematory ovens which burn men alive as Bernard Palissy burned his furniture—to complete an experiment.

And now on the other hand . . . well, on the other hand, there is Jefferson's republic. But Jefferson's republic is harder to talk about precisely because it is not a system and can therefore be defined only by its absolute, its unconditional, its stubborn preference for man, for concrete men of flesh and blood, as against any political system whatever, no matter how theoretically perfect.

But this in no way obscures Jefferson's thought. For him it was a universal law that political systems, all political systems, have an unfortunate tendency to betray the people's trust and enslave them. Reversing the process whereby the law assumes the innocence of an individual until it can prove his guilt, Jefferson would willingly have held every government guilty of tyranny until it had given incontrovertible proof of its innocence. It can be said of a republic, however, that it is still the political system most likely to prove, from time to time, once in a great while, an exception to this universal law of guilt and tyranny. From time to time, once in a great while, the people in republics express their opinions freely, are spared betrayal and deception, obtain what they seek. It can be said that the republican system, instead of always having to conform to what is popularly called today historical determinism, has more chance than any other system of escaping it. But even of this we are less sure today than Jefferson.

If Jefferson was republican, his was not the same kind of republicanism as that of Saint-Just—or of the Soviet Republics. He was republican because he believed that a republic could best respect and accommodate the freedoms of the individual. But his only true concern was for liberty itself and men's enjoyment of it. A totalitarian republic would have nauseated him; he would have settled instead, and without hesitation, for a constitutional monarch. Those formulas of Saint-Just—"As for me, I see no middle ground"; "In Revolution, there can be no half-measures"; "That man must reign or die"—would have struck Jefferson as murderous stupidities. He would have found them stupid because they reveal a blind and wholly Utopian trust in a given governmental system; murderous because they lead to the mass sacrifice of all who disagree. It is with such formulas that Hitler rid himself of the Jews, and Stalin of the "deviationists" and the "bourgeois."

This does not mean, however, that Jefferson's republic was puny and effete. He was well aware that man's liberty must be defended if it is to endure, and that when it is lacking it must be seized, if necessary by force of arms. A Republic of Cockaigne would have seemed to him fated to mediocrity, and ultimately to enslavement. He was no pacifist, even in domestic politics. He believed that the right of rebellion was sacred, that it must not be allowed to atrophy, and that it must always be exercised. "I like a little rebellion now and then," he wrote. "The spirit of resistance to government is so valuable on certain occasions that I wish it to be always kept alive. It will often exercise when wrong, but better so than not to be exercised at all." And again: "If the happiness of the mass of people can be secured at the expense of a little tempest now and then, or even of a little blood, it will be a precious purchase. *Malo libertatem periculosam quam quietem servitutem.*" Jefferson well knew that liberty is always dangerous and he liked it the way it is.

It is needless to stress that this attitude reveals not the slightest leaning toward Terror. Terror is a system of government. But rebellion, as sanctioned by Jefferson, is directed against government. Its whole purpose is to provide an escape from any political system attempting to put men beneath its yoke.

We always come back to the fact that in Jefferson's mind the mortal enemies of liberty were not this or that particular form of government, as he made clear in the advice he gave Lafayette. They were not even inherent in the colonial system. He would have been quite willing to stay within the British Empire, providing the London government had respected the traditional freedoms of the colonies.

Much later, toward the end of his life, Jefferson expressed, on the future of South America, a view the perspicacity of which no one can fail to admire. This view still helps us to understand what is happening today and what will be happening tomorrow in many parts of the world, in Asia, Africa, or the Near East. "I wish I could give better hopes to our southern brethren. The achievement of their independence of Spain is no longer a question. But it is a very serious one, what will become of them? Ignorance and bigotry, like other insanities, are incapable of self-government. They will fall under military despotism, and become the murderous tools of their respective Bonapartes." What Jefferson prophesied became the history of South America for a century, and will be the history of one nation after another across the world as they shake off the colonial yoke. God knows how many Bonapartes, Hitlers, and Stalins of every hue we see emerging today, all of them anti-colonialists, all of them nationalists, all of them admirers of Jefferson's Declaration of Independence, not one single word of which they understand. The time must not come when we weary of underscoring the difference between the transition from the colonial state to that of an independent nation, and the much more significant and profoundly revolutionary idea implicit in Jefferson's Declaration of Independence.

Jefferson spoke of ignorance and bigotry and other insanities. Among these was the well-intentioned but Utopian stubbornness of Lafayette and his friends. All his life Jefferson fought these insanities, in the defense of liberty and self-government. This was why he placed so great an emphasis upon education. He had learned that everything can turn into fanaticism; today we know it even better. We know that religion can turn into fanaticism, as it did with Torquemada; we know that love of liberty can turn into fanaticism, as it did with Saint-Just; we know that love of a race, of a nation, of a class, can turn into fanaticism.

Life sometimes shows an extraordinary perception of the laws of tragedy by undertaking to round out a conspicuous destiny with a fitting end. We know what happened to Saint-Just. He went to the guillotine to which he had sent Danton, thus consigning to the same executioner's basket the Republic of Sparta and the Republic of Cockaigne. The executioner gave the Paris mob one final look at that graceful and bloodied head which had conceived the puritan, the totalitarian Republic.

Jefferson's epilogue, as tragic as the most terrifying Shakespeare, was staged only after his death. I shall now quote word for word a well-informed man whose integrity is unimpeachable. That man is Alexander Ross, a Canadian who held responsible posts in his own country and was moreover a personal friend of Abraham Lincoln, for whom he performed a number of services. In his *Memoirs* he wrote:

> Thomas Jefferson, the author of the Declaration of Independence, made a clause to his last will, conferring freedom on his slave offspring, as far as the Slave Code of Virginia permitted him to do it, supplying the lack of power by "humbly imploring the Legislature of Virginia to confirm the bequests with permission to remain in the state, where their families and connections are." Two of his daughters by an octaroon female slave were taken to New Orleans, after Jefferson's death, and sold in the slave market at $1500 each to be used for unmentionable purposes. Both these unfortunate children of the author of the "Declaration of Independence" were quite white, their eyes blue and their hair long, soft, and auburn in color.
>
> Both were highly educated and accomplished. The youngest daughter escaped from her master and committed suicide by drowning herself to escape the horrors of her position.

It is not without immense sorrow that one encounters a fact of this kind in the history of a nation. The deed was even more cowardly, and uglier than the murder of King Edward's children, which at least had the excuse of reasons of State. It was the most horrible justification for Jefferson's instinctive distrust of every governmental system. For there can be no doubt that the deed was done in perfect accord with the laws of Virginia, where men had fought to affirm and defend their natural rights and their freedom. Saint-Just wrote, "The most oppressed of all peoples will be the one oppressed in the name of its own rights. For then the crime of oppression becomes a religion." Jefferson was right. There is no end to the task of winning liberty. The republic his heart envisioned would be in a permanent state of revolution.

10

The Declaration of

Independence

Congress had chosen Jefferson to draw up the Declaration of Independence. Later Jefferson himself explained what he had wanted to achieve in writing this most awe-inspiring document of the American nation. He wrote it without consulting texts, quite obviously all in one breath, as it were, making almost no corrections or deletions. He left it to Congress to make corrections. Jefferson did not seek to be original. He was attuned to his people and he wrote this text in the way a violin, touched off by waves of sound that are attuned to it, will begin to sing of its own accord. Among all the delegates, he had been chosen because he was the most sensitive, because he would faithfully reflect all the currents, all the feelings, all the convictions of the nation and would know how to express them with felicity. These are the very words of John Adams, who tells us that Jefferson had "a peculiar felicity of expression." Jefferson wrote with the same spontaneous and simple impulse that impelled the American militia to fight at Concord.

The Declaration of Independence can be divided into two parts, the first a declaration of political principles, and the second the application of these principles to the historical situation which led to independence. It is only the declaration of principles that concerns us here, since this has permanent value, can be applied to every political situation, and is authentically revolutionary. Here then is the declaration of principles:

When in the Course of human events it becomes necessary for one people to dissolve the political bands which have connected them with another, and to assume among the powers of earth, the separate and equal station to which the Laws of Nature and of Nature's God entitle them, a decent respect to the opinions of mankind requires that they should declare the causes which impel them to the separation.

We hold these truths to be self-evident, that all men are created equal, that they are endowed by their Creator with certain unalienable Rights, that among these are Life, Liberty, and the pursuit of Happiness.

That to secure these rights, Governments are instituted among Men, deriving their just powers from the consent of the governed.

That whenever any Form of Government becomes destructive of these ends, it is the Right of the People to alter or to abolish it, and institute new Government, laying its foundation on such principles and organizing its powers in such form, as to them shall seem most likely to affect their Safety and Happiness. Prudence, indeed, will dictate that Governments long established should not be changed for light and transient causes; and accordingly all experience hath shewn, that mankind are more disposed to suffer, while evils are sufferable, than to right themselves by abolishing the forms to which they are accustomed. But when a long train of abuses and usurpations, pursuing invariably the same object, evinces a design to reduce them under absolute Despotism, it is their right, it is their duty, to throw off such Government, and to provide new Guards for their future security.

There follows a long list of complaints, describing in detail the grievances of the Colonies against England, in which the King of England is assigned the same mythical role as the bourgeoisie was to be assigned in the *Communist Manifesto*. The conclusion of the document is of course not as universally applicable as the declaration of principles.

> We must, therefore, acquiesce in the necessity, which denounces our Separation, and hold them, as we hold the rest of mankind, Enemies in War, in Peace Friends.
>
> We, therefore, the Representatives of the United States of America, in General Congress, Assembled, appealing to the Supreme Judge of the world for the rectitude of our intentions, do, in the Name, and by Authority of the good People of these Colonies, solemnly publish and declare, That these United Colonies are, and of Right ought to be, Free and Independent States; that they are Absolved from all Allegiance to the British Crown, and that all political connection between them and the State of Great Britain, is and ought to be totally dissolved; and that, as Free and Independent States, they have full power to levy War, conclude Peace, contract Alliances, establish Commerce, and do all other Acts and Things which Independent States may of right do.
>
> And for the support of this Declaration, with a firm reliance on the protection of divine Providence, we mutually pledge to each other our Lives, our Fortunes, and our sacred Honor.

Considered apart from its historical context, the Declaration can be summed up as follows: It is God Who created nature, and, in that nature, man. All men are created equal. From that initial equality derive rights and also obligations —obligations which, though not explicitly defined, are yet clearly implied.

The rights come first: life, liberty, and the pursuit of happiness.

The obligations are to God, to Whom, as Creator, we pay religious homage; Who, as Judge, rewards good and punishes evil and, as Providence, directs the whole natural order He created, mankind included, and each individual in that natural order, to a just end. There are also men's obligations to their fellow men, to whom they pay "a decent respect."

All this is established immediately, accepted as self-evident truth, accepted as an order of things that cannot be denied or compromised without grave offense to God and human reason, without unsettling nature itself. All this comes ahead of any political organization. Political organization comes, and can only come, afterwards, and then not to oppose or impede this natural order in any way whatever, but rather to conform to it, to ensure it, to strengthen it, and if necessary to protect it. The validity and the justice of every political system, of all institutions, their essential legitimacy, are thus measured by the degree of their conformity to this unchanging and sacred natural order. The natural order comes first, then the political order, subordinate to the natural order. The political order has no inherent validity. It is valid only to the degree to which it conforms to the natural order.

Therefore, when a political system opposes and jeopardizes the natural order instead of preserving it, there is a sacred right, there is even a religious duty, to alter and to abolish this system.

Since the Declaration is the basis of all American political philosophy, I shall sum it up once more, in other terms, to make sure that its many aspects are clarified.

The whole natural order is created by God, and within that order man himself. Certain fundamental and inalienable rights of man derive from it: life, liberty, and the pursuit of happiness. In the exercise of these rights, man need account only to God, Creator and hence Providence and Judge of all nature and of man himself.

In order that these rights may be better exercised, the whole political order is created by men, for men, to serve men. Man is above the political order, as God is above the natural order. Since it is man who is the creator of the whole political order, he is in turn its providence and its supreme judge. Man may delegate the right to govern, but it is first and foremost to men that governments have obligations; it is to men that governments are accountable.

To reverse this political order, to enslave men rather than to serve them, to transform into absolute despotism the power they originally delegated, is an offense against the whole natural order, against all humanity, against God Himself; it is blasphemy. In such case, resistance and rebellion are more than a right; they are a duty and a religious obligation.

An analysis of the Declaration of Independence reveals extremely distinctive features, above all its essentially religious character. I use the word religious; I do not use the word ecclesiastical. There is no reference in the Declaration to revelation of any kind, no reference even to the Bible or to that Christianity with which nevertheless America is so deeply imbued. The Declaration is not at all in the spirit of Bossuet—"a political concept drawn from Scripture." Still less, of course, is there reference in it to any church whatever. It is entirely concerned with nature, with God, the Author of nature, and with self-evident truths. It follows then that it is God, and God alone, Who, as Creator, establishes men's equality with one another and guarantees the inalienability of their rights and the validity of their governments. Without this foundation in God, Creator, Providence, and Judge, everything—the political order, the fundamental rights, men's equality with one another, and ultimately all political justice—crumbles. When I say that the Declaration has an essentially religious character, it is to underline its emphasis upon the fact that the whole political and social order depends by its very nature upon the sovereignty of God, and is a participation in God's rule over nature.

The Declaration is also essentially democratic. All power and all political justice reside first in the people themselves. This means that governments either represent the popular will and consent or they are not legitimate. On this point it is most interesting to note that the Declaration, though never vague, keeps to general principles. It is not a strictly republican Declaration. It rises above all political systems (republic, aristocracy, monarchy) to define political legitimacy. In fact, the Declaration nowhere even indirectly suggests that there was ever a time when the King's authority over the Colonies had been illegitimate. In breaking with England the Colonies were not breaking with their past. The young American nation could always turn back to its past and look at it without shame. Even under the authority of the Kings of England and within the union of Empire, it had never been a slave. That very authority of the Kings of England had always stemmed only and exclusively from the consent of their subjects. Once the subjects withdrew this consent, the authority over them ceased to exist.

A few years later, in France, the Jacobin Grégoire was to declare the opposite: "Kings, in the moral order, are what monsters are in the physical order, and the history of Kings is nothing but the martyrology of nations." For a nation which has lived through long centuries under the rule of monsters, there can therefore only be shame. The French Revolution deliberately imposed on France a complex of shame with regard to its past and its infancy as serious as the worst neuroses described by psychoanalysis. The Russian Revolution has also insisted on a total break with Russia's past, and that decision will go on weighing upon the nation's destiny for a long time to come. The American revolutionaries were much wiser.

But whatever may be said about the legitimacy of all other political systems—a legitimacy which the American Declaration does not question—it is very evident that so precise an affirmation of men's equality with one another, of the people as the primary seat of political power, and therefore of the essentially delegated and representative character of all political power, constituted an urgent demand for the actual establishment of government by representation, for a democratic society, and ultimately for a republican form of government.

At this point it becomes more and more clear that the American political ideal is a republic which recognizes only God as higher than the dispersed but solidly entrenched authority of a nation of citizens. It shows how the tradition of the first New England Puritans, enriched and matured, had perpetuated itself.

The word "fraternity" does not appear. But the affirmation of God as Creator, Providence, and Judge, and of the universal equality of men with one another implies fraternity. The Declaration defines the essential obligations of that fraternity: "a decent respect" for the opinion of others, and —since men's interests do not always coincide—in peace, friendship; in war, enmity.

A further characteristic of the Declaration I would like to call political relativity. Political reality and political power never are, and never can become, absolutes. Their validity is entirely relative, first to God and the natural order, then to men; they are justifiable only as they serve men and as men consent to them. The Declaration of Independence is not lacking in eloquence; but it is totally devoid of ideological fanaticism, empty abstractions, all excess. Just as it takes care not to make a *tabula rasa* of the past, so it also refrains from making a heaven of Utopia. Here, perhaps, is where it is at its most revolutionary. If Jefferson had been asked which comes first, the nation or its citizens, the question would not have made sense to him. And, in fact, it makes no sense. A nation does not exist apart from the men who constitute it; it is they who create it by the continual renewal of their mutual consent; it is they who stand guard over it; they are its judges as they are its witnesses. The nation is created by them and for them, not they for the nation. Men come first, before the nation. The mere fact of declaring independence creates a nation. The Declaration of Independence, as such, and because it is one, is also a declaration of national unity, and that unity is based upon a mutual pledge: "We mutually pledge to each other our Lives, our Fortunes, and our sacred Honor." Free, always and wholly dependent on consent, this community of lives, fortunes, and sacred honor —this, and only this, is a nation. Upon due consideration, it is much, but it is in no sense an idol to be worshiped.

The sentence inscribed on the wall by the French Convention as a preamble to The Declaration of the Rights of Man and of the Citizen—"The citizen is born, lives, and dies for his country"—is blasphemy; it is a profession of idolatry in the sense that it endows something created and created by man—the nation—with divine right over the individual. The American Declaration of Independence is at the other extreme from such idolatry. According to this Declaration man is born, lives, and dies free, created by God for happiness; he lives and dies under God's Providence, awaiting His judgment. The Declaration does not define the happiness for which man is created. Each must seek it as his heart dictates. What seems to me most admirable, most priceless, most true, and also boldest, is that equality and liberty are bestowed from the start, at each man's birth, together with life itself. It is not the nation that bestows them, but God, and He bestows them without discrimination, upon the wicked and the good alike, as He bestows His sunlight and His rain. It is only in order to make more sure of these primary, elemental values that men create nations; it is only to preserve these fundamental and inalienable rights that nations are born and live. Nations die when, instead of preserving these rights, they abandon or violate them. This is exactly what the Americans had seen happening. England died as their mother country when it failed to respect their innate rights. The American nation was born and endures to protect these rights, to respect them, and to make them respected.

Last of the essential rights of man listed in the Declaration is the right to the pursuit of happiness. The Declaration does not say "the right to happiness." Here again it sounds that characteristic note of relativity and restraint, so contrary to all Utopias. Though men are alive, equal, free by right of birth, their happiness is not a birthright; yet all men desire happiness and they have the right to desire it. The nation cannot bestow happiness, but is there to help men pursue it. Whenever the common good of a nation becomes no more than the sum of individual ills, the very idea of a nation is betrayed.

Nations, however, created and constituted by men and for men, have rights of their own: the right to war or peace, to commerce, to alliances, and above all to equality of rank among other nations. And men also have duties to their nations. So that nations may safeguard their peoples, men sacrifice to them, when the need arises, their fortunes and their lives. It is upon this willingness to sacrifice that the unity and the strength of a nation are founded. It is this willingness to sacrifice, not strength or wealth, that gives a nation equality of rank and honor with the others.

But men not only have duties to their nation. They also have a right, a terrible right, and it too is imprescriptible. It is the right to rebellion. On this subject the Declaration shows a certain tempered humanity which is perhaps insufficiently noted. The Declaration recognizes the influence of custom, traditionally one of the most vital and legitimate sources of justice and the law. It qualifies with prudence the

right to rebellion. It takes into consideration the fact that
men's suffering, endurance, and patience are also political
realities. But it affirms that limits to this patience must be
set, since there is a point where patience becomes nothing
but cowardice, and endurance dishonor. When these limits
are surpassed, rebellion is the most sacred obligation of all:
"liberty or death."

Such is the American Declaration of Independence and
national unity. This first analysis of the famous document
already shows how vast, how concretely human, how firmly
balanced was the political concept of Jefferson and his peers.
Now we must go on to study its historical context and then
its prophetic and revolutionary significance.

11

Congress and the Declaration

Jefferson was lucky with his style, but perhaps even more lucky with his ideas. The analysis of his philosophy leads to a disillusion amounting almost to dismay. Jefferson had the ideas of his century, and though it called itself the century of philosophers it was certainly not the century of philosophy. Philosophy, having spread into every field, had lost all distinction, and even its identity. Newton was considered a great philosopher. Franklin spoke of his discoveries in electricity as though they were discoveries in philosophy.

The philosophy of the eighteenth century, over-confident and greedy, considered itself the complete opposite of medieval alchemy, but these opposites have a family resemblance. Alchemy sought to master nature by the application —outside its proper sphere—of the purely philosophical principle of Aristotle's theory of matter and form. Eighteenth-century philosophy claimed that it could understand, explain, and dispel all mysteries by the application—outside their proper sphere—of the purely rational principles of Newtonian mechanics or, still worse, of Rousseauesque sentimentality. The universe was nothing but an immense mechanism, though certainly a very complicated one, and God was nothing but the Watchmaker. What could be more reassuring? By hard work, concentration, patience, and the strict application of already proven laws, man would move ahead step by step and eventually come to understand the infinite complexities of the machine. Once he understood it, he would control it. The skill of the Watchmaker was of course admired, but what God was in Himself and what He might have to say to us was not, after all, very interesting. In His creation, in nature, He had said once and for all everything that could possibly interest us. Perhaps some day, when men knew as much about all the workings of the machine as God, it might even be possible to do without Him altogether. Since, according to the Gospel of Jean-Jacques, no one doubted the inherent and fundamental goodness of man, man had only to know nature better and better in order to become more and more divine. Evil was only a temporary disorder in the mechanism; therefore things could be set right as soon as the faulty gears were located. With evil eliminated, suffering would soon be eliminated too, and perhaps even death itself.

This philosophy, crude, blustering, slothful, uttering the most unpardonable lies, since it awakened hopes it would not fulfill and made promises it could not keep, was the philosophy of a century that prided itself on being the Age of Enlightenment. Prevalent in France, England, and all Europe, this philosophy was to dominate the nineteenth century. It was, alas, the philosophy of educated people in America as well. Reread Thomas Paine and Benjamin Franklin; reflect upon the strange remark that Jefferson himself once made—"Why should I go in search of Moses to find out what God said to Jean-Jacques Rousseau?"—and you will realize that the signers of the Declaration of Independence, or at least those of them with a superior education, and especially Jefferson, were intoxicated by this fashionable philosophy. It is on account of the handicap of their philosophical background that I say these men were lucky, because, beyond shadow of doubt, they were far better than their philosophy; because in their character, in their thinking as Americans, they were far better than when they thought in the European style of the day; because the Declaration of Independence is far more the product of their character and temperament—in short, of a national tradition—than it is the product of their philosophy.

A comparison of Jefferson's rough draft with the final text as voted by Congress illustrates and confirms what I am trying to say. For purposes of critical interpretation, nothing speaks as eloquently as corrections on a text. The chief corrections made by the Congress, those worth noting because they profoundly affect the meaning of the Declaration, concern God and slavery. Among the complaints listed in the Declaration, Jefferson had included a long paragraph on slavery in the Colonies, blaming England. Congress, yielding to the Southern delegates, struck this out. On the other hand, it inserted several extremely significant references to God. Without making too extensive a comparison, let us look at Jefferson's wording and then at the wording of the Congress, on this most important of points.

Jefferson: "We hold these truths as self-evident, that all men are created equal and independent; that from the equal creation they derive rights, inherent and unalienable, among which are the preservation of life, liberty, and the pursuit of happiness."

Congress: "We hold these truths to be self-evident, that all men are created equal, that they are endowed by their Creator with certain unalienable rights, that among these are Life, Liberty, and the pursuit of Happiness."

Jefferson: "We, therefore, the representatives of the United States of America, in General Congress, Assembled, do, in the name and by the authority of the good people of these States . . ."

Congress: "We, therefore, the Representatives of the United States of America, in General Congress, Assembled, appealing to the Supreme Judge of the world for the rectitude of our intentions, do, in the Name and by the Authority of the good people of these Colonies . . ."

Jefferson: "And for the support of this declaration, we mutually pledge to each other our lives, our fortunes, and our sacred honor."

Congress: "And for the support of this Declaration, with a firm reliance on the protection of divine Providence, we mutually pledge to each other our Lives, our Fortunes, and our sacred Honor."

There is no doubt in my mind that Congress and Jefferson had different concepts of God, and a serious difference on such a point as this implies two profoundly divergent philosophies. While it is true that Jefferson made a reference, at the start of his own text, to "Nature's God" which Congress left as it was, this reference did not commit him to much. Nature's God, in the context of the reigning rationalism, which was also Jefferson's, remained as mistily, as vaguely defined as possible, like Rousseau's God in the *Vicaire Savoyard*, like Voltaire's Great Watchmaker, the God grotesquely endowed by the French Declaration of the Rights of Man, and later by Robespierre, with the title of Supreme Being.

Obviously, too, neither the reigning philosophy of the day nor his own attitude inclined Jefferson to recognize God as personal and distinct from nature; as Creator, Providence, and Judge; as the absolute Master of history, Who has always governed and always will govern the world here below, in His utter wisdom and efficacity. The American Congress admired Jefferson's skill with the pen but did not accept his philosophy. Doubtless most of the members of that Congress had not read Rousseau; Moses and Jesus meant more to them.

They had read the Bible and they believed in it. In the end, these were the men who determined the character of the Declaration, and even its philosophy. The Congress was in the tradition of the first New England Puritans, and in the Declaration this tradition prevailed over the philosophy of the period.

The greatest luck of all for the Declaration was precisely the divergence and the compromise between the Puritan tradition and what Jefferson wrote. Had the Declaration been written in the strictly Puritan tradition it would probably not have managed to avoid an aftertaste of theocracy and religious fanaticism. Had it been written from the standpoint of the lax philosophy of that day, it would have been a-religious, if not actually offensive to Christians.

The only conclusion to draw from all this is that one must take the American Declaration as it is, without trying to find for it an explanation or an immediate justification in the philosophical context of its time; it must be viewed as a more profound accomplishment. It is in no sense a corollary or a conclusion; it is a prophetic and revolutionary beginning. Like the great masterpieces of art, in which luck is strangely fused with genius, it radiates its own irrefutable light.

12

The American
Revolution

The Declaration of Independence actually expressed the American people as a whole, the nation, even more than it did the American elite. The American Revolution was not made by an elite or a minority; it was not an indoor revolution, sprung full-blown from one man's brain, like the philosophical revolution created by Descartes as he sat by his stove or the social revolution planned by Marx as he sat in his London attic. It was an outdoor revolution, a hardy plant springing up from a seed that God had sown. Since the political sovereignty of the people derives from God, and revolution is the ultimate expression of that sovereignty, all authentic revolution, though it too derives from God, originates in the people and can be carried out only by them.

I say the people; for it is the people who make revolutions, not the kings, not the ecclesiastical bodies, not the philosophers, not the intellectuals. Revolution, of course, excludes none of them. All of them can perfectly well use their powers to support revolutions and upon occasion have done so, but their support has never been of primary importance. Since it is the people who make revolutions, a revolution, to be valid, must be made not only with the people but by them. A revolution against the people will always be a fraud, a betrayal, and a defilement of the terrible majesty of revolution.

Revolution, like so many other Western concepts, comes to us from the Judeo-Christian tradition. It is a transposition to the sphere of politics of what the ancient Jews called the Apocalypse. We must therefore rid ourselves of any hasty, preconceived notion of the Apocalypse and define its exact historical meaning. By Apocalypse the Jews meant both the fulfillment and the end of a world, an era, a cycle, and at the same time the dawn of a new order, a new world, a new era, a new cycle. Apocalypse has three essential elements—a fulfillment, an end, and a beginning. Christianity, always so insistent upon its links with Israel, constitutes, in its relation to Israel, a truly Apocalyptic event. For Christianity fulfilled the prophecies, abolished the ancient law, and established the new law, the law of grace. In the same way, in politics, revolution abolishes the old regime, fulfills an ancient and a latent desire, inaugurates a new order and a new hope. To judge a revolution and determine how radical it is in character, as well as whether it will be beneficent or fatal in effect, the following questions must be asked:

Does what it accomplishes deserve to be defended and completed?

Does what it abolishes deserve to be abolished? Does it perhaps abolish too much, or not enough?

Is the hope it inaugurates justified? Is this hope lofty enough, universal enough? Does the revolution expand rather than narrow man's destiny?

What the American Revolution accomplishes

Nothing in the West is as old as the tradition of political freedom. This tradition, come down to us from the Roman Republic and the Greek republics, has suffered many assaults across the centuries, but even when most cruelly betrayed in practice it has survived in theory almost uninterruptedly, through declarations of principle, teachings of the scholars, and literature. Originally it was believed that even the power of emperors and kings was delegated by the people. At the beginning of the third century the great Roman jurist Ulpian, no doubt anxious to prevent any interruption of legitimacy between the ancient Roman Republic and the Empire, explained, *"Quod Principi placuit, legis habet vigorem, utpote cum populus . . . Ei et in Eum omne suum imperium et potestatem conferat."* "What has pleased the Prince has the force of law, since the people have vested in him and devolved upon him their own sovereignty and power." It is therefore the people who are originally vested with political sovereignty, since it is they who can delegate it. To Ulpian, as to Jefferson, it was self-evident that "the justice of political power derives from the consent of the governed."

Some centuries later, Pope Gregory the Great pointed out that the difference between the Emperor and the barbarian kings lay in the fact that one governed free men while the others ruled over slaves. Early in the eleventh century Saint Peter Damian, Bishop of Gubbio, an austere man in whom there was surely no trace of what we would call today a "liberal," wrote his matchless formula:

> *Potestas est in Populo*
> *A Summo data Domino.*

"All political sovereignty derives from God, but resides essentially in the people." This formula was restated in approximately the same words on October 2, 1945, by Pope Pius XII. "The people themselves hold the original title to civil power which derives from God."

Saint Peter Damian's formula dates back, I repeat, to the start of the eleventh century. It seems to me to have epitomized, in advance, the Declaration of Independence, which reaffirms that there is no political legitimacy except in the consent of the governed and also that God is Creator, Providence, and Judge of mankind and of the world. The American Declaration follows the true course of a tradition, and it is the most ancient, the most venerable tradition in the political thinking of the West, since it is linked to Judeo-Christian Revelation with its concept of God, and to Rome and to Greek philosophy, with their concepts of the city state and of man. The quest for a philosophy that can explain the Declaration of Independence leads far beyond the mediocre philosophy of the eighteenth century, even beyond Locke. The American Declaration, made under specially favorable circumstances, was a moment in a *politica perennis* of the West. It is in the *philosophia perennis* of the West that its philosophical justification must be sought.

The Declaration of Independence is not a Utopian document. Entirely unlike the Cartesian or Jacobin Revolutions, it made no *tabula rasa*. It is therefore in the traditional philosophy of the West, deriving from Greek philosophy, Roman law, and Judeo-Christian Revelation, and not in a philosophy of *tabula rasa,* that the meaning and the wording of the Declaration is best illuminated. This is the philosophy that best explains God to us, as Creator of nature, Providence, and Judge. This is the philosophy that best defines nature as it exists, particularly human nature, its rights, its duties, and its destiny. This is also the philosophy that best explains the sacredness of life and honor ("our Lives," "our sacred Honor,") that best teaches us the use of the things of this world ("our Fortunes"). As man's ultimate goal this philosophy names beatitude ("the pursuit of Happiness"). It gives to this pursuit of happiness all its heart-rending poetry and its cruel ambiguity, since we learn from it that man aspires as much to eternal as to earthly happiness. This is the philosophy that best defines man's freedom and the whole scope of his responsibility. This is the philosophy that makes most manifest the equality of all men in their natural and supernatural dignity as children of God and as brothers, having in common one Father and one Judge. I said that the Declaration of Independence must be taken as it is, and that is what I mean. But what it is and what it says will be best understood by being read in the light of this traditional philosophy. Nothing could serve better to define the prophetic, and hence revolutionary, import of the Declaration of Independence than to set it face to face with this traditional philosophy.

The men who signed the Declaration, as I have said, were better than the philosophy of their day. It must also be said that the Declaration itself is superior to the men who signed it; prophecy is always superior to the prophet. In fact, it is absolutely astounding that the eighteenth century produced such a document. It is like a proof of the ceaseless workings of God's providence. Just as it stands, this Declaration is so complete, so perfect, that it has the quality of a natural revelation, almost indeed as though a Divine grace had been conferred upon the American nation. In any case, it is the loftiest expression of the American vocation.

What age before the eighteenth century could have produced this Declaration? If it can be said that the Declaration was the fruit of a tradition, and that this tradition was the most ancient, the most venerable, the most constant in the Western world, it must also be pointed out that before the Declaration this tradition had declared itself for the most part only in books. And the abyss between theory and practice in the field of politics is no less wide and deep than the abyss between, for example, an excellent treatise on horsemanship and the fact of winning the Derby, or between a tract on the laws of painting and the fact of painting the ceiling of the Sistine Chapel. For the first time in the history of humanity a vigorous young nation, established on the shores of a continent, was to undertake on a vast scale the practical experiment of government by the people. Earlier experiments of this nature, such as the ancient Roman Republic, the little Greek republics, the first Germanic tribes, the free cities of the Middle Ages, had been anomalies, and, because of their limitations in time and space, had established no pattern. In the eighteenth century there was a universal conviction that no great nation could be a republic. Saint Peter Damian's admirable formula was a carved ivory of speech, a prophecy by that time, moreover, quite forgotten. An unfulfilled prophecy is only an empty dream. But the fulfillment of a prophecy, its actual realization, is always a greater marvel than the prophecy itself, precisely because it has ceased to be a formula, however beautiful, and become a fulfillment. It is like the little seed the Gospel speaks of which, nothing or almost nothing in itself, yet grows, if someone is minded to cast it to the ground, into a great tree.

What the Declaration abolishes

Every successful revolution involves the abolishment of something outlived, some Old Testament henceforth without purport. What the Declaration of Independence abolished was, in short, "divine right" in politics. I repeat, it abolished the divine right in politics, and not merely the divine right of kings, although historically of course the first concern was with the powers of the king. But what do we mean by "divine right" in politics?

In the West, it was originally well understood and agreed to in principle that the people derive political sovereignty from God and that they alone have the unqualified right to exercise it. It was indeed upon the very exercise of this sovereignty of the people that the power of kings was based. As Ulpian said, the people delegated their sovereignty to the prince, and this prince, emperor, or king exercised, in the name of the people and for the well-being of the *res publica,* the powers delegated to him. Sovereignty, therefore, followed this chain of succession: first came God, fount of all right and justice; next came the people, in whom was vested the natural right to all political sovereignty; then came the king, to whom sovereignty was delegated and who exercised it in the name of, and for, the people; and then, again, at the end of the chain, came the people over whom this sovereignty was exercised. The people were thus considered at once the sole source of political sovereignty and the subject of that sovereignty. The ritual of a king's consecration clearly illustrates this chain of authority and every link in the chain. Indeed, the ritual itself makes clear that the king is king only by the authority of God, as expressed in the people's consent. So far, nothing could be more legitimate. The power of the king is still essentially a delegated power. The people plainly have the right to delegate their sovereignty to whomever they please, even to a king, even for the whole life of a king, even to the eldest son of the queen, and so on, indefinitely. Logically it follows that the people can also take back their sovereignty. The legitimacy of a king's power therefore depends essentially upon the continued consent of the people.

The very stability of the monarchy, the respect with which it was surrounded, the power it commanded and the pride power gives to anyone who has it, gradually obscured the fact that the king's power originated in the people. In the logical chain of God, the people, the king, the people, the link between God and the people disappeared, and the chain became God, the king, the people. The people were recognized no longer as holding political sovereignty, but only as subject to that sovereignty. Kings became convinced that their authority in the political order was vested in them directly by God. It was then that the theory of the divine right of kings was born. The professors of Cambridge University expressed it perfectly in a declaration to Charles II: "Kings derive not their authority from the people but from God. . . . To Him only are they accountable." It would hardly be possible to reject with greater arrogance the Magna

Charta and the English tradition. But at least those Cambridge professors said exactly what they meant.

Henceforth kings were to assume the attributes of divinity
in the political realm, and first among these were infallibility and omnipotence. The people owed their kings the blind
and trusting obedience we owe to God. Though this right
was called divine, it had little to do with God, or at least with
the true God. To make government responsible only to God
was to admit that here and now, on this earth, government
was subject to no control whatever. To the extent that a king
had a Christian conscience, that conscience might temper his
rule. But the State itself was essentially freed from all responsibility to the people, while the people's subjection to
the State was made absolute. Therefore, should the time ever
come when the State rejected God Himself, it would no
longer be bound by conscience in any way. There would no
longer be limits to its power, since it would certainly not
abandon the attributes of divinity it had claimed. To endow
men with the prerogatives of God is an act of idolatry. Beyond any doubt, it is this divine right of kings that lies at the
root of modern totalitarianism. When the State constitutes
itself creator, providence, and judge of its people, it constitutes itself their god. This is a return to the time of ancient
barbarism, when each nation had a god and idols of its own.

The American Declaration restored and solemnly re-
affirmed the earlier chain of political succession: God, the
people, government, with government responsible to the
people and the people subject to the laws they made and government protecting these laws. In so doing, the Declaration
uprooted and destroyed divine right in politics with its inherent totalitarianism.

This is where, in my opinion, the American Revolution is
infinitely more radical than the French. When the French
Declaration of Rights proclaimed that "the origin of all sovereignty resides essentially in the nation," it was not abolish-

ing divine right; it was merely transferring it, extending it, and strengthening it. The French Declaration extended divine right because it was careful not to confine itself to political sovereignty; what it said was "all sovereignty." It strengthened divine right, since it did not recognize any sovereignty above its own. All it accomplished was to transfer divine right, having extended and strengthened it, from the person of the king to the nation. The way was now open for the nation to become, from one day to the next, totalitarian, and this in fact is what it became.

A nation can also turn into an idol. Strange indeed is the notion that tyranny has only one head; like the Beast of the Apocalypse, tyranny can have many heads, continually reborn, and when the tyrant has many heads tyranny becomes omnipresent and universal. It was still possible in the eighteenth century to believe in the infallible innocence of the people. But today, now that we have seen the great totalitarian democracies, it is no longer pardonable to ignore the fact that democracies can become tyrannies. After all, Hitler would have accepted the principle that "all sovereignty resides essentially in the nation." He believed that he was the incarnation of his country's will to power, as indeed he was. And Communism transfers the divine right in politics to the proletariat, just as the French Convention transferred it to the nation.

To abolish divine right in politics—and this is where Congress was right and Jefferson was wrong—it is not enough merely to give the people full sovereignty. It must also be recognized that men's inalienable rights, upon which their sovereignty is based, derive from God, Creator, Providence, and Judge. It is true that the people have rights, and that those rights are imprescriptible and inalienable; but not every right is theirs. They have no right to deify and worship themselves. Since their rights derive from God, they can exercise them only according to God's will. In their very sovereignty the people are subject to God. Without religion even democracy is exposed to all the perils of tyranny. The American Declaration carefully avoided making a philosophical absolute of the people; it did not give the people precedence over God in the chain of succession; it maintained the traditional chain of succession and traced back men's imprescriptible rights to God, the source of all justice and all rights. It recognized and it stated that all political realities, even the most sacred, are ultimately relative, because they too are created by God and dependent on Him. It was upon this harmony of relationship between man and his God that the Declaration solidly established both its principles of equality and freedom, and the majesty of the law. It eliminated all possibility of anarchy as well as tyranny. In this chain of political sovereignty the people are always subject and at the same time always free and sovereign. They are subject to their own laws and to God's justice. They are free because they obey only their own laws. They are sovereign because their sovereignty is part of the sovereignty of God.

> *Potestas est in Populo*
> *A Summo data Domino.*

A new political system

The Jacobin Utopians believed that they were making a *tabula rasa* and ridding themselves of divine right, but all they actually achieved was to give divine right a new disguise. The American revolutionaries, having instinctively rediscovered the most ancient tradition of the Western world, eradicated divine right from political society and founded a new political system. They inaugurated on their continent an era of freedom that was then considered unattainable and is still so considered in most of the world today.

Totalitarian despotisms, like those of Hitler and Stalin or like that of the Russians in Hungary, present a twofold danger. They can take over any society; everyone recognizes this clear and present danger, and it appalls all free men. The other threat is not so obvious. Glaring examples of brutal despotism blind us to the fact that there are many less violent ways whereby freedom can be lost. At this point let me quote Tocqueville, since no one could say it better.

> Above this race of men stands an immense and tutelary power, which takes upon itself alone to secure their gratifications and to watch over their fate. That power is absolute, minute, regular, provident, and mild. . . . For their happiness such a government willingly labors, but it chooses to be the sole agent, the only arbiter of that happiness; it provides for their security, foresees and supplies their necessities, facilitates their pleasures, manages their principal concerns, directs their industry, regulates the descent of property, and subdivides their inheritance; what remains, but to spare them all the care of thinking and all the trouble of living? . . .
>
> A great many persons at the present day are quite contented with this sort of compromise between administrative despotism and the sovereignty of the people; and they think they have done enough for the protection of individual freedom when they have surrendered it to the power of the nation at large. This does not satisfy me: the nature of him I am to obey signifies less to me than the fact of extorted obedience.

Nor would it have satisfied the founders of the American Republic. They were wholly concentrated on continually broadening the rights and responsibilities of the individual, and on exercising the most vigilant control over the state. They had no wish to see the nation they were founding become a nation of slaves—still less a nation of courtiers or a herd of sheep. And they took every precaution to see that this would not happen. Their revolution went further than any other, not only in destroying despotism but also in safe-guarding the individual against the encroachments of administrative control.

The State always discovers excellent excuses for depriving the individual of his rights or for narrowing his exercise of them. One of the most persuasive excuses is the claim to be acting for the common good and for national unity. The founders of the American Republic believed that the best way to safeguard the common good and national unity was to entrust them as far as possible to the private initiative of free individuals. In this they were truly original. They were convinced that no political system in the history of the world had relied enough on the resources, the intelligence, and the good will of the individual. They knew the risk this involved, and a terrible civil war was to justify their fear. Yet they considered even the risk of civil war less dangerous to the common good of Americans and to national unity than any curtailment of freedom, and that is why they insisted upon the right to rebellion as an essential part of their political concept. They have been proved right. All the administrative controls and all the despotisms together cannot build so united, so powerful a nation as liberty. This experiment of theirs has universal import. I feel certain that if the day comes when the European nations, instead of moving toward more and more centralization, move toward more and more individual autonomy and give private initiative the greatest possible scope, Europe will once again astound the world. This faith in freedom would no more impede European unity than it impeded the unity of the United States. On the contrary, it would advance that unity, provided the experiment were carried out wholeheartedly and with conviction.

I have already emphasized the fact that in the American Revolution life, human life, men's equality with one another, and a complete and perilous liberty, were all there at the start, were all implied from the very beginning, bestowed by

God, Whose gifts are sacred, inviolable, accorded once and for all. Never again can these rights be put into question. They do not end a history; they start a history, and set its course. The rights are there; society must make its peace with them, no matter what it entails. The risk for men and for society itself is immense, yet it is only within the framework of this risk that society is human and the future can be a truly human future. The Declaration of Independence places squarely on the shoulders of the individual the full responsibility, the full burden of his destiny, and not only of his own personal destiny, but of his common destiny with all other men in its ultimate fulfillment.

This, in my opinion, is the striking difference between the American Revolution and a Marxist revolution. The Communists also speak of liberty and equality. But for them liberty and equality must await the end of the revolution. Liberty and equality are no more than hypotheses in the Marxist revolution. I use the word hypotheses because we have no certainty that they will ever be achieved. And meanwhile, the Marxists ask us to hand over our human liberty, our right to human equality and fraternity, our lives—if need be—and our honor, in exchange for a promise which, for all we know, may be a fraud; in exchange for a draft on future happiness which, for all we know, may be returned for lack of funds. Before this promise can be honored, an infallible dictatorship is to create the perfect society from which will one day emerge infallible man. That will be the day when the leap is made from the necessary strictures of revolution into freedom.

But how can we be sure that freedom will not be forgotten along the way? How can we be sure that, by the time we reach the goal, we will not have lost our taste and our desire for freedom? Marxist reasoning ends in a paradox: any resistance to revolution and its unavoidable demands imperils the liberty and equality that revolution alone can bring. The liberty of today must be violently suppressed to ensure the liberty of tomorrow; the Terror of today is justified in the name of the liberty of tomorrow.

The American Declaration, on the contrary, affirms that liberty and equality can never wait, that without them life has no human dignity. The American Declaration affirms that chaos itself is better, with liberty and equality, than the most harmoniously designed political and social order without them. It recognizes that man comes ahead of society. Man creates society; he is not created by society. There is no limit to man's revolutionary hope.

This, then, is the American republic. Above and before all, it is the free republic of free Americans. The devotion America inspires has been given by the people of their own free will, and from this the nation has forged its strength. It is the very republic that Montesquieu envisioned when he wrote, "There is nothing more powerful than a Republic in which the laws are obeyed, not out of fear, not out of rationality, but out of passion, as in Rome or in Sparta: for then, to the wisdom of good government is added all the strength that any faction could ever call upon."

PART II

*The Industrial
and Social Revolution*

13

Once More Montaigne— but Other Cannibals

Montaigne, in that same famous essay of his on America, tells about the visit of three Indians to Rouen when Charles IX, then still a child, was there with the Court. Their observations, preserved for us by Montaigne, included one which brings up, in simple and even brutal terms, the question I intend to consider in this second part of my book. Montaigne first explains that the Indians "have a way in their language of speaking of men as halves of one another," a graphic and striking expression of man's essential solidarity and equality with his fellow man. They said, Montaigne tells us, that "they had noticed that there were among us men full and gorged with all sorts of good things, and that their other halves were beggars at their doors, emaciated with hunger and poverty; and they thought it strange that these needy halves could endure such injustice, and did not take the others by the throat, or set fire to their houses."

Those American aborigines had unerringly detected the evil which was to poison Europe throughout modern history. That evil is the Social Question. No satisfactory solution for it has so far been found in Europe, but I believe that twentieth-century America offers an answer worthy of consideration, a more advanced, a more complex answer than could

have been furnished in Montaigne's time, yet one supplied
by a people who feel exactly the same shock that those Indians felt, their same indignation in the face of injustice. In
short, those savages had grasped the fact that the contrast
between extreme luxury and extreme poverty stems from
man's exploitation of man and is an economic form of canni-
balism. But this time the cannibals were on another continent.

Obviously, the economic and social conditions that the first
colonists found were most exceptional. To say that the land
they came to belonged to the Indians would not be accurate.
The Indians were a nomadic people, living off bird and beast
and fruits of the earth. They had no agricultural tradition
and no industry; they never became one with the land on
which they lived. Politically, as I have said before, this land
was truly a *tabula rasa*. But it was also a *tabula rasa* from the
economic and social standpoint. It was, at the time of its discovery, a land that really belonged to no one, or rather belonged to anyone at all, to anyone who settled it.

Even now, here and there in the Middle West, two wagon
wheels thrust into the ground on either side of the entrance
to a private property still speak eloquently of that early
period. When the first pioneers from Boston, New York, or
Virginia reached their destination, after a journey of many
weeks or months on scarcely marked and little-known trails
along which they moved at the slow pace of the covered wag-
ons that carried their families, their tools, and all they had,
and found at last some unclaimed piece of forest or grassland
that pleased them, they stopped, unfastened their wagon
wheels, and dug them into the earth so that whoever passed
that way would know that this piece of earth, which till then
had belonged to no one, this *res nullius,* was henceforward
theirs, their land, their property, *res domini.*

There they settled, and by the sweat of their brows cleared
forest or grassland, dug wells or drew off springs, felled trees

to build their houses, plowed, sowed, and reaped. They carved out and shaped their land, their property; to them their property and their sweat were one. They became proprietors of what before had been virgin land, never surveyed or registered by anyone; in their remoteness from any central government they were free.

There was nothing more natural and there was therefore nothing more legitimate than that proprietorship rooted in toil and that liberty rooted in solitude.

Needless to say, however, this state of affairs did not last. First the several Colonies, and later the federal government, claimed and exercised the right to enforce law and to control the pioneer settlements. But the very fact that in America, and not so long ago, property was not inherited but earned, and earned only by the initiative, daring, and toil of the individual in a land still uninhabited, on a frontier where anyone could settle, means that even now in America the word property still evokes the idea of chance, work, and individual effort, as it never does in Europe. America, rejecting "divine right" in government, also rejected it in the economic and social domain, and, thanks to this tremendous advantage, has been spared the great revolutionary convulsions to which Europe and Asia are still prey. America remembers that the American earth and its fruits have not always belonged to those who now possess them; that in the past, in the not so distant past, the land was God's and God's alone, that others might have settled it, that for everyone beneath the sun there must be some piece of land, since land itself was created by God to nourish all mankind. If the great revolutionary battle cries that raise such havoc today in Europe had so infinitesimal an effect upon America, it is primarily because they were not understood. To Americans they seemed to be coming from another planet.

14

Jefferson against Hamilton

Once the war with England was over and Independence, fought for and won, had become an established fact, the new nation came face to face with the harsh realities of sovereignty; it began to experience economic difficulties. There is no doubt that the towering figure of that period was Alexander Hamilton, Secretary of the Treasury in Washington's first Cabinet. Son of a Scottish father and a mother of French Huguenot descent, this American had a clear understanding of the immediate problem confronting the young Republic, certainly a far clearer understanding than that of Jefferson. Indeed, he took brilliant advantage of Jefferson's lack of experience in economics, and later Jefferson would bitterly regret having let himself be used as a tool for operations whose full and to him inherently harmful import he had not grasped at the time. The debate was long and vehement.

What was America in its first days of Independence? America was three million people, widely scattered along an extended coast behind which the land stretched away indefinitely, little known and almost entirely unexploited. Even some of the most populated coastal regions, such as New England, were poor. Money was scarce; there was practically no industrial equipment; the national debt was enormous and, for that day and time, crushing. Financially, America, though victorious and independent, was starting out bankrupt. When Hamilton became Secretary of the Treasury he found himself in the peculiar position of being entrusted with the administration of finances which did not exist. He was determined, at no matter what cost and also, unfortunately, by no matter what means, to find money for the nation. He had the mind of a technician and the attitude of an adventurer. His genius lay in having completely understood both the nature of money and the economic conditions of the young Republic. He had the imagination to realize that money is not only an index of goods in circulation, but also, and perhaps even more, the means by which purchasing power acquires mobility. He understood that the shortage of currency threatened the country with complete paralysis, for when there is no money in circulation purchasing power is immobilized, goods cease to move, and production itself comes to a halt.

Only by putting money, even for the time being fictitious money, in circulation, could production, the primary source of wealth, be revived. To save so anemic an economic organism demanded a blood transfusion. Hamilton performed the transfusion and it was an unqualified success. In my opinion, he saved America. Without that transfusion, America would have sunk farther and farther into economic anemia, grave disorders would have arisen from increasingly widespread poverty, and the very unity of the young nation would have been endangered.

Hamilton clearly perceived the logical progression from cause to effect that exists between economic prosperity and national unity, and he made this perfectly plain. His entire financial system, he said, was planned to "cement more closely the union of the States." It was by no means accidental that Hamilton and his friends the Federalists were the chief advocates of the Constitution. They were the men who had drafted it, they had got it ratified. And now Hamilton was consolidating that federal Constitution, integrating it not only with the laws and customs but with the common economic interests of the nation.

Other nations, such as France, were able to achieve their unity because they were constantly threatened with invasion and were therefore compelled to recognize the law of the nation-in-peril as supreme. But Hamilton saw that, in an America no longer threatened with invasion, the best way to ensure unity was to organize the nation as a commercial society which would draw all its diversified parts into the close-knit system of a single, common market. Thus the law of supply and demand served to consolidate the unity of America as the law of the nation-in-peril had served for centuries to consolidate the unity of France. Actually, however, the reason why Hamilton considered this law of economic centralization so overwhelmingly important was that he realized that, for America, it was indeed no other than the law of the nation-in-peril. He was fully aware that if he could not revive production, if he failed to create a common market for the whole nation, America would fall apart. In enforcing this law of economic centralization, he was as rigid, as merciless, and perhaps, too, as unjust, as the Committee of Public Safety would later be in France. I say this because Hamilton, with the cold-bloodedness of a surgeon amputating a limb to save a life, deliberately sacrificed that part of the nation which seemed to him a dead weight.

It so happened that what he sacrificed was the largest segment of the population. In those early days America was almost entirely a nation of farmers. Hamilton believed that money should be channeled only to those who keep it circulating—to tradesmen, shipowners, and manufacturers. He was unquestionably the first to envision a great industrial future for America. He did everything in his power to promote the business and industrial class, small as it then was, at the expense of the farmers. By his handling of the public debt, by commercial bills, and by banks, the farmers were stripped of what little they had for the benefit of the speculators. The transfusion that resuscitated the American economy came from "the blood of the poor." According to Hamilton—and his philosophy is shared by many economists today—an ailing economy, in the case of severe and protracted crisis, can be cured only at the cost of countless individual bankruptcies. "Destitution to the poor" is the modern version of the "Woe to the vanquished" of antiquity.

Hamilton did not distinguish between production and speculation. Perhaps he could not, or perhaps he was unwilling to distinguish between them. Determined to encourage production and trade, he had to place the purchasing power in the hands of those who would make the most effective use of it. He therefore encouraged speculation, and encouraged it quite deliberately. Speculators could create industry, they could extend trade, they could keep money in circulation; in short, they could forge the young republic into a dynamic and prosperous economic society.

With this in mind, it becomes easier to understand the antipathy, not to say contempt, that Jefferson felt for Hamilton. The two men opposed one another in everything. It was above all an opposition of principles, one which must be clearly understood, since the same opposition of principles still exists in American society today.

As a new nation, America had more need of England than ever before. Independence had simply meant ceasing to be a political colony, to become an economic colony instead. Hamilton encouraged this state of dependence because he believed it to be unavoidable. One cannot run before learning to walk, and in order to learn to walk it is necessary, for a time, to be supported and guided by someone of greater size and strength. The young American nation could not be economically self-sufficient. For Hamilton, that fact settled the question. It would be from economic colonization that America would learn the arts of industry and commerce until the time came when it could stand on its own feet and even compete with England. There is no doubt that Hamilton was right. But it was Jefferson who continued to strike the heroic note of the Declaration of Independence. Speaking of the English, he wrote:

> When we take notice that theirs is the workshop to which we go for all we want; that with them center, either immediately or ultimately, all the labors of our hands and lands; that to them belongs either openly or secretly the great mass of our navigation; that even the factorage of their affairs here, is kept to themselves by factitious citizenships; and these foreign and false citizens now constitute the great body of what are called our merchants, fill our seaports, are planted in every little town and district of the interior country, sway everything in the former places by their own votes, and those of their dependents, in the latter, by their insinuations and the influence of their ledgers; that they are advancing fast to a monopoly of our banks and public funds, and thereby placing our public finances under their control; that they have in their alliance the most influential characters in and out of office; when they have shown that by these bearings on different branches of government, they can force it to proceed in whatever direction they dictate, and bend the interest of this country entirely to the will of another; when all this, I say, is attended to, it is impossible for us to say we stand on independent ground, impossible for a free mind not to see and to groan under the boundage in which it is bound.

No one has defined more clearly or with more precision what it means to be an economic colony. But even as President, Jefferson himself could do nothing to change the status he so deeply resented. For a nation to free itself from this kind of dependence it takes more than a Declaration; it takes more even than a victorious war; it takes a self-sufficiency that can be achieved only through autonomous production, and that is why America could not throw off England's economic yoke until it, too, became a great industrial nation. Hamilton was right. But to win economic emancipation would take America a hundred years.

Jefferson's attitude was no doubt somewhat sentimental. Like Rousseau, he was persuaded that God lives in a garden, that man can remain innocent only in the country, can remain free only in the depths of the forest, as remote as possible from cities and industrial civilization. This dream of the romantics has never quite faded away; it even cast its spell upon so recent a writer as Bernanos. To Jefferson, industry, business, and above all, banks were the very works and pomps of the Devil. About banks, at least, Henry Ford was to agree with him.

But there was more to Jefferson's attitude than mere sentimentality and romanticism. To him industrial production inevitably entailed financial speculation; to him it was therefore stained with the blood of the poor. A man of fundamental honesty such as Jefferson was revolted by the thought that the manipulation of money makes the rich richer and impoverishes the poor. A remarkable exception even for his time, Jefferson himself left public life poorer than he had entered it. In the industrial and commercial development of the young nation, he saw a danger to morals and a threat to the spirit of democracy. Yet when he became President he did not abolish Hamilton's banking system; all he did was to keep it under strict control. In the long run America derived inestimable benefit from the fact that Hamilton was able to play a role in government and that he played it when he did. For by the time Jefferson reached the Presidency, America had already gone so far along the road to economic unity and a single common market that no retreat was possible. A solid foundation for national unity had been laid.

By character as well as by conviction, Jefferson tended to put individual liberty ahead of national unity. It was not that he was indifferent to national unity. It was he who had written, "We mutually pledge to each other our lives, our fortunes, and our sacred honor." But for him the American republic and its unity were primarily based upon individual liberty. Jefferson foresaw that the development of an industrial society would inevitably endanger individual liberty. Although today Hamilton's ideas have won out over those of Jefferson so completely that even agriculture itself is industrialized and America has become the greatest industrial nation in the world, we would nevertheless do well to turn back to Jefferson's warnings and consider them. It is undeniable that the vast and complex machinery of industry is a threat to individual liberty. There can be no question that, if it is not impossible, it is at least most difficult, to remain faithful to the spirit, or even to the letter, of the Declaration of Independence in a society dominated by mass production and mass distribution, where the individual runs the continual risk of being submerged in a conformity all the more tyrannical because it is unconscious. It is certainly easier to remain an individual in a primitive agricultural society where every man can cultivate his own garden and live on what he grows. Jefferson's fears were by no means groundless. He had instinctively foreseen what was to become the key problem of the modern world—the problem of how the individual, who has more or less freed himself at last from the tyranny and the terror in which nature and its elements once held him, can now free himself from the tyranny of society itself.

15

Karl Marx, America, and
the Hippocratic Oath

As to how Marx and Engels appraised economic and social conditions in America, there is no need for conjecture. They made themselves perfectly clear. We have their correspondence with fellow socialists in America over the years between 1848 and 1895. That correspondence makes a thoroughly fascinating book. I shall start out by quoting from one of these letters which seems to me to go far toward defining the nature of the problem I intend to consider in this chapter. It was written by Karl Marx to Weydemeyer, and dated London, March 5, 1852.

. . . Finally, in your place I should tell the democratic gentlemen that they would do better first to acquaint themselves with the bourgeois literature before they presume to yap out their contradictions of it. . . . Before they try to criticize the critique of political economy they should acquaint themselves with the first elements of political economy. One has only to open Ricardo's great work, for example, to find these words on the first page: "The produce of the earth—all that is derived from its surface by the united application of labor, machinery, and capital—is divided among *three classes* of the community, namely, the proprietor of the land, the owner of the stock or capital necessary for its cultivation, and the laborers by whose industry it is cultivated."

That bourgeois society in the United States has not yet developed far enough to make the class struggle obvious and comprehensible is more strikingly proved by H. C. Carey (of Philadelphia), the only American economist of importance. He attacks *Ricardo*, the most classical representative (interpreter) of the bourgeoisie and the most stoical adversary of the proletariat, as a man whose works are an arsenal for anarchists, socialists, and all the enemies of the bourgeois society. He accuses not only him, but Malthus, Mill, Say, Torrens, Wakefield, McCulloch, Senior, Wakley, R. Jones, etc., in short the economic masterminds of Europe, of tearing society apart and paving the way for civil war by their proof that the economic bases of the different classes must give rise to a necessary and ever-growing antagonism between them. He tries to refute them . . . by attempting to demonstrate that economic conditions—rent (landed property), profit (capital), and wages (wage labor)—are conditions of cooperation and harmony rather than conditions of struggle and antagonism. All he proves, of course, is that he takes the "undeveloped" social conditions of the United States to be "normal" conditions.

As for me, no credit is due me for discovering either the existence of classes in modern society or the struggle between them. Bourgeois historians had described the historical development of this struggle of the classes long before me, and bourgeois economists had portrayed their economic anatomy. What I did that was new was to prove:

1) that the *existence of classes* is bound up only with *specific historical phases in the development of production;*

2) that the class struggle necessarily leads to the *dictatorship of the proletariat;*

3) that this dictatorship itself only constitutes the transition to the *abolition of all classes* and to a *classless society*.

Ignorant louts like Heinzen, who deny not only the struggle, but even the existence of classes, merely prove that, despite all their blood-curdling yelps and humanitarian airs, they regard the social conditions under which the bourgeoisie rules as the final product, the *ne plus ultra* of history, and that they are merely the servitors of the bourgeoisie. And the less these louts themselves comprehend the greatness and the temporary necessity of the bourgeois regime, the more repulsive is their servitude. [The italics in this text are by Marx himself.]

In all Marx wrote, few pages are as clear as these, few more important to ponder. In all the sociological literature of the world, few pages can be of greater help to us in understanding America and what it has become.

In this letter Marx unhesitatingly affirmed his direct line of descent from the bourgeois and capitalist tradition of political economy. This point is of the utmost importance; it makes it possible to do Marx justice. Perhaps, too, it makes it possible to do justice to others, for instance to Henry Charles Carey, of whom Marx spoke above. To the extent that Marx was right, to the extent that he was logical, he was logical and right within the capitalist economic tradition, and he was logical and right only within that tradition. For example, on the basis of the so-called economic law formulated by Adam Smith and restated by Ricardo, which holds that "high and low wages and profit are the causes of high or low prices," it is obvious that a society geared to maximum profit and founded on competition is inevitably forced to keep prices down as far as possible in order to meet competition and to reduce wages as far as possible in order to increase profits. Within these terms Marx was a thousand times right, and labor conditions must indeed sink lower and lower. Even today, Marx can be effectively refuted only if Adam Smith, Ricardo, Malthus, and every other leading economist of the capitalist tradition is rejected at the same time, as Henry Charles Carey seems to have fully understood. All Marx did was to carry on that tradition, develop it, and draw certain new conclusions. He never departed from it, he recognized it as his own, he respected it intellectually, he considered it irrefutable. Even while attacking the bourgeois system and trying to bring about its downfall, he still meekly accepted all its rules. His attitude was that bourgeois capitalism had its own unquestionable *grandeur,* and that it was a *necessary,* but at the same time a *transitional,* phase of economic development. According to him, the great theoreticians of capitalism had made an admirable analysis of the anatomy of the larva, but had unfortunately failed to realize that the larva must one day change into a butterfly. Marx, however, was sure that the change would take place, and this was the essence of his discovery. As the swallow is the harbinger of spring, so Marx was the prophet of the resplendent socialist butterfly that was to emerge from the larva of capitalism. Marx clearly saw and explicitly stated that the study of both larva and butterfly belong to a single science, entomology. That is why he insisted that between him and the traditional bourgeois economists—Malthus, Ricardo, and the others—there was no break in "scientific" continuity.

No less insistently, however, Marx made plain, in the letter to Weydemeyer, what he considered his own contribution. He had proved, he claimed, that "the existence of classes is bound up only with specific historical phases in the development of production." This proposition seems quite acceptable at first sight, yet it is anything but clear. It shows Marx's almost habitual inability to distinguish between *cause, contingency,* and *effect.* For instance, it might be asked, did the military aristocracy in medieval Europe become the ruling class because it owned the land, or did it own the land because it had already become a ruling class as the result of its role in war? To take another example, in the democracy that France is today, French intellectuals could be called a ruling class, although they do not own the means of production. To this, many of them would of course reply that they are proletarians, and in a way they would not be wrong, since most of them are poor and underfed. But are people proletarians because they do not own the means of production, or is it because they do not belong to the ruling class? There can perfectly well be a ruling class that does not own the means of production.

Marx further claimed to have proved that "the class struggle necessarily leads to the dictatorship of the proletariat." In his book *The Poverty of Philosophy* he explained very clearly how, under capitalism, labor conditions must continually deteriorate. He quoted Ricardo: "*Diminish the cost of production* of hats, and their price will ultimately fall to their new natural price, although the demand should be doubled, trebled, or quadrupled. *Diminish the cost of subsistence of men,* by diminishing the natural price of food and clothing, by which life is sustained, and wages will ultimately fall, notwithstanding that the demand for labourers may very greatly increase (Ricardo, Vol. 2, p. 253)." It is Marx who italicized the words and gave the reference. "Doubtless," Marx commented, "Ricardo's language is as cynical as can be. To put the cost of manufacture of hats and the cost of maintenance of men on the same plane *is to turn men into hats. . . . The cynicism is in the facts and not in the words which express the facts.*" This time it is I who underline Marx's description of a condition which to him, as to Ricardo, seemed unavoidable. To both of them it seemed certain that in direct proportion to the increase in production the workers would be forced down to the level of existing only "as the most suffering class," stripped of all human dignity and left to the mercy, like Ricardo's hats, of a fluctuating market. What is harder to understand in Marx's reasoning is how a class reduced to such abject misery could ever rise to the power of dictatorship. Here it seems to me that none of Simone Weil's objections can possibly be refuted. "Not a day passes," she wrote, "but what Marx's formula, by which the State would give birth to its own gravediggers, is proved shockingly false; and indeed, one wonders how Marx could have believed that slavery breeds free men. No slave regime in history has ever yet been overthrown by its slaves. The truth, as has been unforgettably stated, is that slavery so debases man that he ends by loving it, that freedom is precious only in the eyes of those who actually possess it; and that a completely inhuman regime, . . . far from molding men capable of erecting a human society, shapes all those at its mercy in its own inhuman image—the oppressed no less than the oppressors."

In Marx's letter to Weydemeyer, the third and final discovery he claimed to have made was that "this dictatorship itself only constitutes the transition to the abolition of all classes and to a classless society." The term "classless society," which has met so strange a fate both in America and in Russia, may no longer mean very much. In America it seems to mean that everyone can own property; in Russia, that no one can own property, except society itself. But the fact remains that in America those who actually control either money or the means of production have a power that other Americans have not, while in Russia, as Milovan Djilas has explained, those who control the State actually own the means of production and therefore have a power all the more absolute because competition is precluded.

Marx declared, not in the Weydemeyer letter but in his frequent arguments with Bakunin, that once the Proletarian Revolution had been achieved, once the whole bourgeois civilization had been liquidated and the means of production placed entirely in the hands of the people, the State, its role fulfilled, would of its own accord wither away. There can be no doubt that this vision reflected Karl Marx's deepest feeling. But today, forty years after the October Revolution, we have the opportunity, denied to Marx, of confronting that intuition with reality. The scientific spirit, which Marx always claimed was his, should not fear such a confrontation, but on the contrary should welcome it. As Claude Bernard, the great French physiologist, wrote, "The experimental method, the free thinker's method, seeks only scientific truth. *Feeling,* from which everything emanates, must keep its complete spontaneity and all its freedom for putting forth experimental ideas; *reason,* also, must preserve that freedom to doubt which forces it *always to submit ideas to the test of experiment. . . .* Genius is revealed in a delicate feeling which correctly foresees the laws of natural phenomena; but *this we must never forget,* that *correctness of feeling and fertility of idea can be established and proved only by experiment.*" (The italics are mine.)

As Mr. Djilas has pointed out, the Proletarian Revolution, instead of abolishing social classes, has merely created a new propertied class, entrenched in its privileges, and anyone can see that, far from having done away with the oppression of the State, the Revolution has extended its power by making it totalitarian. That there are good reasons for this, Mr. Khrushchev has been at some pains to explain. But a fact is a fact. Forty years have passed since the October Revolution and now, confronting Marx's feeling and his idea with the facts and submitting them to the test of experiment, it is only scientific to ask whether good reasons will not always be found for putting off indefinitely the total abolition of classes and the withering away of the State; it is only scientific to ask if Marx's feeling was "correct" and if his idea was "fertile," or if, after all, his so-called scientific theory was no more than another of those Utopian hypotheses which have cluttered the path trod by science across the centuries and which science has always had to abandon in order to advance. It is only scientific to ask if the dictatorship of the proletariat has not enslaved the workers, rather than set them free.

Marx was born in 1818. Napoleon, prisoner on the island of Saint Helena, was still alive. Looking back at so recent a past, Marx was under no illusion about the French Revolution. He saw, as clearly as Jefferson had seen, its Utopian and disastrous nature. In fact he openly declared that the Revolution had given the French not Liberty, Equality, and Fraternity, but Infantry, Artillery, and Cavalry. Why should we be less frank than Marx in declaring that the October Revolution has brought the world, not the fulfillment of all it promised, but the State, with its Police, its Army, its Terror? Of course, this is not what Marx hoped or planned. But neither did Saint-Just or Lafayette hope or plan for Napoleon, yet they unquestionably helped to create him.

But Marx's letter to Weydemeyer, which has led to all these reflections, has a very special bearing on my subject. For here is Marx, who went out of his way to speak with the utmost contempt of all those who dared contradict him, actually referring with respect to an American economist, Henry Charles Carey, as "the only American economist of importance." Coming from Marx, this was honorable mention indeed and should have been enough to send American universities scurrying to find out who Carey was and above all what were his ideas on economics. It has been my experience, however, that even specialists in the field scarcely know his name and I have not met a single one who recalls the letter in which Marx discussed him. Judging at this point only from what Marx said of him, it seems to me quite obvious that this Henry Charles Carey "(of Philadelphia)" had what Claude Bernard would have called unusually perspicacious economic and sociological *ideas* about America and an unusually *correct feeling* as to the direction in which it was to evolve. He saw the diversification of society that would result from a

highly developed industrial production as an element conducive to harmony rather than to conflict, and of still more
importance is the fact that he was not afraid to attack head-on
Marx's "scientific" gods—Malthus, Ricardo, and the whole
classic school of capitalist economy, "in short the economic
masterminds of Europe." Ah, what a great man he was, and
how Americans should cherish him. . . .

Carey seems to have realized perfectly what neither Marx
nor Engels realized, what Mr. Khrushchev does not yet realize, that America was moving toward an economic and social system entirely different not only from Communist socialism *but also and at the same time* from the classic capitalist system defined by Malthus, Ricardo, and Adam Smith.
"He tries to refute them . . . ," Marx added in his letter,
". . . by attempting to demonstrate that economic conditions are conditions of cooperation and harmony rather than
conditions of struggle and antagonism." This extraordinary
appraisal of Carey by Marx was made more than a hundred
years ago, on March 5, 1852. Slow as the course of history may
run, surely a century is a sufficiently solid experimental basis
upon which to judge who was right and who was wrong—I
say experimentally, but Marx would say "scientifically" right
or wrong—between Marx and Carey, in their conflicting
views of conditions in America. Marx, dogmatic as usual, concluded that "all he [Carey] proves, of course, is that he takes
the 'undeveloped' social conditions of the United States to be
'normal' social conditions." One could wish that Marx had
shown a little more self-doubt, had been more "scientific," in
the spirit of Claude Bernard's maxim: "The one fundamental rule of scientific research is doubt."

The fact is that now, after a century of experimentation, it
is almost impossible to maintain any longer that social conditions in America are still "undeveloped." For the past hundred years American society has been advancing, although
with inevitable lags and even with setbacks, in exactly the

direction Carey foretold, Marx's predictions to the contrary notwithstanding. America has been moving toward harmony, and not toward struggle between the classes, as I shall attempt to explain in the rest of my book. It is always easy enough to say that a condition that does not fit in with a preconceived theory is not a "normal" condition, that it is only "temporary." But by the time a century has passed, this reasoning becomes somewhat threadbare, or else—what amounts to the same thing—people begin to suspect that it is just one more way of putting them off till doomsday, the last recourse of the Utopians.

Nothing makes one despair of intelligence as much as the Marxists' persistent misunderstanding of America. Catholic theologians were less stubborn; not one of them, a hundred years after Galileo was condemned, would have dared uphold the scientific validity of the astronomy of Ptolemy and Genesis. And yet I am sure that even today, on the authority of Marx alone, Mr. Khrushchev would condemn Henry Charles Carey's books. Engels, whose analysis of American conditions was admirable right up to the point where he began to think in terms of doctrine, wrote, on June 3, 1886:

> America after all is the ideal of all bourgeois: a country rich, vast, expanding, with purely bourgeois institutions unleavened by feudal remnants of monarchical traditions, and without a permanent and hereditary proletariat. Here everyone could become, if not a capitalist, at all events an independent man, producing or trading, with his own means, for his own account. And because there were not *as yet* [Engels' italics] classes with opposing interests, our—and your—bourgeois thought that America stood *above* [Engel's italics] class antagonisms and struggles. That delusion has now broken down, the last Bourgeois Paradise on earth is fast changing into a Purgatorio, and can only be prevented from becoming, like Europe, an Inferno by the go-ahead pace

at which the development of the newly fledged proletariat of America will take place. . . . I only wish Marx could have lived to see it.

It is indeed too bad that Marx is dead, too bad that he did not have the physical stamina of a Methuselah to await the fulfillment of his predictions about American society. The very words inferno, purgatorio, and paradise belong to the Utopian vocabulary. Good, plain Americans like Henry Charles Carey have always known that no human society is ever a paradise, that it can and must be prevented from becoming an inferno, and that our duty is simply to make it habitable for the mortals that we are.

Let us come back to Carey. Only a man of exceptional intelligence could have perceived, as far back as that, the need to reject at one and the same time both the traditional capitalist economy and the Marxism which stemmed from it. Between Marx and Carey, between Marx and America, the distance is as great as that between Euclidian and non-Euclidian geometry. Ricardo was the Euclid of political economy. Marx remained Euclidian. But Carey and America broke with Euclid altogether. Until the nineteenth century, the world never suspected that there could be any development in geometry other than the one based on Euclid's postulates. Lobachevski was the first to invent a non-Euclidian geometry, and it has been doing well and making progress ever since, despite the sarcasms heaped upon it by the Euclidians. In that same period, Carey, the American economist, had the courage to break away from the postulates of Ricardo and Malthus, taken up and studied and developed by Marx with the diligence of a conscientious schoolboy. Indeed, Carey anticipated the course America was to take, a course which diverged as much economically and socially from that charted by Smith, Ricardo, Malthus, and Marx as did Lobachevski's geometry from that of Euclid. Needless to say, Marxists, and even European capitalists, resent this, refusing to admit even the possibility of such a divergence, just as the Euclidians resented Lobachevski.

All this is quite understandable; in fact it is natural, or, as Marx would have said, "normal." To Marxists, Marx and Ricardo are more important than truth. Political economy stands today where medicine stood a hundred years ago, when Claude Bernard wrote:

> Medicine is still in the shades of traditional practice, and suffers the consequences of its backward condition. . . . Superstition and the marvelous play a great part in it. Sorcerers, somnambulists, and healers by virtue of some gift from Heaven are held as the equals of physicians. The medical personality is placed above science by physicians themselves. They seek their authority in tradition, in doctrines, and in medical tact. This state of affairs is the clearest of proofs that the experimental method has by no means come into its own in medicine.

Bernard made another caustically accurate comment:

> But it happens further quite naturally that men who believe too firmly in their own theories do not believe enough in the theories of others. So the dominant idea of these despisers of their fellows is to find others' theories faulty and to try to contradict them. . . . They make experiments only to destroy a theory, instead of to seek the truth. At the same time, they make poor observations, because they choose among the results of their experiments only what suits their own object, neglecting whatever is unrelated to it, and carefully setting aside everything which might tend toward the idea they wish to combat. Thus men are led . . . to falsify science and the facts.

It is neither by accident nor simply for the pleasure of the surprising relevancy that I so gladly quote from Claude Bernard, the matchless theoretician of the experimental method in medicine. For to me there is a deep and most enlightening analogy between medicine and political economy. The goal of political economy is the health of the body social, as the goal of medicine is the health of the individual physical body. The same difficulties, the same disputes which cause confusion as to the nature, methods, and aims of medicine, also cause confusion as to the nature, methods, and aims of political economy. Both these disciplines involve the same temptations, the same dangers, and perhaps the same moral obligations.

Again, it was Claude Bernard who wrote, "The experimental method and experimentation were long ago introduced into physico-chemical sciences which owe them all their brilliance. . . . Our one single aim is, and always has been, to help make the well-known principles of the experimental method pervade medical science." Marx, too, had the avowed aim of discovering the laws of production and making political economy into an exact science. But Bernard was fully aware that, in medicine, that goal was still remote. "Each kind of science," he wrote, "presents different phenomena and complexities and difficulties of investigation peculiarly its own. This makes the principles of experimentation . . . incomparably harder to apply to medicine and the phenomena of living bodies than to physics and the phenomena of inorganic bodies." Ricardo and Marx were far from having so cautious an attitude. And yet social phenomena are just as complex and delicate as the phenomena submitted to medical investigation; they are perhaps even more complex; they offer greater resistance to analysis. Moreover, as physicians themselves are prepared to admit, even today medicine still works on the basis of hypotheses, tentative generalizations and assumptions, but not yet, except perhaps in biochemistry, upon the basis of laws. In the same sense, at a time when political economy was even more backward than medicine, the fundamental error of Ricardo and Marx, the one from which flowed all their other errors of judgment and prophecy, was to have claimed that their formulas were laws. In the realm of science, when laws are not supported by facts, they are not laws at all, but merely systematic postulates which do more to hinder the advance of science than to hasten it.

This was the nature of Marx's economic postulates, which included the postulates formulated by Ricardo and the English capitalist school. Yet the ultimate aim of Marx and Ricardo was legitimate. It is to be hoped for political economy that it will some day emerge from empiricism and dogmatic system to become a science, as it is also to be hoped for medicine. Meanwhile, however, neither political economy nor medicine are sciences, and surely political economy is still less of a science than medicine. Both are as yet no more than arts; both depend on recipes, on observation, on experiment, and on chance, but not on what can properly be called laws. Medicine, at least, frankly recognizes this situation, yet without in any way renouncing its scientific ideal. Indeed, on the contrary, since Claude Bernard's time, medical laboratories have multiplied all over the world, and so have medical discoveries. Never before have the life and health of mankind been better protected. But political economy suffers from delusions of grandeur; it has tried to run before learning to walk. There is something appalling in the thought that men as intelligent as Ricardo and Marx could invent ideas which they believed to be scientific and objective in a realm as vast and delicately complex as that of economics. Of course, even in this realm there must be no renouncing of the scientific ideal, yet here, as in medicine, the ideal must be pursued with humility, with complete submission to fact, and with tireless research, before there can be the slightest hope of establishing laws. Only an ignoramus or a charlatan would attempt to create a body of laws in a realm still wholly immersed in traditional ideas.

The analogy between medicine and political economy goes even beyond that methodical doubt and that patient humility which in both realms are the suitable and indeed the only honest way of implementing a great scientific ideal. After all, even if medicine is not yet a science, it has existed and been practiced for a long time now as an art, the aim of which is to preserve health and cure illness. But, *from a scientific point of view,* this avowed and accepted aim of medicine is an oddity. To deliberately undermine health, to provoke illness or death, is not the function of medicine, or at least not its aim, though illness and death are often provoked in laboratory experiments on animals. It must therefore be further specified that the aim of medicine is to preserve *human* health and to cure illness in *human beings.* The introduction of the specifically human element into the essential aim of medical art endows it with a *moral* character. To be purely and exclusively scientific in medicine *is not permissible.* Even if the experiments made by German doctors in concentration camps helped to further the general advance of medicine, they will always remain a *medical* monstrosity. Since the adoption of the Hippocratic Oath, the physician no longer has absolute freedom of action, even in seeking to advance medical science. At this point it seems fitting to quote from that famous Oath:

> The regimen I adopt shall be for the benefit of my patients according to my ability and judgment, and not for their hurt or for any wrong. I will give no deadly drug to any, though it be asked of me, nor will I counsel such. . . . Whatsoever house I enter, there will I go for the benefit of the sick, refraining from all wrongdoing or corruption, and especially from any act of seduction. . . .

It may well be that, since the beginnings of human society, that which has been most lacking in political economy throughout its history and that which, by its absence, has caused the greatest number of catastrophes, is a Hippocratic Oath, which would have brought to those who practiced the art of economics the same tradition of disinterestedness, devotion, and concern for mankind that exists among the practitioners of medicine. This does not mean that all physicians live up to the Hippocratic Oath, yet none dares attribute any other aim to medicine than the one Hippocrates assigned it. Here is where political economy seems to me to lag far behind medicine. Here, also, is where Karl Marx seems to me superior to Ricardo and the English capitalist school, inasmuch as Marx looked forward to a day, once the economic evolution had been completed, when man would at last be reconciled with man. Meanwhile, however, man is no more than a guinea pig on whom to test laws. Marx was wrong about those laws, as he was wrong about that evolution, but at least his concern for the future, no matter how Utopian, was that of a humanist. Ricardo's was not.

16

"The Chapter of
the Hats"

Before undertaking an analysis of the American political economy, which seems to me the least dogmatic of them all, I would like to clear the air by showing the havoc that dogmatism has wrought upon political economies in general. Once again, Marx has eased my task.

Comparing Ricardo to Hegel, Marx wrote, "If the Englishman turns men into hats, the German turns hats into ideas." This remark is without doubt the neatest and most comic caricature ever drawn of capitalist economy and Hegelian philosophy. Like all good caricatures, this one too, alas, contains some truth. But if political economy has become no more than a machine for turning men into hats, Marx must bear his share of responsibility. Needless to say, this machine does not appear to be much concerned with human values.

Now, forty years after the October Revolution, critics of Communism are not lacking. Faced with the awful chasm between the socialist dream and its historical reality, the question arises of who is to blame. Most critics, and they include no less a personage than Mr. Khrushchev, hold Stalin responsible. Some, and among these is Milovan Djilas, even go so far as to blame Lenin as well. But when it comes to Marx, the critics hesitate. The good intentions and disinterestedness of that old graybeard are so unmistakable that there is a certain reluctance to defame his memory and desecrate his tomb. And yet it is not a question of desecrating his tomb, or even of defaming his memory. Only his judgment and, still more, his "scientific" pretensions, are at stake. Marx's gestures, vocabulary, and arrogance, and those of all the characters, solemn or comic, who have succeeded one another on the Marxist scene and have invariably been so sure of themselves and their own infallibility, seem strangely familiar. They remind us of characters we have seen somewhere before. Suddenly, it dawns on us who they are: none other, of course, than those legendary physicians in Molière. But if Mr. Khrushchev seems more like Sganarelle, poor Marx is indeed a blood-brother to Monsieur Diafoirus and Monsieur Purgon.

I mean this seriously. Perhaps Molière himself, who was mortally stricken on stage while playing Argan in *The Imaginary Invalid* and who refused, as he had sworn he would, to call a doctor, did not intend his portraits of those grotesque but dangerous characters, the physicians of his time, to be taken as lightly as people think. In writing *The Imaginary Invalid* or *The Physician in Spite of Himself,* the author of *Tartuffe* and *The Learned Women* was quietly but dauntlessly exposing still another form of hypocrisy and pedantry; he was dauntlessly exposing those who professed to be scientists though they were not and could not be scientists in the pre-scientific medicine of that day; he was dauntlessly exposing a new kind of Tartuffe, who took advantage of the universal fear of death, as Tartuffe himself had taken advantage of the believers' fear of hell. Undoubtedly Molière, two hundred years in advance, paved the way for a Claude Bernard in medicine, and made such a figure possible. With fearless irony, he was already defending the work Claude Bernard was to do.

What political economy most needs now is another Claude

Bernard to adapt the theory of the experimental method to its problems. If political economy has not yet had its Bernard, it is, I believe, because the whole field is rank with pseudo-scientific theories, pedantry, and hypocrisy, and also because it has not yet had its Molière to pierce and deflate the bombast and conceit of those who cut off an argument the way Molière's physicians cut off an arm.

All the humor of Molière's physicians stems from a fallacy, and that fallacy is grim. Molière's physicians claim to have the science and the power to cure illness and prevent death. In reality they have neither that science nor that power, but rather than abandon their pretensions, their prestige, and the money it brings them, they would look on the death of a patient with indifference, for they are without sense of responsibility. It is exactly the same with the so-called "scientific" economists, who widely proclaim that they have the science and the power to save mankind from poverty while in reality they have neither this science nor this power, nor can they possibly have them, and their pedantry finally induces in them a profound indifference to the fate of man, to human misery, oppression, terror, and mass murder. All they want is to be everlastingly right and so highly respected that no one dares to contradict them. If Sganarelle's famous declaration of faith were put in the mouth of Lenin, Stalin, Mao Tse-tung, Tito, or Khrushchev, it would sound a sinister, but undoubtedly authentic, note.

SGANARELLE: . . . I think it's the best trade there is, for whether you do well or badly you get paid just the same. We never get blamed for doing a bad job; and we cut the cloth we work on to please ourselves. A cobbler making shoes can't spoil a piece of leather without paying for the damage; but in this job we can spoil a man without its costing us a penny. The blunders aren't our fault: they're always the fault of the man who dies. In short, the nice thing about this profession is that dead men have a most marvelous decency and discretion; you never hear a dead man complain of the doctor who killed him.

LÉANDRE: It is true that the dead are uncommonly polite on this subject.

In his solemn address on the fortieth anniversary of the October Revolution, Mr. Khrushchev was brazen enough to remind his listeners of the Hungarian uprising. He might just as well have used the words of Monsieur Purgon, the Molière physician: "That is a very great audacity, and a very strange revolt of a patient against his physician. . . ." And again, how easy it would be to imagine Marshal Zhukov, at the time of the uprising, using the language of Monsieur Purgon to reassure the Central Committee of the Party on Hungary's fate: "Don't worry, I have remedies which are proof against everything. I am waiting for her to come to her death agony. . . . The patient either will die or she'll be yours—or I'm no doctor." Today's physicians of the social body have far more power than the physicians of Molière; they use far more drastic remedies. But they have the same self-assurance in the practice of their art.

It is Marx, however, Karl Marx himself, who was responsible for making them all so marvelously dogmatic. And it is Marx, more than any of them, Marx with his apocalyptic prophetic vision, who recalls the Molière physicians: "What I want is important diseases, good long fevers with delirium, fine high fevers with purple eruptions, good old plagues, nice, well-formed dropsies, splendid pleurisies with inflammation of the lungs. That's what I like, that's where I triumph. And I should be delighted, sir, if you had all the diseases I have just named, and if you were given up by all the doctors in desperation, in your last agony, just so I could show you the excellence of my cures, and my earnest desire to render you service." To which, like Argan himself, we are supposed to respond, "I am obliged to you, sir, for all your kindness to me."

Nothing is more coldly, more obstinately, more unconsciously cruel than pedantry. Nor does anything propagate itself so readily. Karl Marx has fathered more disciples than have either Claude Bernard or Molière. Today, every hope of discovery or advance in political economy is obstructed in the name of Marx or Hegel, just as in the seventeenth century the Sorbonne condemned the use of quinine in the name of Aristotle. The names of the authorities have changed, but the fanaticism is still here, and so are pedantic nonentities. One of these is described by Molière: "He is firm in dispute, obstinate as a mule in his principles, he never alters his opinions, and he follows a line of reasoning to the last confines of logic. But above all what I like in him is that, in following my own example, he accepts without question the opinions of the great Ancients, and he has refused to listen for a moment to the arguments and experiments concerning the alleged discoveries of our own time . . . and similar nonsense."

"Even in America," wrote Engels on January 29, 1886, "the condition of the working class must gradually sink lower and lower." If today, more than seventy years later and now that this surprising prediction has been completely belied by the facts, a Communist were asked to explain so flagrant a refutation of Engels' prophecy, he would have no qualms about replying, in the words of Sganarelle, "Such good health is alarming." For the past hundred years, Marxists have been trying to convince us that America is on the decline. America is "The invalid imagined by Marxists," and what they cannot forgive is that their patient refuses to admit that he is ill.

CLÉANTE: Sir, I am delighted to find that you are up and to see that your health is better.

TOINETTE: What do you mean, his health is better? That's not true. Monsieur is always sick.

CLÉANTE: I had heard that Monsieur was getting better, and I think he is looking very well.

TOINETTE: What do you mean, he's looking well? He's looking very badly, and anyone who says he's looking better is crazy. He's never been so sick.

ARGAN: That's very true.

TOINETTE: He walks, sleeps, eats, and drinks like anybody else. But that doesn't keep him from being very sick.

ARGAN: That's very true.

CLÉANTE: Sir, I am shocked indeed to hear it.

Let us leave it to others to be shocked about America.

In the same Molière play there is also an excellent analysis of the dictatorship that Marx so ardently desired for the proletariat. The brief dialogue I am about to quote may help the reader to understand how it can be possible, even today, for a certain well-known French writer to praise both humanism and Terror at one and the same time. Here is the scene in which Molière's physician tries to stir up in the patient's body an antagonism between its various parts that can end only in class consciousness, and the struggle to defeat and eliminate such parts as prevent the others from profiting.

TOINETTE [*disguised as a doctor*]: What the devil are you doing with that arm?

ARGAN: What?

TOINETTE: There's an arm I would have cut off immediately, if I were you.

ARGAN: Why?

TOINETTE: Don't you realize that it draws all the nourishment to itself, and it prevents the whole side from profiting by it?

ARGAN: Yes, but I need my arm.

TOINETTE: You've got a right eye there that I would get rid of, if I were in your place.

ARGAN: Get rid of my eye?

TOINETTE: Don't you see that it incapacitates the other eye and deprives it of nourishment? Believe me, you should get rid of it as soon as possible, and you will see much better with the left eye.

ARGAN: There's no hurry.

. . . . . .

BÉRALDE: There is a doctor who seems to know his business.

ARGAN: Yes, but he goes a little too quick.

BÉRALDE: All great physicians are like that.

Heaven forbid that I should for a moment question the greatness of Sorbonne professors, and I am well aware that, although the centuries pass, the Sorbonne will endure forever. It is still today what it was in the time of Molière, what it was even in the time of Joan of Arc. I can only hope that, along with that learned and powerful institution, there will always be a Molière as well. Today, perhaps, Molière is a Hungarian boy, too young to know about the Sorbonne, but old enough to watch the Russian helmets go by on the streets of Budapest. And perhaps he watches them with the impertinent air with which the little Poquelin observed the pointed hats of the Learned Doctors of his day. It has always been the aim of great comedians to make people laugh at their own misfortunes. But perhaps the new Molière will find this harder to achieve than his predecessor; perhaps it will prove difficult to make the Hungarian people laugh.

Molière did more than condemn human folly; he laid bare its causes. Here I must quote at some length the admirable passage in which Béralde takes the side of reason against his brother, Argan, who is befuddled with remedies and the jargon of pedantry. It shows how little can be done against the fanaticism of pseudo-science. To prove the fanatic wrong is useless, since it is not the truth that he seeks, but a confirmation of his faith. The mere fact that in Western Europe today there are workers willing to be Communists after the massacre of their Hungarian brothers is proof enough of my thesis. But now, let Argan speak for himself.

ARGAN: So doctors don't know anything, according to you?

BÉRALDE: . . . All the excellence of their art consists in a pompous jargon, in a fine-sounding lingo, which gives you words for reasons and promises for results.

ARGAN: But after all . . . everybody calls in the doctors.

BÉRALDE: That's an indication of human weakness, not of the genuineness of their art.

ARGAN: But the doctors must certainly think their art is genuine, since they use it on themselves.

BÉRALDE: The fact is that there are some among them who accept the popular delusion, by which they profit, and others who profit by it without accepting the delusion. Your Doctor Purgon, for instance, doesn't know any better; he is . . . a man who believes in his rules more than in all the demonstrations of mathematics, who would think it a crime to venture to examine his rules. He doesn't see anything obscure in medicine, or anything doubtful or difficult. With his impetuous prejudice, his rigid self-confidence, his brutality in what he thinks is reasonable, he never pauses to consider anything. You shouldn't hold any grudge against him for anything he may do to you; it's with the best faith in the world that he will finish you off, and in killing you he will do just what he has done to his wife and children, and what, if the occasion should arise, he will do to himself. . . . It's our disquiet, our impatience which upsets everything; and most men die of their remedies, and not of their illnesses.

ARGAN: But you must agree that we can aid nature in certain ways.

BÉRALDE: Dear heaven, these are mere ideas that we like to befool ourselves with. Men have always been full of fine fancies which we come to believe because they flatter us, and because it would be very nice if they were true. When a doctor talks to you about aiding, supporting, relieving nature, about taking from nature what interferes with her and supplying her what she lacks, about restoring nature and making her function properly . . . he is telling you medicine's fairy tale. But when you come down to truth and experience, you find nothing of all that. It's like one of those lovely dreams which leave you, when you wake up, only the distress of having believed them.

The physician of today would be gravely mistaken were he to hold any grudge against Molière. It was with Molière that there began that trend in modern medicine which makes it possible to hope that it may some day become a science. It was with Molière that physicians began to give up "medicine's fairy tale" and "come down to truth and experience." Looking at political economy in the light of "truth and experience," it is equally obvious that when Marx, to paraphrase Béralde's tirade against physicians, talks to you about aiding, supporting, relieving society, about taking from society what interferes with it and supplying it what it lacks, about restoring society and making it function properly . . . he is telling you the "fairy tale" of political economy. It is impossible to hold any grudge against him, since he is so obviously sincere, but nothing is more dangerous than the sincerity of pedants, for it spreads like the plague.

"It's our disquiet, our impatience which upsets everything," wrote Molière. But disquiet is legitimate enough in those dying of hunger; and impatience is a hundredfold justified in the oppressed. There can be no question of denying the ills of capitalist society as Marx observed them at first hand in London. Marx claimed to be able to cure those ills, but we are more likely to die of the cure than of the ills. The chain of causes to which Marx attributed those ills was entirely the fruit of his imagination. Alain, the late French moralist, made a brilliant analysis of that chain of causes— oddly enough, in writing about Argan. This is the example he used: "The infant pricked by a pin howls as though he were desperately ill because he has no idea of the cause or of its cure. And sometimes he even makes himself truly ill by his howling, whereupon he howls louder still. But this illness must still be called imaginary, for while imaginary ills are as real as real ones they remain imaginary in the sense that we bring them upon ourselves by our own actions, while at the same time blaming them upon outside things. It is not only infants who make themselves ill by their howling."

Even a pinprick is always painful. But Ricardo's ruthless capitalism was more than a pinprick; it was a spear thrust into the heart of human dignity. If the infant knew the cause and its cure, that is to say, if he saw things as they are, if he had the ability to reason correctly and the intelligence to follow his line of reasoning to its logical conclusion, he would simply remove the pin. This is what the Americans have always tried to do. But Marxists refuse to recognize real causes and real cures; they howl and squirm and perpetuate their ills by their own actions. They create a "fairy tale" out of the pin or the spear, instead of removing them. Marx may be the Balzac of political economy. But the fiction of political economy is no more interesting than medicine's fairy tale. No one in the world can force me to like this kind of fiction. And when, in addition, I am informed that it is "scientific," I can only laugh.

17

"The Only American Economist

of Importance"

Who was Henry Charles Carey, whom Karl Marx called the only American economist of importance?

His father, Mathew Carey, born in Ireland in 1760, was the son of a rich baker and received an excellent education. It was the fashion at the time to give young men manual skills, and Mathew Carey became a printer. He started a newspaper which he printed himself and in it he violently attacked English rule. For this he was sent to prison, and eventually into exile. In Paris he met Benjamin Franklin, who was then the ambassador of the young American Republic. Franklin appointed him printer to the embassy.

Mathew Carey must have followed Franklin to Philadelphia, since that is where we find him some years later. By this time he had met Jefferson, Madison, and Hamilton. Lafayette had advanced him funds to start a printing establishment of his own. The printing of the Catholic and Protestant Bibles (the Douai and King James versions) made him a wealthy man. He repaid Lafayette in full. Meanwhile he had also become one of the most influential pamphleteers in America.

His son, Henry Charles, was born in Philadelphia in 1793. Franklin had been dead for three years. Washington was still

President. Jefferson was fifty. When Henry Charles Carey died, in 1879, Marx still had four years to live; Samuel Gompers, founder of the American Federation of Labor, was twenty-nine; Henry Ford was sixteen. Thus Henry Charles Carey constituted, if only by the long span of his lifetime, a link between the great generation of Americans of the Independence era and the America of our day. But by his thinking also he linked the two periods. Carey's works, more than any others, enable us to understand how that same dynamic, optimistic, individualist, and enterprising spirit, which had found such powerful expression in the political realm, came to be embodied in the economic and social realm as well.

Undoubtedly Mathew Carey had deeply influenced his son. He had handed down his hatred of England. He had also awakened his son's social conscience. In the high-flown language of the day, Mathew Carey had entitled one of his pamphlets, "Appeal to the wealthy of the Land, Ladies as well as Gentlemen, on the Character, Conduct, Situation, and Prospects of Those Whose Sole Dependence is on the Labour of their Hands." It is plainly stated in this pamphlet that political economy has its limitations and must never be allowed to reach the point where that concern for the poor which is essential to the health of the social body is abandoned. "Whoever passes this line of demarcation," wrote the elder Carey, "is guilty of the heinous offence of 'grinding the faces of the poor.'"

Henry Charles Carey's life was characteristic of a peculiarly American tradition which still exists today and is most difficult for Europeans to understand, since it is almost unknown in Europe. What kind of boy was Henry Charles Carey at the age of ten? Undoubtedly he was an intelligent, brave, hard-working, and very promising child. His father's writings and wide cultivation had made him one of the best known and most respected men in America. He counted among his friends the finest names of the Independence era. His printing establishment and his publishing enterprises had built him a fortune. What would a man in his position be likely to hope for a son? A French father's greatest hope would be for his son to get the best education possible in the best possible schools.

Yet we learn that Henry Charles Carey left school for good when he was ten or eleven years old. He made the decision himself; he thought school a waste of time. But what is so astonishing is that his father made no objections. Americans are not necessarily convinced that school is the one and only, the indispensable, means of obtaining an education. Everyone who knew Henry Charles Carey has testified that he became one of the best educated men of his time. He spoke and wrote excellent French. At sixty he taught himself German. He was an omnivorous reader of everything that he could lay his hands on, from philosophy and history to novels, poetry, fairy tales, and science. Later in life he was to say that he owed his unusual erudition to his father. His father, he said, had given him both his love of reading and a sharply questioning and practical attitude toward life. Soon after he left school, when he was still only twelve years old, his father made him a businessman. He sent him out into the business world on his own, to direct the Baltimore branch of the publishing firm.

Business, the ruthless discipline of business, in which the law of cause and effect is implacably reflected in the balance sheet, gave Henry Charles Carey his education. Americans believe that nothing can replace the experience of earning a living, just as our forefathers believed that a youth could not be knighted till he had won his spurs in battle. And after all, in an industrial and commercial society the struggle for daily bread is as bitter as any of man's battles. The education acquired in that struggle gives men judgment and strength. And this is what counts in the end. To be educated in the school of harsh reality, whether on the field of battle or in the arena of production and commerce, broadens the mind and forges the character, developing a toughness and resilience that no school can ever provide. For the school is still the cocoon of the human larva, and only when that cocoon has been shed can the boy become a man. Henry Charles Carey turned precociously soon into a man.

To Carey, business, into which he was plunged at so early an age, was primarily a means of making money, as it is all over the world. And since he was an excellent businessman, he rapidly became, if not rich, at least very comfortably off. Besides his publishing firm, he had investments in leading Pennsylvania industries. He owned a town house in Philadelphia and a country place in New Jersey. He led the pleasant and easy life of a man of wealth. But to this American, business represented far more than a means of making money; what he sought from business was independence, and thus the possibility of devoting himself wholly to what he believed to be his vocation. In 1835, at forty-two, in the full tide of health and strength, Carey retired from business in order to elaborate and complete a theory of political economy.

Again, this is characteristically American. I have often met American businessmen who, despite an unbroken record of success, dream only of the day when they can retire, not to take a rest, but to devote their minds and talents to work of a more altruistic nature that will benefit mankind in general, even beyond the frontiers of their own country. Moreover, a great many leading American businessmen, indeed almost all of them, seem to spend nine-tenths of their time running a vast number of intellectual, social, or humanitarian enterprises, while still taking full responsibility for their own business.

Henry Charles Carey retired completely, leaving to others the management of his publishing firm. From then on he led the life of a philosopher and writer. Just as in boyhood he had scorned going to school, so he remained aloof from the universities. Yet, in his own way, he was a teacher. He wrote for the newspapers, and for some years was one of the chief editorial writers for the New York *Tribune,* at the time the most influential paper in America in economic affairs. He published a prodigious number of pamphlets, and frequently lectured to businessmen's clubs. He also wrote several books, of which the most important are *Principles of Political Economy* (3 vols., 1837-1840); *The Past, the Present and the Future* (1848); and his masterpiece, *Principles of Social Science* (3 vols., 1858-1859). Besides all this he corresponded constantly, not only with fellow countrymen but with many Europeans. He was a member of the Swedish Royal Academy, the American Academy of Arts and Sciences, and a number of other learned societies.

He felt about politics as he did about universities. He had no desire to enter them. He refused to be a candidate for governor of Pennsylvania or of New Jersey. He was even spoken of as a potential candidate for the Presidency, but he never let himself become involved. Yet it has been generally acknowledged that his influence on the politics and legislation of his day, though indirect, was considerable. He was on friendly terms with some of the most powerful members of Congress, as well as with several Presidents, including Abraham Lincoln, who consulted him on pending legislation and even on appointments to the Cabinet.

Moreover, everyone of any importance in America sooner or later appeared in Carey's house in Philadelphia. Sunday afternoon was his day at home, and people came from as far as New York and Washington, knowing that in Carey's house they would meet both Americans and foreigners with authoritative opinions on current problems and also on questions of a more general philosophical interest. Talk flowed freely, feeling ran high, but the manners were those of the civilized world, and Carey's hospitality was enhanced by wines which he chose with the care of a connoisseur.

If I have lingered over the details of this man's life, it was in order to help the reader to form a just opinion of his work. For those with Marxist leanings the fact that Marx himself considered Carey "the only American economist of importance" should be enough. Those, on the other hand, who are inclined to lean in the opposite direction, could hardly fail to find his standing in American society impressive. Whichever side the reader takes, Carey's work merits consideration.

I have said that Carey is almost forgotten today. Nevertheless two books have recently been written about him, one in 1931* and the other in 1951.† The book by Arnold W. Green is the more important of the two, although unfortunately it can only confirm the American public in its belief that Carey's work has no value. I am completely convinced that the contrary is true. I have no hesitation whatever in admitting that his work contains flaws, grave flaws. Indeed, to admit the flaws is the only possible way of saving that part of his work which has validity and stature. But Carey, in many ways, was a great man.

Henry Charles Carey belonged to his times. Like Marx and so many other of his contemporaries, he too suffered from the cult of the pseudo-scientific, from the fashion for extrapolation and premature generalization, and from the prestige of Newtonian physics. And yet, along with all this and in the very face of it, his work teems with brilliant and profoundly accurate intuitions. It is in his intuitions, and in them alone, that his greatness lay. But beyond any doubt, he had these intuitions, and they put an intolerable strain upon the whole structure of the alleged science of political economy. They were like a tree that grows in the wall of a house

* Kaplan, A. D. H., *Henry Charles Carey. A Study in American Economic Thought* (Baltimore: Johns Hopkins Press).

† Green, Arnold W., *Henry Charles Carey, Nineteenth-Century Sociologist* (Philadelphia: University of Pennsylvania Press).

and ends by bringing down the house altogether. A tree of this kind is a living tree, sound and sturdy, and that is precisely why it demolishes whatever stands in its way. Carey's supposedly scientific structure belonged to his day and was in no sense original; since Descartes, Europe had been cluttered with faulty structures such as his. But the tree that demolished these structures was not European; it was American. This is where Carey was original.

Carey had certainly found the analogy between political economy and medicine. He was on the right road, even if he did not follow it very far. "The physician," he wrote, "though not required to treat the man who is in the enjoyment of perfect health, invariably commences his studies by ascertaining what is the natural action of the system—having done which, he feels himself qualified to examine into the disturbing causes by which health and life are constantly destroyed. Physiology is the necessary preliminary to pathology; and this is as true of social as it is of physical science." It remained for him to introduce the experimental method into the social sciences, as Claude Bernard introduced it into medicine. But it was Carey's misfortune that Claude Bernard came after him. Carey's great work, *Principles of Social Science,* appeared in 1858. Claude Bernard's little book appeared in 1865. But even before Claude Bernard, medicine certainly had fewer pretensions than political economy.

It can be said of Carey that, even when he was carried away by his enthusiasm for Newton and the law of universal gravity, he had no illusions about the state of social science. "Social science can scarcely be said to have an existence. . . ." he wrote. "Political economy can bear only the same relation to social science that the observations of the Chaldean shepherds bear to modern astronomy." In other words, political economy was still in its stammering infancy. At about the same time, on February 1, 1859, Karl Marx was writing, "I hope to gain a scientific victory for our party." I prefer

Carey's Chaldean shepherds. Without them, no science can ever come into its own. It is always with the shepherds that everything must begin. Unhappily, Carey, in his impatience, sometimes forgot that his place was at their side. Too often he let himself be led astray by the countless demons of economic dogmatism.

And now, what is political economy? What is its aim?

This is how Adam Smith, revered patriarch of capitalism, defined it: "The great object of the political economy of every country is to increase the riches and power of that country." No definition could be more clearly expressed. To me it is strictly nationalist and imperialist, no less so than were Napoleon's dreams. The only difference is that the lever of commercial imperialism is not war but wealth. Yet, since it behooves us to be as fair as possible to those we dislike, I must hasten to add that Adam Smith's view of political economy was limited, and that he saw it as only one element in the art of government, as only one of the many elements that go to make up the whole body of knowledge with which anyone administering the national economy should be familiar. In all fairness, therefore, it was not Adam Smith, but his successors, who made of political economy the science of civilization itself. It should be added that Smith was something of a humanitarian and that he actually did seek the welfare of the workers. This may be the very reason why Carey never attacked Smith, though he was pitiless in his criticisms of Ricardo, Malthus, and the other theoreticians of capitalism. But in Smith's mind, the logic of his system conflicted with his humanitarian ideas, and so in the end, once again, a rigid system was to triumph over good intentions.

Let us now look for a moment at Carey's concept of political economy. At the very least, it must be admitted that he immensely broadened the scope of the debate. He saw things on a grand scale, a very grand scale, and in this he was in the best American tradition. He began by pointing out that man's whole life is "a contest with nature." Man's life is indeed a battle, a battle on more than one front. There is the strictly metaphysical battle between being and non-being, which takes place within the soul. There is also the ageless debate which man carries on with God. But what concerned Carey was man's contest with nature, and his dominion over it, the *Imperium Naturae* of Francis Bacon. Carey believed that society owed its existence to this contest with nature, since the strength of any one man alone was so disproportionately small that unless he associated himself with his fellow men he was doomed from the start. Nothing could be more real, less abstract, than this association of human beings with one another; it is an association in which men unite their strength for power over nature, and an association encompassing literally not only all the regions of the earth but also all the centuries of man's existence on it. As I roll along in my car, I am inseparable from him who long ago discovered the principle of the wheel; and as I light my pipe, I am still bound to him who once discovered and mastered fire.

The concept of the struggle for power over nature as the goal of mankind can hardly be called original. But where Carey was so characteristically American was in his insistence that this association of men's strength and power had a more distant, loftier aim, a more imperative goal than that of mere power over nature. "The ultimate object of all human effort," wrote Carey, in a truly remarkable statement, "[is] the production of the being known as *Man* capable of the highest aspirations." Here Carey took a decisive step of his own. Nowhere in the theoreticians of the capitalist school, nowhere in Marx and Lenin, can any such words as these be found. Basically, all that concerned Carey was man, and the process whereby man becomes more and more civilized. What Carey sought to create, beyond a theory of political economy, was a theory of civilization itself. For him, man was not only greater than the whole of nature, but even above the victory he won over it. With this victory civilization began, but it still had far, far indeed to go. It still faced the obligation to fulfill man's "highest aspirations."

In the last analysis, therefore, Carey's ambition was to construct a philosophy of civilization. Unfortunately, however, he was not equipped for the task. He did not distinguish between the degrees of knowing, or even between moral philosophy and Newtonian physics. This was an error common to his time. Kant himself confused Newtonian physics with the philosophy of nature. Nevertheless, despite this inadequacy of Carey's, whenever he turned to "truth and experience" he overflowed with original and profound ideas, and his work contains a profusion of invaluable clues to an understanding of American society and civilization.

Carey very clearly saw that neither all the victories over nature nor all the wealth accumulated by toil can avail, unless those victories and that wealth are then put to man's service, for him to use for his own, his human aims. Just as the nature of man is above that of the beasts, so his highest aspirations and his ultimate ends transcend the realm of the material. Man is more important, he has more intrinsic value, than the whole of nature, more even than his dominion over nature, more than society. Carey was a true Jeffersonian.

What Carey could not forgive in the English school of political economy, which after all must historically be called the capitalist school, and what he particularly could not forgive in Ricardo and Malthus, whom Marx so profoundly respected, was that they assigned to civilization the role of pursuing not happiness but wealth and power; that they debased man by directing him toward an aim that was beneath him, since power and physical satisfaction are also the aim of the beast; that they forgot to take man and man's nature into consideration when they established their so-called laws which reduced him to the level of the beast. Quoting Madame de Staël's friend Sismondi, Carey asked, "What then, is wealth everything, and is man absolutely nothing?" And he went on to say, "In the eyes of modern political economy he *is* nothing, and can be nothing, because it takes no note of the qualities by which he is distinguished from the brute, and is therefore led to regard him *as being a mere instrument to be used by capital* to enable its owner to obtain compensation for its use." With this bitter pronouncement Carey was merely recognizing the true significance of capitalism. Here Carey saw eye to eye with Marx. No one who has read Ricardo could fail to agree with them.

While it is a fact that Carey hated England, it would be exceedingly unjust to say that this hatred explains his anti-capitalism. It was his perspicacity that made him anti-capitalist. He saw that, like the physical body, the social body also has maladies that doctors must attend. When, in the sixteenth century, the spread of syphilis across the whole of Europe struck at the very sources of life, the English called this plague the "French disease," the French called it the "Neapolitan disease," the Italians called it the "Spanish disease," each country thus blaming another for the scourge. But a no less destructive disease, a disease of the social body which falsifies the aim of economic production by subordinating man to that which he produces, found its theoretical justification in the English capitalist school and has now spread over more than half the face of the earth in that phase of its development known as Marxism. It is immensely to Henry Charles Carey's credit that, in his time, he was shrewd enough to attack this social disease at its focal point. So far as I know, he never mentioned Marx, yet he was undermining Marx's whole position by his constant attacks on the English capitalist school. It would be possible to go on quoting him indefinitely. His life work was actually one long, mercilessly documented and pitilessly honest indictment of the appalling system formulated by the English economists and swallowed hook, line, and sinker by Marx.

Such is the course of modern political economy [wrote Carey], which not only does not "feel the breath of the spirit" but even ignores the existence of the spirit itself, and is therefore found defining what it is pleased to call the natural rate of wages, as being "that price which is necessary to enable the laborers, one with another, to subsist and perpetuate their race without either increase or diminution" (Ricardo)—that is to say, such price as will enable *some to grow rich* and increase their race, *while others perish of hunger, thirst, and exposure.* Such are the teachings of a system that has fairly earned the title of the "dismal science."

This American was immeasurably more radical than Marx. He would never have conceded what Marx conceded so readily in his letter to Weydemeyer—"the greatness and the temporary necessity of the bourgeois regime." Carey saw nothing great, nothing even temporarily necessary, in bourgeois capitalism as defined by the English school; he saw it quite simply as a loathsome malady, a social disease to be fought and conquered. And today there is still no other way of refuting Communism except by denouncing at the same time the form of capitalism that gave it birth. In Carey's indictment, moreover, there can be detected the first intimations of an original American philosophy of labor and production.

Such being the tendency of all its teachings, it is no matter of surprise that modern English political economy sees in man only an animal that *will* procreate, that *must* be fed, and that *can be made* to work [Carey's emphasis]—an *instrument to be used by trade;* that it repudiates all the distinctive qualities of man, and limits itself to the consideration of those he holds *in common with the beast of burden or of prey;* that it denies that the Creator meant *that every man should find a place at His table,* or that there exists any reason why a poor laborer, able and willing to work, should have any more right to be fed than the cotton-spinner has to find a market for his cloth; or that it assures its students that "labor is a commodity."

Let me say again that it would be a mistake to imagine that so grave a denunciation of English capitalism showed nothing but hatred of England. The division of the world into beasts of prey and beasts of burden is quite enough to explain the tide of revolutionary and anti-colonial ferment of which Marxism is taking full advantage. But that division was not created by Marx; he found it ready made.

To use the familiar language of parables, once upon a time the world was told a story, the story of the wolves and the sheep, and there were two versions of it. Here is the first version, as told by Ricardo and the capitalist school:

"Mankind," they said, "is divided into wolves and sheep. The wolves can subsist and increase their strength only by eating the sheep. But to do this requires scientific organization. If the wolves were to eat up all the sheep at once, or if on the other hand they were to give the sheep nothing whatever to eat, they themselves would starve to death. So the wolves must allow the sheep to propagate and survive, they must give them just enough to eat to enable them to do so, and they must calculate as exactly as possible how many sheep it is necessary to keep alive so that there will always be sufficient prey for the wolves."

And now here is the second version of the story, as told by Marx:

"Unfortunately it has been scientifically proved, and is therefore indisputable, that humanity is divided into wolves and sheep and that it is in the nature of the wolves to eat the sheep. But I intend to change all that. I propose to convince the sheep that there is no more miserable fate than to be perpetually doomed to be eaten. Thus I shall awaken the sheep to class consciousness. Sheep of all countries, unite. Together we shall bring about the Revolution of the sheep and establish the dictatorship of the sheep. Then the sheep will eat the wolves. When all the wolves have been eaten, there will no longer be the need for a dictatorship, there will no longer be the need for a State, there will be only sheep. It will be what I call a classless society. And the free development of each sheep will be the condition for the free development of all."

It must be admitted that this story is more consistent in its capitalist than in its Marxist version. For it is somewhat hard to understand how the sheep, even by uniting, can ever eat the wolves, unless they themselves become wolves, in which case it would be the same story all over again, as Milovan Djilas seems to have understood.

To continue with my parable, Carey, the American, having heard the two versions of the story, then said:

"That story of yours is abominable. I refuse to accept either the capitalist version or the Marxist improvement on it. I cannot deny that among man's instincts there are some that impel him to behave like a beast of prey. Nor can I deny that his weakness exposes him to exploitation. But because of what is specifically human in man, he is neither wolf nor sheep; he is man, and, as such, stands far above both beasts of prey and beasts of burden. What is specifically human in man keeps him from exploiting others as it keeps him from letting himself be exploited by them. And man is fully aware that his greatest source of strength, indeed the very guaranty of his liberty as an individual and of his power over nature, lies in association with his fellow men. Only by dominating his predatory instincts and overcoming in himself the craven weakness that makes servitude acceptable to him, can man remain man and form a society with other men for the purpose of producing enough nourishment for all and a greater common happiness."

But now, without parable or circumlocution, I shall restate these same fundamental positions. According to classical cap-

italism, as defined by the English school, the supreme goal
on earth is to increase wealth and power continually through
the exploitation of natural resources and the subordination
of labor and the workers to capital and money. This creates
a society of master and slave. History has seen just such a society, which has been historically responsible for repeated
and specific crimes at home and in its colonies. There is always a danger of societies of this kind. What I mean is that
no society can be infallibly immunized against the social can-
cer of the exploitation of workers by those who own the
means of production.

According to Karl Marx, on the other hand, the supreme
goal on earth is a harmonious and fraternal City of Man in
which men will at last be reconciled to one another. This
City of Man will come into being when the Revolution "violently overthrows the old system of production." The role of
hero and builder of this Revolution will be played by the
proletariat. The proletariat is composed of all the victims of
capitalist exploitation. It is under capitalism that the proletariat becomes a class; it is only within the capitalist system
that it can exist, and it exists within that system only as "the
most suffering class." Marxist revolution is therefore inconceivable except under the capitalist system. Under no other
system could it possibly take place. With the coming of the
Revolution, the proletariat "destroys at the same time as the
system of production, the conditions of class antagonism, it
destroys classes in general, and, in so doing, its own domination as a class." At that moment, the harmonious and fraternal City of Man will be achieved. Historically, however,
everything goes to show that Marxism always falls far short
of its goal; that it not only never attains its ultimate goal of
man's reconciliation with man, but that it creates, by revolution, exactly what it claims to destroy, that is, a new class,
which in turn takes possession of the means of production
and pitilessly exploits both labor and the workers. Milovan

Djilas has made this very plain. The fact is that the adventures of the unhappy Marxists are exactly like those of poor Don Quixote with his lady love, Dulcinea del Toboso. Needless to say, Dulcinea is the loveliest and most noble of princesses, just as the Communist City of Man is obviously the most harmonious and fraternal of Utopias. But malevolent sorcerers always appear from somewhere to keep Don Quixote and Dulcinea apart, and when at last he reaches her it is only to find that they have transformed that "peerless and great lady" into the ugliest of scullery maids. Yet this does not cause Don Quixote to waver in his unalterable admiration and fidelity.

But Carey rejected both the capitalist postulate and its Marxist corollary. He clearly understood the diversity of economic functions, a diversity which becomes greater and greater with the advance and extension of production, and he considered this diversity as necessary to social harmony as the various physiological functions are necessary to health, and in no way conducive to antagonism and class struggle. Refuting Ricardo and Malthus, he proved that it is not only possible but inevitable for the economic conditions of the workers to improve through the dynamic and fertile association of labor and accumulating capital. He thought of labor and capital as existing on the intellectual and spiritual planes as well as on the material plane; he saw them as much in terms of their continuity in time as of their extension in space. The ultimate objective of all human effort, according to Carey, was not just the accumulation of the things of this world, but the achievement of civilization itself, in other words, the creation of a more and more civilized mankind— "the production of the being known as Man capable of the highest aspirations." The one way by which to achieve a higher civilization seemed to him, not by revolution (as in Marx), not by the fierce systematic exploitation of the poor by the rich (as in the capitalist system), but by the association of all men for this common purpose. I believe it to be a matter of historical fact that this is not just the ideal of a man named Henry Charles Carey, but that it is characteristically American, and to the extent that any ideal can ever be realized it is the ideal to which the whole of American society aspires. I must now prove this theory of mine in my next chapters, and prove it according to Claude Bernard's formula that defines experimentation as a process of reasoning by which we methodically submit our ideas to the test of the facts.

This is in no sense a complete analysis of Carey's work, which is as labyrinthine as it is luxuriant. I shall not even attempt to reduce this labyrinth to the classic order of a French garden. Rather, I mean to give a summary view of it.

Carey made use of the myth of Robinson Crusoe to explain his economic and social ideas. He began with man, alone in the face of nature, and went on to show man's need to associate with other men and the evolution of the economic organism. But he did not depend on myth alone. He also made use of a unique experience completely outside that of either Ricardo, Malthus, or Marx—the experience of pioneer life on the American frontier. Basing his arguments upon it, he demolished the postulates of the English school on the origins and development of human societies. That part of Carey's work, founded as it was on actual experience, still seems to me irrefutable today. He was aware that his were not the accepted methods of approach, and he felt the loneliness of his position, but he knew that he was right. "Social science," he wrote, "as taught in some of the colleges of this country and of Europe, is now on a level with the chemical science of the early part of the last century; and there it will remain so long as its teachers shall continue to look inwards to their own minds and *invent* theories, instead of looking outwards to a great laboratory of the world for the collection of facts with a view to the *discovery* of laws." I believe that this distinction between invented theory and discovered theory is exceedingly useful. It makes the difference between a Molière physician and a Claude Bernard. It may even make the difference between a Lenin and an American labor leader, but I shall come back to this later. Carey was indeed in a lonely position, but he had no doubt that he was on the right path. With the disarming candor found in all the great American Puritans, he said, "Salvation, salvation is in me and in my books."

To a degree rare for his time, Carey seems to have recognized the equivocal nature of society. He was well aware that economic necessity brings about a servitude which can be surmounted only if men join together in some form of society. But that very organization of society can itself bring about a new servitude, a social servitude this time, which must in turn be surmounted by a society at once more comprehensive and more tightly organized. Carey had a sense of the continuity of progress which was peculiarly American and profoundly contrary to the concept of all-or-nothing and of Utopian, nihilistic, and totalitarian revolution.

In the beginning, man lived by hunting, fishing, and gathering the fruits of the earth. Whatever he acquired, he acquired by plunder. He did not in any true sense possess the earth, but he was wholly dependent on it. He was its parasite as well as its slave. Property, as such, did not exist; there was only appropriation. Between these two words, *property* and *appropriation,* Carey made what to my mind is another very important distinction. He believed that there cannot be property except where there is labor and productivity. It is property when a man reaps only because he has sown. It is appropriation, on the other hand, when a man reaps what he has not sown, and this is true at every step on the economic ladder. When a speculator makes a fortune on the stock market at the expense of countless investors, this too is a form of parasitism and appropriation. Carey came close to defining not property, but appropriation, as theft.

In the second stage of man's economic development came property. Men associated themselves with the earth by labor and production. Then, to make labor less difficult and to increase production, they entered into an association with one another and shared the common tasks. The more production was increased and diversified, the easier and more remunerative their labor became, especially when their tools had been perfected. This primary and basic association of men for the increase of production and general welfare was what Carey called "commerce." By commerce he meant all interchange of goods, ideas, services, and tools, wherever in space and whenever in time this interchange took place. People have ridiculed this stretching of the word commerce to make it an all-inclusive synonym for society and civilization. But to me it seems, on the contrary, very fine, very intelligent, and moreover actually traditional. It is we, in our day, who have shrunk the word commerce, as indeed we have shrunk many other words. As late as the eighteenth century the Encyclopedists called the exchange of ideas, the reading of good books, the correspondence of Voltaire and Frederick II, a commerce. And in the liturgy of the Church the Incarnation of Christ, through which God associated himself with man, is called *admirabile commercium*.

Because of the diversity of production, everyone is at the same time a producer in one field and a consumer in all others. In this connection, Carey drew still another distinction, this time between *commerce* and *trade*. Commerce consists in making all that is produced available to everyone. Between producer and consumer, however, there exists an obstacle, the obstacle of distance. Distance creates a need for transportation. Of all the taxes imposed on production, Carey considered the tax of transportation the heaviest. The collector of that tax is the trader, the middle man, who comes between the producer and the consumer. Carey did not deny that trade was necessary, but he looked upon it as a servitude to be lightened as much as possible. The ideal solution would be to keep diminishing the distance between producer and consumer, to disperse production, to bring the market to the door of the producer, and to create as close an association as possible between the farmer's plow, the weaver's loom, and the blacksmith's anvil. Carey envisaged an industrial society which, although exceedingly widespread, would remain an organic whole, with an almost complete economic autarchy of small communities within the large, general community of civilization. The traveler in present-day America cannot help wondering whether this great dream that Carey described a hundred years ago has not now become a reality.

Carey's contempt for the trader and the middle man knew no bounds. He recognized the need for trade and transportation, and how could he do otherwise? But he urgently stressed the danger inherent in the period of transition from the producer to the consumer, for it was during this period that both producer and consumer were robbed. The aim of the trader is to buy at the lowest price he can and resell at the highest. He can do this only because of the distance that lies between consumer and producer. To both consumer and producer that distance represents a servitude. But to the trader it represents a living, and as a parasite he grows rich by exploiting it. Trade and transportation alike are necessary, but once trade obtains a monopoly, once it corners a commodity, once it starts speculating with a view to paying the producer less and charging the consumer more, it becomes theft.

The distinction that Carey made between commerce and trade was both general and profound. It underlay his thinking along every line. He condemned the abuses of trade, speculation, and monopoly at all levels and in all realms; he condemned them in whatever they affected, whether finance and banking or raw materials and manufactured goods; but first and foremost he condemned them where they affected that most sacred of assets, labor itself; he condemned them not only on the local market, but even more on the national and international markets. Upon this premise he built a philosophy of war, of the role of the State, and of colonization which is far more intelligent than anything to be found in Marx. Perhaps these theories of his are somewhat lacking in subtlety; perhaps he should have been better able to see that a war can be just, that the State has its own legitimate role to play; and his attitude toward colonization I will take up later in this chapter. But in his ingrained mistrust, on principle, of war, of the State, and of colonization, he was truly American, a true descendant of Jefferson.

> War and trade [wrote Carey] regard man as the instrument to be used, whereas commerce regards trade as the instrument to be used by man. . . . To the dealer in cotton or sugar, it matters little whether his commodities grow on hills or in the valleys, on trees or on shrubs. To the dealer in slaves, it is immaterial whether the chattel be male or female, parent or child; all that he requires to know being whether, having bought it cheaply, he can sell it dearly. . . . The soldier desires labor to be cheap, that recruits may be readily obtained. The great land-owner desires it may be cheap, that he may be enabled to appropriate to himself a large proportion of the proceeds of his land; and the trader desires it to be cheap, that he may be enabled to dictate the terms upon which he will buy, as well as those upon which he will sell.

This analogy between trade and war led Carey to express an opinion which I have not seen expressed elsewhere and which must seem, to anyone familiar with French history, admirably just. He held that the two men who had the most

catastrophic effect on France were Napoleon and Louis Philippe. Napoleon took workers who should have been producing and plunged them into his wars. Louis Philippe surrendered the nation's wealth to the greed of speculators and
shopkeepers. Both of them gave the State an ever greater monopoly not only on the work of men's hands but also on the
work of their minds. It was thanks to those two that the
French State became that monstrous, octopus-like middle
man, that parasite of production and consumption which,
with its titles, licenses, taxes, diplomas, and monopolies, forever comes between teacher and student, between reader and
writer, between peasants and those who eat and drink, between manufacturers and those who buy clothing, travel,
marry, work, and inhabit a house. The fact that the middle
man, instead of being a small shopkeeper, had now become
the State, in no way changed his parasitical nature, nor did it
impose less of a servitude upon the people; on the contrary,
he became even more dangerous, more parasitical, more of a
monster. As a parasite, the middle man inhibits production
more and more. People do not seem to be sufficiently aware,
for instance, that the great modern school of French painting
has developed not merely outside but even against the official teaching of the Beaux-Arts. Not one of the great painters
who constitute the glory of the Paris school owes anything to
the State and its official instruction. For, in all fields, production attains greatness only to the degree that it escapes from
the monopoly of middle men and its servitude to them, only
to the degree that it is untrammeled and free. This is what
Carey so thoroughly understood.

Carey began by giving warm support to free trade in the
form that England was then advocating. At first sight it
seemed to fit in very well with his general theory of commerce, in which the aim was to remove every obstacle to
trade. But upon reflection, he changed his mind completely
and became the champion of protectionism for America. It

had become clear to him that free trade, as actually practiced at that time by the English, was nothing, despite its name, but the instrument of a monstrous monopoly and an economic colonialism; that instead of constantly diminishing the distance between consumer and producer it only increased that distance inordinately; that instead of setting men free it made them the slaves of a system that fed upon them. The English bought raw materials all over the world as cheaply as they could, brought them back to their island, and charged the seller for the cost of transportation; then they sent back these raw materials all over the world in the form of manufactured goods, sold them at high prices, and this time charged the purchaser for the cost of transportation. Carey saw as clearly as Jefferson that, although America was politically independent, this economic colonialism threatened the young nation with servitude. He came to the conclusion, justifiable in my opinion, that *no trade can be truly free except as between producer nations,* and that therefore America must build up its own independent industry in order to enter eventually into free competition with England. Meanwhile, in the period of transition, the only solution was protectionism which would compel America to industrialize its production.

Carey's attitude toward the problems of the American Civil War was even more typical of his thinking. He had little sympathy for Lincoln; their viewpoints were diametrically opposed. Lincoln thought primarily in terms of politics; his chief concern was with the Rights of Man. Carey was firmly convinced that whoever invented the chain pump had done more than Saint Paul to abolish slavery. He saw little use in giving the Negro political freedom, only to have him engulfed in the still more horrible slavery of the economic proletariat. In Carey's view, the solution was to hasten the industrialization of the South. If the South were industrialized, it would no longer depend on selling its cotton on the English market or on buying England's manufactured goods. The resulting prosperity would bring continually increased economic benefits to both planter and Negro, and would therefore very soon make possible the emancipation of the slaves. Before the Civil War began, and even while it was going on, Carey kept pressing Lincoln to construct a great highway across the whole South, linking it to the North and thereby establishing closer economic relations between the two regions. If one can resist the seductions of political romanticism and look at the situation objectively, it is impossible not to see how right Carey was. Of course, this does not mean that Lincoln was wrong. Yet the Civil War did not solve the Negro problem, it undoubtedly could not have solved it, and it is only today, and because of the advance of industrialization in the South and throughout the nation, that the condition of the American Negro is now rapidly improving with the greater diversity of economic choices opened up to him by industrialization. Emerging at last from his proletarian servitude, the Negro is better able than ever before to defend and exercise his rights. This evolution has taken a hundred years. Carey had instinctively understood— and here again he was characteristically American—that in human affairs the all-or-nothing is always a false solution, and that the only true solution lies in continued progress.

Today, belatedly, though it is never too late to do right, the French government has also at last understood that it must hasten the industrialization of Algeria. France has realized that if the war is to end, it will be ended not so much by firing guns as by building roads, bridges, and factories, planning cities, industrializing agriculture, planting forests, and also establishing schools and emancipating the Moslem women. But to do this requires time, and the all-or-nothing policy which has such a fascination for so many members of the United Nations does not seem to me particularly clear-sighted under the circumstances, nor does it seem to be of much assistance to the peoples involved.

It is extremely interesting to note that during the Civil War, at the very same time that Carey was repeatedly calling for the construction of a great highway across the South, Karl Marx, speaking in the name of the European working classes, sent Lincoln a solemn pronouncement, written in exactly the same style as *Don Quixote* and those tales of chivalry which had turned the head of the Knight of the Sorrowful Mien. Here is how Marx described the American Civil War in his message: "Was not the contest for the territories, which opened the dire epopee, to decide whether the virgin soil of immense tracts should be wedded to the labor of the immigrants or prostituted by the tramp of the slave driver?" To this piece of literature Lincoln modestly replied, "The government of the United States has a clear consciousness that its policy neither is nor could be reactionary, but at the same time it adheres to the course which it adopted at the beginning, of abstaining everywhere from propagandism and unlawful intervention. It strives to do equal justice to all states and to all men, and it relies upon the beneficial results of that effort for support at home and for respect and good will throughout the world. Nations do not exist for themselves alone, but to promote the welfare and happiness of mankind by benevolent intercourse and example. It is in this relation that the United States regard their cause in the present conflict with slavery-maintaining insurgents as the cause of human nature. . . ." If I am to judge by Carey and Lincoln on the one hand, and Karl Marx on the other, I shall end by believing that the most truly distinguishing feature of the American character is the natural modesty with which it expresses itself.

Just as Jefferson had clearly seen the danger of political independence for nations without education, so Carey saw a similar danger for nations without autonomous production. He would have been far less anti-English, however, had England, instead of exploiting its colonies to further its own trade, made an effort to help them develop their production and industry. But we cannot afford to let ourselves be intimidated by words, no matter how unpopular. The word *colonialism* must be scrupulously re-examined whenever it is used. In each specific case, we must ask what lies behind it. Carey and even Lincoln himself would surely have drawn a distinction between the Opium War waged by the English against the Chinese to compel them to buy a lethal drug they no longer wanted, and the conquest of the French Congo by Savorgnan de Brazza who handed over to France a vast territory peopled with barbarians whom France has been slowly but surely industrializing and civilizing ever since. The process must take time; in this realm, whoever tries to make haste will only break his neck.

After Carey's death, in 1890, Charles H. Levermore wrote, "Carey and his friends never captured our colleges; but, for a generation, they have dominated five-sevenths of the newspaper offices, a pulpit far more influential than the professorial chair. The arguments to which Carey gave form and eloquence are in the mouths of more than half the businessmen and farmers of our country."

It is not, alas, too surprising that American universities neglected Carey during his lifetime and have now all but forgotten him. Academic circles are always inclined to be timorous, somewhat behind the times, and conservative. In the early Middle Ages, French institutions of learning did little but repeat Saint Augustine by rote; and even today, the Sorbonne often shows undue affection for time-worn ideas. But it is not only conservatism that accounts for the attitude of the great American universities toward Carey. It took a war for America to win political independence. It took a century of

effort, after that had been achieved, for America to win economic independence from England. Now, two centuries after
Jefferson, I do not believe that America has yet won complete
intellectual independence. I am convinced that in many areas
of its intellectual life America still remains a European colony, with all that this condition entails in the way of inferiority or superiority complexes, overbearing nationalism, or
undiscriminating "liberalism." I say this with no intent to
offend. A serious book is not written either to offend or to
flatter; it is written in an attempt to understand the facts and
make them understood. I shall therefore try to be extremely
precise and weigh each utterance, hoping that the reader will
also make some effort to be objective, and not allow his sensi-
tivities to influence his judgment.

Needless to say, it would be not only unjust but completely
false to maintain that in all areas of intellectual life America
is still a colony. A scientist such as Oppenheimer, a novelist
such as Faulkner, a composer such as John J. Becker, some
of the younger painters, a constellation of brilliant architects, a large number of journalists, a few motion-picture
producers, a labor leader such as George Meany, certain
theoreticians in economics, and undoubtedly many other
outstandingly gifted people in other fields would do honor
to any great country and have put America in the front ranks
of the world's contemporary intellectual and artistic achievement.

But, and I emphasize this *but* advisedly, there are two
quite characteristic American attitudes which seem to me to
justify my contention that America is still an intellectual colony.

In the first place, America does not always give its own
creative minds the recognition due them. Indeed, it sometimes ignores them altogether. This is so often the case that
an observer as casual as the average European traveler in

America finds it only too easy to assume that in certain fields there are no creative minds. The proof is that even I, who have lived in the United States for eight years, would never have heard of Carey, had I not read about him in Karl Marx. It was Gertrude Stein who explained Picasso to the Americans, and they listened to her; today, a Picasso exhibition draws millions of visitors in the United States. But if Picasso, as great a painter as we know him to be, had been American, if he had been born and had painted in Missouri, Gertrude Stein might never have taken an interest in him, or if she had, America would not have listened to her or believed her. This is a characteristically colonial attitude and constitutes a major obstacle to the development of young indigenous painters. In their hearts, Americans do not believe that there could ever be found among them men of such stature as Stravinsky, Picasso, and Bergson.

In the second place—and if what I am about to say seems to belie what I said above, it must be remembered that opposites are often two sides of the same truth—there are Americans who, abandoning all hope of competing with Europe on the artistic and intellectual level, turn to something that they feel is within their reach, such as an obvious practical achievement, and unhesitatingly declare that it indicates a quality of civilization far superior to anything that Europe has ever been able to create.

But the American universities must be judged apart. They have, it seems to me, a peculiar responsibility toward the nation's past and its continuity. The task of the artist is to create, experiment all the time with new forms, to live in the future. The task of the scientist in the laboratory is to discover nature's secrets. But the task of institutions of learning is to preserve the past, to instruct youth in it, and also to detect what is great in the nation's present. American universities are not controlled by the federal government, and are in that respect vastly better than the French government-controlled university system. But what do they do with their freedom? Intellectual freedom means curiosity, challenge, creative doubt, the critical spirit. I cannot help wondering whether the fact that Henry Charles Carey's works have fallen into oblivion may not simply mean that none of the great American professors dare believe that an American who was not afraid to attack the whole school of English economists head-on, together with what Marx called "the masterminds of Europe," could possibly have been right.

18

The Prophet of a New Messiah

In 1890 Charles H. Levermore wrote that half America's businessmen and farmers accepted Carey's ideas. Henry Ford was then twenty-seven years old. He was young and poor, but he knew exactly what he was going to do with his life. More than anyone else, he was the man who would transmute Carey's ideas into concrete form. It would take time. For many years to come, America's laws and social structure would still be much the same as those of Europe.

"You see," Thomas Edison wrote in 1912, "getting down to the bottom of things, this is a pretty raw civilization of ours—pretty wasteful, pretty cruel, which often comes to the same thing, doesn't it? And in a lot of respects we Americans are the rawest and crudest of all. Our production, our factory laws, our charities, our relations between capital and labor, our distribution—all wrong, out of gear. We've stumbled along for a while, trying to run a new civilization in old ways, but we've got to start to make this world over." If these words recall Marx or Lenin, this proves not that Edison was Marxist but perhaps that Marx was not wholly original in proclaiming the collapse of capitalist civilization. It is true that by 1914 capitalist civilization was bankrupt and everyone knew it. But in 1912, when Edison made his astounding statement, Marx had been dead less than thirty years. Pavlov was sixty-three, Freud fifty-six; Lenin was forty-two, Stalin thirty-three; Einstein thirty-three; Mussolini twenty-nine; Hitler twenty-three. The world was about to be rebuilt.

Edison's words were not in themselves revolutionary, but they sounded the unmistakable premonitory note of revolution. There are moments in history when it becomes all too evident that a civilization has arrived at a turning point. What is to come, or how it will come, may not be very clear, but it is clear enough that society is about to undergo a violent change. These are stirring and dangerous times, when nations stand uncertain at the very brink of disaster; they can take the road to progress, they can create and dare, or they can fall into chaos, madness, and suicide. Sometimes their choice is made by one man, one man alone. Lenin chose for Russia, as, in part at least, Henry Ford chose for America. I do not claim that America would have chosen a different road had there been no Henry Ford, but Ford certainly gave America the impetus to move faster and he saved it considerable time.

In 1912 capitalism, in America, as in Europe, was still developing along traditional lines, hungry for profit, preoccupied with production, engaged in weathering the successive crises that shook it, and pitilessly exploiting labor. America had just won industrial independence from Europe, but it was still an integral part of the capitalist system. Adam Smith, Ricardo, and Malthus had defined it, and Marx, accepting their definition as a postulate, had denounced it. In this system money was king, money alone made the laws, money dominated the market and the fate of the working man. In Europe the movement toward social emancipation was to be interrupted, betrayed, and shattered by the First World War, and then profoundly corrupted by the October Revolution of 1917. In America the condition of the worker was, if possible, even worse. Trade unionism, violently attacked by management and helpless in the face of existing laws, was unable to formulate its aims, let alone organize and unite. The mass immigration of recent years had flooded the continent with wretched, illiterate workers who were defenseless against the worst kind of exploitation and ripe to become a Marxian proletariat with "nothing to lose but its chains."

The difficulty in evaluating Henry Ford is that most of his methods, in his own country at least, have been so generally adopted that people no longer realize how enormously original they were and how extraordinarily fruitful they have been. Nowadays, we have an unfortunate tendency to remember only Ford's personal eccentricities and that hardness of his which so marked the last years of his life. But in 1912 he was not yet fifty and had only recently become the head of an enterprise which so impressed an Irish writer that he said, "When you study the Ford Company, you have before you a great State, perfect in every particular—the nearest that anything on the face of the earth has got to Utopia." Such a comment proves how revolutionary Ford appeared to his contemporaries.

Henry Ford was born in 1863 on a farm near Detroit. His father, an immigrant of peasant stock, fully intended that his eldest son should also stay on the land, and in fact Henry Ford did not definitely give up farming to become a mechanic until 1891, when he was twenty-eight. For the rest of his life this background was to give him a Puritan asceticism, a strong feeling for nature and solitude, for trees and birds, together with a truly revolutionary determination to lighten the farmer's burden of toil and someday ease his fate. This he achieved, more than anyone else in the world.

Yet his true vocation, the only thing he loved, was machinery. His schoolwork had been mediocre, and he never lost his contempt for books. The strength of his genius—for he had genius—lay in his passion for anything mechanical, for

any kind of machine, from the movement of a watch to a locomotive. Later he was to say of his childhood years, "My toys
were all tools—they still are." And again he said, "Machines
are to a mechanic what books are to a writer. He gets ideas
from them and, if he has any brains, he will apply those
ideas." He was a born mechanic; he was never anything else
but a mechanic, an inventor in mechanics. This was both his
strength and his limitation. The social upheaval which Edison believed to be necessary, the emancipation of worker and
peasant for which Marx longed, Ford also kept constantly in
mind. But he was convinced that the machine itself, the increase of mechanization, could at least make possible, if it
could not actually bring about, that upheaval and that emancipation. Today it is obvious that all the countries in the
world are attempting to industrialize themselves, that Russia's prestige among backward nations derives less from its
Marxism than from its industrial achievement, and that true
national independence is no longer conceivable without industrialization. But if this is now self-evident, it was less so
in 1889, when Henry Ford announced to his bewildered
young wife that he was going to build a horseless carriage,
that horses were obsolete, and that within a few years horseless carriages would jam New York's Fifth Avenue. Oddly
enough, Henry Ford always detested horses, and it seems
that his feeling was reciprocated.

In any wholly new undertaking there is a long period of
growth between the germ of the idea and its fruition. On
Christmas night, 1893, in the kitchen of his Detroit home
and with the help of his wife, Henry Ford successfully tested
his first internal-combustion engine. In 1896 he put an engine in his first quadricycle. He did not sell his first automobile until 1903, when he was forty years old. And it was only
some ten years later, after he had brought out his Model T,
expanded his factories, integrated production and distribution, and made the famous decision to pay his workers $5 for

an eight-hour day, that Ford realized his lifelong ambition and won both fame and fortune. Until then no one but his wife had really believed in his genius. The story goes that when he built his first automobile and drove proudly home to the farm, his father received him coldly. No doubt the old farmer felt that a man of thirty-three with a family, who left his grocer's bills unpaid for three months, had better things to do than waste time and money toying with mechanical contraptions.

In 1903, when Henry Ford was looking for stockholders for the third time and went into partnership with a coal dealer named Malcomson, he had a hard time getting anyone to believe in him. Allan Nevins and Frank E. Hill, in their book *Ford: the Times, the Man, the Company,** wrote: "What men *did* know was merely that Malcomson was an impulsive plunger, that Ford had one business failure and a withdrawal from a second venture behind him, and that automotive manufacturing already seemed dangerously overcrowded." All in all, Ford was able to raise only $28,000. Not another cent was ever paid in from the outside to increase the original capital. For several weeks the new company teetered on the edge of bankruptcy. From the 7th to the 11th of July, 1903, with bills coming in and not a single automobile sold, the company had only $223.65 in the bank. At last, on July 15, the first Ford was sold to a Chicago doctor named Pfennig. This was the turning point. By August 20, the company had more than $23,000 in the bank. Ten years later, on March 1, 1913, it had already paid out to its stockholders more than $15,000,000 in dividends, and its properties were valued at more than $22,000,000.

Although these details belong in the story of America's greatest industrialist and show that his life was not, after all, an entirely easy one, this is not my only reason for mentioning them. I have a more important reason. At the very same

* New York: Scribner, 1954.

time that Ford was making his stockholders rich, he was involved in a continuous and bitter quarrel with them. People who think of a given enterprise only in terms of the money it brings them are of a peculiar stupidity and a monumental gullibility. Ford's stockholders accepted their monthly dividends as manna from heaven, stubbornly refusing to consider the earthly source whence this manna came. At the very same time that Ford was making them rich, one automobile company after another was going bankrupt. It might conceivably have occurred to Ford's stockholders that this monthly manna was coming to them because Ford's ideas and methods were superior to those of the other industrialists—a simple case of cause and effect. But this elementary step in logic they never took. Right until the end, until Ford had completely bought them out, the stockholders refused either to understand or accept Ford's wholly new concept of industry in general and of the automobile industry in particular. I know of no more perfect illustration of the fable about the goose that laid the golden eggs.

Certain words may sound absurd and even distasteful when applied to industry, yet one cannot avoid using them. While Ford's stockholders thought of the company strictly in terms of profit and loss, he envisioned its role as essentially apostolic and missionary. Success soon proved the truth of the idea. Ford actually thought of himself as a kind of Saint Paul, charged with the burden and anxious care, not of all the churches, but of all the regions of the world, sending out to all peoples everywhere, not epistles, but automobiles, trucks, tractors, and engines; carrying to every nation of the earth, not a message of supernatural hope, but a promise of progress and liberation. Henry Ford considered himself, and was, prophet and apostle of the machine, its witness and its martyr. Such a conviction, held with such intensity, offended, shocked, and profoundly disturbed the purely mercenary temper of the capitalist world. According to the most deeply rooted, the most revered, the absolutely sacrosanct bourgeois tradition, prophets and apostles can be tolerated as quaint epiphenomena of civilization, but one must never, never in the world, bring them into a meeting of the board of directors.

Henry Ford was not only on the Board of Directors of his company but also ran the company and managed and organized its factories. He was determined to make it serve his prophetic vision. Inevitably, he was not understood; inevitably, there was conflict. Whatever the impact and success of their message, prophets live and die alone. The loneliness and intransigence of those last years which caused Henry Ford to make so many sorry mistakes stemmed not only from his obstinacy and pride but also from his conviction that he had always been able to see what others had failed to see, what others had consistently refused to see, and from his feeling that for so long, against everyone and quite alone, he had been right.

I am quite sure that in all this I have not denatured or exaggerated Henry Ford's thinking. In his book *My Philosophy of Industry* (1921) he calmly called his opening chapter "Machinery, the New Messiah," and it is very clear that he considered himself the prophet of that new Messiah. In describing the renascence this Messiah heralded, he used the language of the Apocalypse itself; he spoke of a new heaven and a new earth. This explains Henry Ford's whole life, his patience, his tenacity, the stubbornness in the first long, difficult years which he had spent—others said he had wasted them—on costly experiments with machinery; the endless poverty that counted for nothing so long as one day the engine turned, and finally the immense fortune that also counted for nothing so long as the wheels of the factories turned and production continued. When he was a billionaire, a journalist asked him an impertinent question. "Mr. Ford, how much are you worth?" "I have no idea," Ford replied, "and moreover I don't care." We are condemned to a complete misunderstanding of Henry Ford's personality if we fail to believe that when he said that, he was speaking the naked truth.

If I am to say where money stood in the scale of Henry Ford's values, I say it stood last. First came work, and man's power, through work, to create. In work Ford saw life's joy and purpose. Work was not a livelihood; work was life itself. "Thinking men," he wrote, "know that work is the salvation of the race, morally, physically, socially. Work does more than get us our living; it gets us our life." As a true Puritan, Ford was essentially a moralist, and again as a true Puritan, he reduced all morality to the practice of a single virtue— work. Just as the devout Christian finds the highest expression of his faith in martyrdom, so Henry Ford found the most perfect expression of man's labor and productivity in industry, and held it to be sacred and honorable. He had no use for art, and in that, too, he was a true Puritan.

Ford saw, however, and as clearly as Marx, that certain conditions of work can degrade rather than ennoble. We remember Marx's well-known statement on the "degrading distinction between intellectual and manual labor." I do not suppose this statement would have made much sense to Ford, had he come upon it, for he had long since reconciled any such distinction in himself. Essentially he was a man who had always worked with his hands, first on a farm, then in a factory. He had never ceased to be a mechanic, yet at the same time he had always been a reflective man—a thinker, if you will, and why not? Indeed, he even claimed that his years of manual labor, his passion for tools and the raw material they transform, did more to sharpen his intelligence than books ever could for self-styled intellectuals. In Ford's view, manual labor led—by a path different from that of intellectual or artistic intuition, but just as directly, just as surely—to the fulfillment of what Simone Weil has so superbly called "the original pact of the mind with the universe."

Ford had the zeal of an apostle. It was not enough for him to have solved a problem to his own satisfaction; he wanted to bring his solution to the entire world. Upon close examination, the whole originality of Ford's discovery consists in his penetrating and thoroughly practical vision of the vast role that mechanization can play in emancipating human society. Long ago Aristotle foresaw that the development of the machine would one day make it possible to abolish slavery and that a time would come when men ceased to enslave other men and had "mechanical slaves" instead. Henry Ford carried out Aristotle's prophecy, and did it deliberately, too. This is what made him great; this is what made him infinitely more revolutionary than Marx, who was only an intellectual. The Russians obviously understood this, since they sent their engineers to be trained in Ford's factories and requested Ford engineers for Russia. Time after time, and even as a young man, Henry Ford spoke with unmistakable clarity about the emancipation that the machine would bring. "The machine and not the man," he wrote, "would be the drudge." It was imperative, he said, "to lift . . . drudgery off flesh and blood and lay it on steel and motors."

The linking of Henry Ford to Aristotle leads to even wider implications. Aristotle accepted slavery because it benefited a minority of free men, relieving them of servile tasks and enabling them to consecrate their lives to philosophy, art, and the government of the republic. There was no other base for an aristocratic society except slavery. But Henry Ford saw that if the burden of slavery were shifted from man to the machine, there would be time for leisure and creativity for all mankind, and that therefore the development of machinery would tend to create its own aristocratic society, for, although society is based on the dialectic of master and slave, with the advent of the machine all men can become masters. Thus, through the mastery of nature, man will at last be reconciled to man. Needless to say, this is an optimistic and visionary view. Experience has taught us that the machine also creates oppressions, and Ford was fully aware of it. Yet I firmly believe that this optimistic and visionary view was his and that he devoted his life to the attempt to realize it.

People think of Henry Ford as the automobile king, and it was of course in the automotive industry that he was most brilliantly successful. But his industrial theories applied to every kind of production, or at least to the production of all commodities, and they also applied to the sale and distribution of goods. They also applied to making war, and, in Ford's private vision, perhaps even to making peace. "There are three basic industries," Ford said, "to grow, to manufacture, to transport." Agriculture, manufacture, transportation, everything had to be industrialized. "Never do for yourself what a machine can do for you better, faster, in greater quantity, and at lower cost." If these were not Ford's actual words, they surely express his guiding principle.

But that was not all. Henry Ford saw the process of industrial production itself as a machine, and his partner, James Couzens, saw the organization of sales and distribution as a machine—in other words, mass production, mass distribution, the assembly line. Nevins and Hill, speaking of mass production in their history of the Ford Company, wrote:

> We shall do well to note at this point the meaning of the term "mass production." Had an ordinary American been asked in 1915 what was the greatest achievement of the Ford Company, he would have erroneously replied: "The universal cheap car, the Model T." Its most remarkable exploit was actually the creation of the womb in which modern industry was to be reshaped, mass production. If asked to define mass production, the ordinary citizen would again have replied

erroneously: "It means large-scale production by the use of uniform interchangeable parts." Indeed most people still confound mass production with quantity production, which is only one of its elements. Actually, Henry Ford himself wrote, mass production is the focussing upon a manufacturing operation of seven different principles: power, accuracy, economy, continuity, system, speed, and repetition. When all seven are used to make a car, tractor, refrigerator, airplane, or other complicated commodity, mass production throws open the door to plenty, low prices, and an improved standard of living. Among a people, in peace against want, in war against enemies, it becomes an instrument to alter radically the shape of civilization.

Henry Ford did not invent this system. He perfected and popularized it and he saw its universal application. But mass production had existed long before Ford. What is printing, after all, if not mass production applied to the art of writing? Probably in the sixteenth century a few conservative monks and cultivated aristocrats damned the printing press for sounding the death knell of the penman's admirable art, the end of illuminated manuscripts and "books of hours." Yet no one dares claim that printing marked a setback for civilization. On the contrary, it is generally credited with having advanced education and the spread of knowledge. Obviously such a discovery, like every new power acquired by man, can lead to evil or to good, and it is for man to ensure that it is used for good. Nor does mass production limit the artist's scope; it actually increases it. The printing of books in itself has long since become an art. The difficulty comes when a method effective in material things is applied to the things of the mind. This, I believe, was the trouble with Descartes. Anyone rereading the famous rules of the *Discourse on Method* will see that Descartes classified, itemized, ordered, and reassembled his thoughts in very much the same way Henry Ford classified, itemized, and reassembled the various processes and the various parts that go into the making of an automobile. But this method that definitively advanced the automobile industry no less definitively debased philosophy.

It would be possible to describe mass production in a few words as a determinism in production which is as detailed and as absolute as possible. This is the principle that Henry Ford grasped and rigorously applied. It is the discovery of the determinism of production that made Ford great, as the discovery of physiological determinism made Pavlov great, and the discovery of psychological determinism made Freud great—and Marx's intuition told him that there was also a social determinism. It was almost inevitable that Ford should be led by his discovery, by the very greatness of his discovery, to certain indefensible and even absurd conclusions. After all, Marx and Freud, not to speak of Descartes, were also led to conclusions which were indefensible because they were extrapolated. Henry Charles Carey fell into the same error. It was the age of extrapolation; it was an age when no one understood that the more precise a determinism the more strictly it must be confined to its own sphere.

Henry Ford was as great in engineering as Freud was in psychology, and the one was as presumptuous as the other when he ventured outside his field. "Rightness in mechanics and rightness in morals," said Ford, "are basically the same thing and cannot rest apart," and this one remark proves my point. This is a serious statement, very serious; it is totalitarian in concept. How truly it shows Ford to be a man of our times! Of course, no one can deny that some mechanical reactions enter into human behavior. Nor can anyone deny that in the behavior of both the individual and society there is, as Pavlov proved, a physiological determinism; as Freud proved, a psychological determinism; and, as Marx guessed, a social determinism. But what is essentially human in man's behavior lies beyond his mechanical reactions, beyond any form of determinism. Carey saw this clearly. Man sets himself free and begins to approach his true human stature only by controlling his mechanical reactions and mastering physiological, psychological, and social determinisms. Determinisms, to be controlled and mastered, must be understood. That is why Freud and Pavlov are so useful. But in defense of these great men, one might say what Roland Dalbiez said of Freud: "In all fairness it must be admitted that he who explores a new world cannot be expected to draw a map of it," for he has yet to learn its contours and its limits.

Ford was an explorer, and that is why he so often lost his way. It is curious that Ford has been so much more criticized than Freud for going astray, since the cause of both men's errors was the same. Pascal defined it perfectly when he said, "Desire for domination outside one's own sphere is tyranny."

Marx himself was well aware of the threat to human dignity inherent in the subjection of the worker to the determinism of production. It is obvious that in mass production, where the worker must always stand in the same place in the line, is always assigned the same meticulous task, and endlessly repeats the same motions in a fixed and unalterable rhythm, his role can hardly be called human. He is no more than a cog in the vast wheels of production, and an interchangeable cog at that. Such work induces "a semi-hypnotic state from which the workman's mind emerges only at intervals." By a cruel irony of fate, Ford, who had always so earnestly sought to lift from men's shoulders the burden of servile tasks, created with the assembly line another and perhaps still more inhuman and intolerable kind of servitude. The worst is that this servitude seems to be essential to the system. Marx's argument that all servitude would be eliminated if the workers were given collective ownership of the means of production is merely the clumsy hoax of an intellectual Utopian. An assembly line is an assembly line, in Russia as in America.

But this in no way detracts from all Henry Ford did for the emancipation of the workers. He was never as clear, as positive, as perseverant as when he was stating this goal. Mass production and mass distribution were to be the means to enable him to manufacture automobiles in such quantity and at such low cost that everyone could afford them, and at the same time to raise wages steadily and shorten working hours. Not only was this Ford's goal, but he was also the first to achieve it on a grand scale. He achieved it in the face of every conceivable obstacle, and to do so he had to battle all his life. Once again, let me say that if, as we look at America in mid-twentieth century, Ford's goal could hardly seem more commonplace, it was anything but commonplace fifty years ago. When great battles for economic or social advancement are won, they are won so completely that we even forget that a battle had once to be fought. A "low-cost car" for everyone and a "high wage" for the men who made it—these were the ideas that Henry Ford expressed again and again, from the very beginning of his career. If one were to quote only his major statements on this subject, they would fill a book. Here is the publicity release issued when Model N, forerunner of Model T, was put on the market:

Henry Ford's idea is to build a high-grade, practical automobile, one that will do any reasonable service, that can be maintained at a reasonable expense, and cost as near $450 as it is possible to make it, thus raising the automobile out of the list of luxuries and bringing it to the point where the average American citizen may own and enjoy his automobile.

So in making the price on the 4-cylinder runabout, the question was not "How much can we get for this car?" but "How low can we sell it and make a small margin on each one?—How many cars must be turned out to get the lowest cost per car, and will the demand absorb this tremendous output?"

These have been mighty questions.

But the Ford Company are doing it, and as a result thousands of people will own a good car this year where otherwise it would have been impossible.

Ford's goals were to lower prices, to reduce to a minimum the profit on each unit, to take the automobile out of the luxury class and make it a basic necessity within reach of every pocketbook, and he thought of mass production only as a means to attain these ends. As early as 1903 he had said, "The way to make automobiles is to make one automobile like another automobile, to make them all alike; just as one pin is like another pin when it comes from a pin factory, or one match is like another match when it comes from a match factory." And in 1912 he wrote, "There is no doubt that the man who can produce a car that will be entirely sufficient mechanically, and whose price will be within the reach of the millions who cannot yet afford automobiles, will not only grow rich but be considered a public benefactor as well." And when at last his Model T—the car that would fulfill all his ambitions—was ready, Ford exclaimed in a burst of enthusiasm, "This car sounds the death knell of high prices and high profits."

From the start, Ford's contemporaries realized the full import of this revolution in production. Clearly, it meant the end of the craftsman and of manufacture by hand. It meant the end of a kind of luxury. It meant the end, or at least a postponement, of any preoccupation with esthetics in manufacturing; it meant the enthronement of monotony. In 1950, when I arrived for the first time in New York, a young American who spoke excellent French took me on a tour of the city. After some hours, he became aware that I was tired and possibly somewhat disappointed. "I admit none of this is as picturesque as Spain, or Greece or Italy," he said, abruptly. "But to us Americans, the picturesque is other people's squalor." Now, after eight years in America, I still remember what he said. No one else has helped me to understand America so well. When Henry Ford put America on wheels, he rescued the farmer from his isolation and brought him within reach of railroads to carry his produce to New York or San Francisco and carry back machines and city goods. By bringing the market to the farmer's door as Carey had envisioned, Ford created an unlimited national market. He opened up an immense hinterland rich in untapped resources. He brought the newspaper to every isolated farmer from the Atlantic to the Pacific. Thanks to him, it soon became possible for everyone to get to the motion pictures. He had breached a solitude. One does not sacrifice such a gift of freedom to the esthetic value of a piece of hand-woven silk.

At the San Francisco Exposition in 1915, the Ford Motor Company displayed a replica of the famous Model T assembly line. When the conveyors began to move, and part by part, gear by gear, bolt by bolt, automobiles began to take shape, frenzied crowds broke through the railings. The whole demonstration had to be called off in haste for fear of accident and the spectators sent away. The next day, the barriers were reinforced, the spectators were restricted to a three-tier platform, and the assembly line once again began to move. It was the hit of the Exposition, for there is apparently nothing quite so impressive as a great display of efficiency in the production of this world's goods. Man could now vanquish other people's squalor.

Ford's success in industry would have been enough in itself to ensure his place in America's hall of fame. But extraordinary as it was, his industrial success turned out to be only the modest prelude to a much more profound, much more widespread revolution in the structure of society. His true stature can be seen only in the light of the history of civilization. At

the meeting on January 1, 1914, described by the two historians of the Ford Motor Company, the Board of Directors
reached a spectacular decision which in my opinion has never
yet had the full recognition it deserves. Up to that time, top
industrial wages had never gone above $2.50 for a nine-hour
day, and American wages were supposed to be the highest in
the world. "Ford," write Nevins and Hill, "covered his blackboard with figures. When he set down the totals for the
wages, they seemed too small compared with the anticipated
profits. He kept raising the average—to $3, to $3.50; then,
over Martin's vehement protest but with Wills's support, to
$4 and $4.50. Couzens, according to one account, had been
watching with ill-concealed hostility. 'Well,' he finally
snapped, 'so it's up to $4.75. I dare you to make it $5.' And
at once Ford did so." A few days later the company officially
announced the eight-hour, five-dollar day. It was estimated
that the raise in wages would cost the company another ten
million dollars that year. "This is neither charity nor
wages," Ford said to the reporters, "but profit sharing and
efficiency engineering." That was in January 1914. The same
year would see the opening of the Panama Canal and the
linking of New York and San Francisco by transcontinental
telephone. America was making enormous strides in industrial and social progress. Europe was about to plunge into the
utter madness of war and revolution.

How I wish I could find words to impress the reader with
the importance of that decision of the five-dollar day! It
meant infinitely more than a mere raise in wages. The "tim-
ing," to use the vernacular of the theatre, was a stroke of genius, for the five-dollar day not only undermined the whole
capitalist structure but cut away the ground from under
Marxist revolution. Let me speak plainly: I consider that
what Henry Ford accomplished on January 1, 1914, contrib-
uted far more to the emancipaton of workers than the October Revolution of 1917. The Revolution of Lenin and his

colleagues, however bloody, was still only a literary revolution which never emerged from the mythical political economy invented by Ricardo and Marx. The fact is that Lenin's Revolution was bloody precisely because it was literary. But Henry Ford, in his characteristically American way, cared nothing for mythical or literary revolution. Having covered his blackboard with figures, he moved straight into "truth and reality." What Marx had dreamed, Ford achieved. But he achieved it only because he was far more of a revolutionary than Marx or Lenin. Ford exploded the whole idea of the famous, supposedly immutable "iron law" of wages on which Ricardo believed capitalist economy was founded and which was to provide every proletarian revolution with a springboard.

Like Lincoln in answer to Karl Marx, Ford avoided rhetoric. "The payment of five dollars a day for an eight-hour day," he was to explain, "was one of the finest cost-cutting moves we ever made." And he added, "Well, you know when you pay men well, you can talk to them." Yet he knew exactly what he was doing; he knew exactly how revolutionary he was. "I can find methods of manufacturing," he said, "which will make high wages the cheapest of wages . . . if you cut wages, you just cut the number of your own customers." Customer—that is the key word, the key to Ford's social revolution, a revolution made not in fiction but in the reality of political economy. Just as Ford took the automobile out of the luxury class, made it inexpensive, and put it into the class of basic necessities, so, at his blackboard on January 1, 1914, he took the worker out of the class of the "wage-earning proletariat" to which Ricardo and Marx had relegated him and gave him new dignity as a customer. At one stroke he exploded the theory of the "minimum-subsistence wage" ("turning men into hats") so unjustly and so firmly established as a "law" of economics by Ricardo, so justly and so firmly denounced by Marx. He abolished the "minimum-subsistence wage"—"that price which is necessary to enable laborers, one with another, to subsist and perpetuate their race." He made every worker a potential customer.

Where is the honor, some may ask, where is the special human dignity in being a customer? I wish at this point that we Europeans would finally bury once and for all the historic prejudices we inherit from an essentially aristocratic and military concept of honor. In any case, social and economic questions are of a wholly different order, and in the economic order, with which Marx claimed to be so exclusively concerned, there is no doubt whatever that the word "customer" lends as much dignity as the word "citizen" lends in the political order of a free republic. A man is a customer on the market when he has purchasing power, just as he is a citizen of the republic when he has the power to influence affairs of state. In the last analysis, the customer controls the market and is therefore a free citizen of it. With Ford, the American worker became a customer, and in fact the best of customers. But one cannot be both a customer and a proletarian at the same time, any more than, at the same time and in the same equation, one can be both a master and a slave. The emancipation of the proletariat which Marx could only envisage as the result of a revolution that would "violently destroy the ancient order of production" was achieved by Ford, very simply, without fanfare, in front of a blackboard. In other words, and I shall return to this later, Ford transformed the ancient order of production without violence and yet more radically than Lenin. He was as far outside the Ricardo-Marx dialectic as Carey. Ford, too, was a man who was never bound by any form of Euclidian postulate. Who would dare suggest today that American workers exist only "in the guise of the most miserable class"? The change in the lot of the workers is a tremendous fact that neither Ricardo nor Marx foresaw.

Here let us pause to consider with what remarkable consistency the American Republic has developed. The Declaration of Independence starts with a statement of the three fundamental rights of man: first life, and then the other two rights without which life itself is not worth living—liberty and the pursuit of happiness. In the time of Jefferson and Lincoln, the American Republic bent every effort to establish and secure civil liberties for all; since Henry Ford, it has bent every effort to establish and secure for all the right to the pursuit of happiness. When the New York *World* asked Edison to comment on the revolutionary significance of Ford's decision to pay five dollars for an eight-hour day, he sent the following reply:

> It is such a radical innovation that I cannot at present give an opinion as to its ultimate effect. Some time ago Mr. Ford reduced the price of his wonderful touring car to the extent of fifty dollars. The user of the car received the entire benefit. Now he has practically reduced it another fifty dollars, but this time the men who make them get the benefit. Mr. Ford's machinery is special and highly efficient. This is what permits these results. This is open to nearly every line of business.
>
> Let the public throw bouquets to the inventors and in time we will all be happy.

Happiness may be harder to attain than Edison imagined, but as far as the pursuit of happiness on earth is concerned, to eliminate misery would be a great step ahead.

In 1914, Ford was at the height of his fame in America and throughout the rest of the world. But my portrait of Ford would not be complete if I omitted those flaws in his character which were later to overshadow his fame and destroy his legendary image in the eyes of the world. I have already explained what I believe to have been the original source of Ford's errors, and I quoted Pascal's observation, "Desire for domination outside one's own sphere is tyranny." Henry

Ford thought he could apply the principles of mechanics to politics, banking, philosophy, in fact to everything. But the greatest damage to his reputation doubtless came from his anti-Semitism and his labor policy.

There has always been an element of absurdity in theoretical anti-Semitism, but since Hitler anti-Semitism is no longer absurd, it is abominable. Henry Ford's anti-Semitism preceded that of Hitler and he later publicly retracted it. Yet, absurd as it is, anti-Semitism has its reasons, or at least its causes. The causes of Ford's anti-Semitism are anything but easy to understand; he himself never really explained them. If I may be allowed a hypothesis, it seems to me that to Henry Ford the Jews were a people who stood pre-eminently for the Book and the Law; for the world of speculation in metaphysics, finance, and casuistry; for a whole world that he had always held in contempt and perhaps even secretly envied, a whole world that he did not understand, that he could never have understood, that was closed to him, a whole world that mechanics could never conquer, a world and a power entirely other than that of the engine and electricity. He must have felt, and deeply resented, that the Jewish people carried within them a prophetic vision that was not his. Prophetic vision is totalitarian. To a prophet, all prophets with another vision must surely be false prophets.

Ford was even more paradoxical in his role of employer. It is sad indeed to observe how his labor policy hardened and deteriorated. In 1914 the name of Henry Ford represented, more than that of any labor leader, more than that of Marx or Lenin, the world's most realistic, most solidly founded hope for the emancipation of the workers. Ten years later that same name had come to mean an almost perfect example of industrial autocracy. Yet this development is not altogether surprising. Once the premise is accepted that mechanics and morality are one and the same, it is only too easy to go on to the conclusion that factory workers are mere

cogs in an immense machine, and the machine itself is obviously far more important than any of its parts. I have already
emphasized that Ford's power and success came from his having envisaged and organized production and distribution as
machines. In these machines, men are no more than interchangeable parts. Since the governing principle of mass production is efficiency, a machine is changed or a man replaced,
a machine is checked or a man's every motion timed in order
to obtain maximum efficiency in the assembly line, and the
only thing that has the slightest importance is the ultimate
achievement of this efficiency. Ford himself frankly admitted
that "a great business is really too big to be human."

Let us not be sentimental. In any undertaking that is at
all bold or new, a certain ruthlessness is not only appropriate
but unavoidable. When Ford said, "I pity the poor fellow
who is so soft and flabby that he must always have 'an atmosphere of good feeling' around him before he can do his
work," he was a thousand times right. Nothing of any conse-
quence has ever been achieved by sentimentality. Ford's comment recalls so many passages in those books by Saint-
Exupéry—*Night Flight* and *Wind, Sand, and Stars*—where
he describes the law of absolute selflessness imposed upon fli-
ers in the early days of aviation. There is no doubt that Ford,
in his puritanism, saw the factory as a kind of monastery
where, in place of the rule of charity, there obtained a law
of work which demanded the same obligations of obedience,
the same observances of silence and penitence as the cloister:
no smoking, no drinking, no talking, no sitting down, etc.

But Ford's puritanism, like that of Saint-Just, went even
further, for in his republic, as in that of Saint-Just, virtue—
the virtue of work—was to be safeguarded by terror. His
Detroit factories, that "great State," that "Utopia," followed
what appears to be the law of Utopias and developed all the
distinctive features of a truly totalitarian state. There is
abundant evidence to prove that Ford workers were organ-

ized like the troops of an army, their foremen organized like the members of a party to carry out in detail the general political line of the man at the top, and a police organized to control both army and party. It was thanks only to continual inquisition and purges that the system worked. I do not question Henry Ford's sincerity or even his idealism, but Saint-Just was also a sincere idealist, and so, without doubt, was Lenin. It is quite possible that Mr. Khrushchev is an idealist, too.

Needless to say, the resemblance of the Ford factories to a totalitarian state must not be taken literally. A purge in Detroit did not mean a bullet in the back of the neck or a concentration camp; it meant simply that an employee was dismissed, without right of appeal or explanation. However, the evidence on this autocratic phase is conflicting, at least superficially. Considerable emphasis has been laid on the fact that Ford workers were always enthusiastic about breaking production records. But Russia's five-year plans have doubtless excited just as much enthusiasm in Russia, and a certain degree of enthusiasm is perfectly compatible with totalitarian organization. The comparison of the Ford works with a totalitarian state is therefore legitimate; moreover, it would not have angered Ford. When a reporter asked him, "What about industrial democracy?" he replied, "An industry, at this stage of our development, must be more or less of a friendly autocracy." Unfortunately, the autocrat always considers himself the friend of mankind, and is always convinced that he knows far better than other men what is best for them.

There is, in all this, a great lesson, and that is what I am coming to. The most spectacular side of Henry Ford's discoveries, the universal application of assembly-line methods to the production and distribution of goods—that specifically mechanical and industrial side of his discoveries—is, by its very nature, independent of the social system in which it operates. As a matter of fact, Russia has also adopted Ford's industrial technique, and this has probably done more to consolidate the Soviet regime than Marx's absurd philosophy. Ford's technique is a highly perfected tool for production and distribution, but, like all tools, it can be handled by anyone. His industrial methods have neither nationality nor ideology; they are equally effective in a totalitarian state or in a democracy, just as psychoanalytic therapy is as effective in Paris or New York as in Moscow.

Ford's methods were also to affect the structure of society. Let us not forget how clearly he put this himself. "I can find methods of manufacturing," he said, "which will make high wages the cheapest of wages . . . if you cut wages, you just cut the number of your own customers." This is the essence of his contribution to social change, and that contribution was prodigious. Henry Ford broke the mainspring of capitalism and Marxist revolution, as the mainspring of a watch is broken. After Ford, the systems of capitalism and Marxist revolution were rendered as useless as blunted and obsolete tools. Ford did no more than define his methods and apply them. But this was enough to prove that Henry Charles Carey's ideal of social harmony was eminently practical and practicable. Yet he failed to follow Carey's thought to the end; he failed to see that the final goal of all production must be to civilize, or rather he held too narrowly material and mechanistic a view of civilization. He had no real understanding for "man in his highest aspirations" or for man's uncompromising sense of personal dignity. But this the trade unionists of America were to teach him.

However, before I attempt to describe the American labor movement, I would like to offer at this point a brief interlude which will either amuse the reader or grieve him, depending on his mood and on the natural bent of his sympathies.

19

A Trial of

Orthodoxy

Henry Ford was involved in several famous lawsuits. None threw as much light on his character as the one brought against him in 1919 by the two Dodge brothers. In the trial, Ford revealed his convictions and his prophetic turn of mind in words all the more striking for being entirely unemotional. What Ford said made it clear that his concept of industry was in flat contradiction to that of classic capitalism and a permanent threat to it. In other words, the trial was essentially a trial of orthodoxy. Beyond the interests at stake, and they were considerable, the main purpose was to determine who was orthodox and who was heretic, whose concept of business was right and whose was wrong.

In June 1903, the Ford Motor Company had been incorporated with a nominal capital of $100,000, nearly three-quarters of which consisted of various assets and patents. Only $28,000 cash had actually been paid in. Of the thousand shares the company issued, each of the Dodge brothers received fifty. These shares were in return for work and materials furnished Ford by the Dodge machine shops, plus $3000 cash.

The company had been reorganized several times, some stockholders had been eliminated, and the nominal capital had been increased, but never by money brought in from the outside. In 1916 the company had eight stockholders, with Ford himself holding the controlling interest. Already, by 1915, the Ford Company was estimated to have earned for the Dodge brothers $5,450,000 profit. That same year the company had paid them $1,200,000 in dividends. Meanwhile, the Dodge brothers had founded an automobile company of their own and were counting on Ford dividends to expand their business. Ford, on the other hand, was bent on expanding his own production and was planning the River Rouge plant, which was to be the biggest and most beautiful plant in the world. He needed money. The idea of cutting wages never entered his head. Instead he cut dividends to one-tenth, still leaving, however, the not unattractive sum of $2,000,000 a month to divide among the stockholders. The Dodge brothers were thrown into a panic. They brought suit. At the trial the two leading parts were played by Henry Ford and Elliot G. Stevenson, the Dodge attorney. It was a memorable scene.

To start his company, Henry Ford had had to find money —in other words, stockholders. At the time, given his lack of credit, Ford had been lucky to find any stockholders at all, but, as it turned out later, it was the stockholders who were infinitely luckier to have found Ford. His partner's sister, Rosetta Couzens, who taught school in Detroit, had hesitated a long time as to whether or not to invest all her savings —two or three hundred dollars—in the Ford Company. In the end, she prudently bought one share at $100. That one share was to bring her $355,000. Ford's objection to stockholders was not that he had to pay them dividends but that he had to take into account, if not their opinions, at least their interests, although they had no responsibility whatever for the management of the company and completely disagreed with him on how it should be managed. Ford found himself thinking of stockholders as parasites. To be sure, even a lion has parasites, but aside from the fact that no lion should

allow his fleas to devour him, Ford, with his puritan intransigence, refused to admit that a lion should allow even a single
flea to live at his expense. The first question, therefore, was
one of relationship between management and stockholders.
Who was to have the final say?

But from the start of the trial, it became obvious that
something far more serious was at stake. What was the primary aim of business? Toward what was all business directed? The Dodge brothers and their lawyer, Stevenson,
who stood for traditional capitalism, claimed that business
was essentially and principally aimed at profit, at greater
and greater profit, and therefore at higher and higher dividends. They willingly conceded that Ford's methods had
yielded excellent profits and that so far their dividends had
been rather nice—"lovely dividends," they called them.

But Henry Ford took an entirely different, not to say opposite view of industry and business. He thought of business
and industry first and foremost as a public service. Of his
company's policy he said that "it enables a large number of
people to buy and enjoy the use of a car and . . . it gives a
large number of men employment at good wages. These," he
added, "are the two aims I have in life." In this statement of
his aims there is nothing about money or profits. We shall see
that he sincerely thought of money and profits as the means
but not the goal of business. His own industrial method, he
said, was "to expand the operations and improve the article,
and make more parts ourselves, and reduce the price." For
him, profits were merely what enabled him to keep the factories going, to carry out his plans of expansion, and to
maintain his company's independence. Profits were also the
proof of success, the proof that he was right and that his
methods were sound. "I would not be counted a success," he
said, "if I could not accomplish that and at the same time
make a fair amount of profit for myself and the men associated with me in business." But promptly, and with an em-

phasis that was almost arrogant, he went on: "And let me say right here, that I do not believe that we should make such an awful profit on our cars. A reasonable profit is right, but not too much. So it has been my policy to force the price of the car down as fast as production would permit, and give the benefits to users and laborers, with resulting surprisingly enormous benefits to ourselves."

For Ford to refer to high profits, and therefore to large dividends, as "awful," just after the Dodges had called them "lovely," was to blaspheme God in His temple, and could not be forgiven. This was what lay at the root of the lawsuit. At the trial this dialogue, which revealed the two opposing concepts in all the implacable intransigence of their incompatible orthodoxies, took place:

STEVENSON: Now, I will ask you again, do you still think that those profits were "awful" profits?

FORD: Well, I guess I do, yes.

STEVENSON: And for that reason you were not satisfied to continue making such "awful" profits?

FORD: We don't seem to be able to keep profits down.

STEVENSON: . . . And are you trying to keep them down? What is the Ford Motor Company organized for except profits, will you tell me, Mr. Ford?

FORD: Organized to do as much good as we can, everywhere, for everybody concerned. . . . To do as much as possible for everybody concerned. . . . To make money and use it, give employment and send out the car where people can use it. . . . And incidentally to make money.

STEVENSON: Incidentally make money?

FORD: Yes, Sir.

STEVENSON: But your controlling feature . . . is to employ a great army of men at high wages, to reduce the selling price of your car, so that a lot of people can buy it at a cheap price and give everybody a car that wants one?

FORD: If you give all that, the money will fall into your hands; you can't get out of it.

In all the world's universities all young people seeking some knowledge of political economy should be required to learn this remarkable dialogue by heart. It is as important in economics as the Declaration of Independence is in politics. Like the Declaration of Independence, it marks a kind of Copernican revolution. Business no longer revolves around money; money is only one of the planets revolving around business; business itself exists to serve mankind, just as medicine exists to serve mankind. Indeed, this fantastic dialogue should be looked upon as the business man's Hippocratic Oath.

In their history of the Ford Company, Nevins and Hill are quite right in suggesting that a compromise might have been possible in the lawsuit between Ford and the Dodge brothers and that Ford would have strengthened his position considerably in the eyes of the court, had he been willing to say, "Our entire policy is for the ultimate good of the stockholders. Expansion is purely a business necessity. In the long run, it will be immensely profitable to the company [as, indeed, history proved it to be]. The fact that it provides new jobs and makes possible a lower-priced car is *incidental*. As to dividends, we have already resumed payment of special ones, and as the company's position permits, these will be larger."

But the trial gave Ford a perfect platform from which to proclaim his convictions as prophet and apostle. The loss of a lawsuit meant nothing to Ford. He would have let himself be drawn and quartered for his convictions. To ask Ford to concede on the one hand that profits and dividends were the first and chief aim of business, and on the other hand that the creating of new, highly paid jobs in conjunction with price reduction was only a secondary and incidental aim of business, was like asking a Christian to declare himself Moslem or a doctor to agree that the heart is on the right. How can a man be asked to disavow himself so completely? Had Ford made such a compromise, he would have felt dishonored. It was not in him to do so.

Needless to say, he lost his case. The judge decided that profits were "lovely" rather than "awful." His decision deserves a little thought. The judge was as outspoken as Ford. "A business corporation," he said, "is organized and carried on primarily for the profit of the stockholders. The powers of the directors are employed for that end . . . and do not extend to a change in the end itself, to the reduction of profits or to the nondistribution of profits among the stockholders in order to devote them to other purposes." Blessed be that judge. Blessed be the Dodge brothers and their attorney. Blessed be the trial and the decision. For they have made it impossible, in my opinion, to mistake since then the true nature of the American economy. If it has followed the judge, it is capitalist; if it has followed Henry Ford, it is anti-capitalist. It cannot have followed both. That lawsuit should be retried again and again in American universities to see whether, in the light of present American laws and customs, Ford would still lose today. I doubt if he would.

Even at the time Ford, like Galileo, did not wholly lose his case. First of all, the decision had of course no effect whatever on his ideas. "I must do business on the basis I think is right," he said. "I cannot do it on another." Furthermore, the mere threat that he might leave the company to founder, and set up a new one without any stockholders, caused all the Ford stockholders to sell him their shares. The Dodge brothers received $25,000,000. Ford is said to have danced for joy. Now he was free to move ahead alone, and expand, to go from expansion to complete economic independence, and from complete economic independence to complete autocracy. It should be said in his defense that he was left no choice. Alone in his conviction, he was also right, and this the great fortune that he made would one day prove to the whole world.

But for the purpose of my argument, the most important thing is that Henry Ford won his case at once in the court of public opinion, for this shows how thoroughly America was imbued, like Ford, with Carey's ideas. A new concept of political economy was taking shape in America, and it was the antithesis of the capitalist traditions still officially upheld by the judge. In their history of the Ford Company, Nevins and Hill go so far as to suggest that Ford's stand at the trial was a conscious bid for popularity. This I do not believe. What I think is that Ford, like every preacher, was glad to have an audience. But the fact that the American public listened to him so willingly proves how ripe the nation already was for the anti-capitalist revolution that Ford initiated in business.

And now I hope to regale you with the interlude I promised—a speech which, if the judge who condemned Henry Ford had been a witty and cultivated man and had fully understood all the implications of the case and of his own decision, he might have addressed to the problem child of American industry. It goes without saying that this speech, defining—I believe quite accurately—the respective positions of the accused and the judge, is entirely the product of my imagination. As I see it, the judge would have adopted, in his delivery, the fatherly tone that an old magistrate will so often affect in addressing a young offender whose chances of redeeming himself in the eyes of society he does not want to mar. Here, then, is what the judge would say:

"I have found against you, Mr. Henry Ford, because it was my duty to do so and because I represent in this court a bourgeois capitalist society of which you not only violate the laws, but of which—and this is far more grave—you threaten the very orthodoxy. If I may be permitted here to express my private sentiments, I would like to say that my verdict was not prompted by ill feeling of any kind. On the contrary, I like you, Mr. Ford; I like you very much. To tell the truth, my heart is torn. How am I to forget, for one thing, that you are already a rich man, that you are to become before very long a fabulously rich man, indeed one of the richest men in the world? How, then, could I fail to like you? With my mother's milk I imbibed a love of money. My chosen profession of judge in a capitalist society has served only to confirm me in this love. I am proud to represent a society based on profit, and your profits are enormous, Mr. Ford, enormous. I beg you to note that I used the word 'enormous'; that profits should be termed 'awful' I will not brook. And here, Mr. Ford, we are reaching the crux of our dispute, or rather of your dispute with capitalist bourgeois society. I like you, but I cannot respect you.

"You will concede that mine is a tragic plight. I had not supposed that at my age I might still be called upon to play the part of a hero torn between love and duty and at the same time unable wholly to respect the object of his tragic passion. I find myself caught up in a drama by Corneille, and it looks as though you were entirely unmoved. Not only that, but here, in this courtroom where I am the judge, it seems to me that our roles are reversed. On the one hand, because of your money, I cannot help liking you, yet on the other hand, to like a man who shows so little of the proper reverence for money fills me with a sense of guilt. Indeed, I seem to have infinitely more feeling of guilt than you have. You do not acknowledge the error of your ways, Mr. Ford, and your remarks reveal the pride of a hardened conscience and an unrepentant sinner. You seem to believe that it is I who am wrong, I, the law, and the capitalist society which I represent and which it is my duty to protect in this court.

"I have no wish to inflict useless humiliation upon so rich a man as you. But after all, Mr. Ford, what do you know of the laws that make for the healthiest economy? When one is ignorant, one should at least have the grace to be modest. Perhaps you have never even heard of Mr. Adam Smith. Let me tell you who he was. Mr. Adam Smith was an English professor, an intellectual, Mr. Ford, who wrote an admirable book called *The Wealth of Nations* which I commend to your attention. In this book Mr. Smith has established definitively the laws on which a healthy economy is founded and which you apparently do not understand. Now, according to Mr. Adam Smith, the aim, the be-all and end-all of political economy, is the continual amassing of wealth and therefore of power, and there is no getting around this fact. The only way to amass wealth is to pile up profits. In this classic definition, Mr. Adam Smith, who knows precisely what he is about, carefully avoids all mention of workers or their wages or the welfare of consumers, or of any theory about doing as much good as possible, everywhere possible, for the greatest number of people possible. Only a poet could be so visionary. And what about Mr. Ricardo? Have you by chance ever heard of Mr. Ricardo? The offenders who appear before us these days are sadly lacking in education, and how shameful it is, too. Mr. Ricardo was a London banker who married money and wrote books which have become classics. You should hear what he has to say about workers' wages. In a healthy economy, wages, like all production costs, whether of hats or any other merchandise, must be reduced as far as possible. And everything over and above is gain, is profit, is dividends, and this is how it should be.

"You must realize, Mr. Ford, that to every reasonable Englishman the authority of Messrs. Smith and Ricardo is as sacred as the wig of the Lord Mayor of London. And it is because the English fearlessly and mercilessly carried out the laws of Messrs. Smith and Ricardo that Queen Victoria was able to reign over the wealthiest nation and the most prosperous empire in the world. How can such achievements as these be overlooked and who are you to dare to set yourself

up against them? Are you not afraid to stand so entirely
alone?

"Even a man like Mr. Karl Marx, another intellectual, German this time, recognized the genius of Messrs. Smith and
Ricardo and the scientific soundness of their system. But
what am I saying? He not only recognized it; he founded
his own system upon it. Please understand that I myself have
no use whatever for Mr. Karl Marx, who lived a life of penury
in London and whose works I consider exceedingly dangerous to society. I am ashamed even to mention his name in
these precincts. For he was revolutionary and he claimed that
the capitalist system of Messrs. Smith and Ricardo would
undergo a complete metamorphosis and become as unrec-
ognizable in its new form as the larva when it has changed
into a butterfly. He too was a kind of poet, but I leave all that
visionary side to you. On the other hand, revolutionary as he
was, Marx still thought he was following in the footsteps of
Messrs. Smith and Ricardo and building on their foundations. Frankly, Mr. Ford, I am more ashamed of you than of
Marx. You do not even respect the authorities he respected
and to me you seem infinitely more revolutionary.

"I shall make my meaning still clearer. Mr. Adam Smith,
the authority we all recognize, stated a law which he knew
to be scientifically sound and which Messrs. Ricardo and
Marx accepted: 'High or low wages and profit are the causes
of high or low prices.' I trust that this law is plain enough for
you to grasp. According to orthodox capitalism, of which Mr.
Adam Smith is the revered Master, upon which our society is
founded, and for which I speak in this court, there is only
one way to cut the selling price of a product, and that is to
cut wages, or profits, or both. Now, since a capitalist, whose
aim is to get rich, cannot reasonably be expected to cut his
profit, he will inevitably be compelled by economic law, if
he wishes on the one hand to reduce prices in order to survive in the competition of the open market and on the other

hand to maintain and increase his profit, to cut wages, to keep on cutting them till they reach that "minimum subsistence wage" below which it is impossible to go, since after all workers must subsist and perpetuate themselves, if the source of that merchandise called labor is not to run dry. This is the way things are. I am aware that it amounts to saying that people can get rich only at the expense of the poor. Mr. Ricardo is satisfied with the way things are; Mr. Marx deplores it. But at least they both admit that things are as they are in obedience to economic law and that this is the foundation of our capitalist society.

"You, Mr. Ford, and you alone, with all the fearlessness of ignorance, dare trample on Adam Smith's law. You claim that it is possible to cut prices and raise wages at the same time, and you do so. According to the law, you should be ruined. But you are not ruined. On the contrary, you are making more and more profits all the time. You are destroying the capitalist system, Mr. Ford, you are turning it upside down. You are standing on your head. You claim that you can get rich, not by making the poor poorer, but by making them rich too. I tell you, you are standing on your head, but the scandal of scandals in all this is that your system succeeds. However, I am allowing my indignation to run away with me, when I should be pointing out to you the consequences of your folly. I beg your pardon.

"A business, Mr. Ford, and in fact any economic or social organization, can be defined by the goal it sets itself. When you change its aim, you change its nature. Now, you are changing the aims of industry and business, and therefore you are changing their nature. Yours is no longer a capitalist business, at least not according to the tradition officially established by Messrs. Smith and Ricardo, and stamped as genuine by Mr. Marx. And if, rich as you are, you are not a capitalist, I would very much like to know what you really are. What I hold most against you is that you confound and

confuse me beyond measure, and that you have no right to
do so.

"You made an unfortunate remark, Mr. Ford, an extremely
unfortunate, not to say downright sinister remark. You had
the temerity to say that money, to you, is only one of the
many links that go into the chain of production, "a part in
the conveyor line," like coal, ore, or one of your numerous
machines. In the capitalist system, the opposite is true. Profit
—money, in other words—is the supreme goal, I was about
to say the idol, while wages, even workers, are only links in
the chain of production, like coal and ore. And now you turn
everything upside down. You look upon your profits as you
would look upon a reserve supply of coal for your factories,
and on the other hand you look upon raising wages as one of
the essential aims of industry.

"Practically speaking, you are heading toward an extreme,
and I believe a highly revolutionary change in society. You
are radically transforming the position of the worker. The
orthodox capitalist system deliberately reduces the worker
to subsistence level and keeps him there, creating what Mr.
Karl Marx rightly calls the proletariat. But by doubling the
wages of your workers, Mr. Ford, you have made it impossible
to maintain a proletarian class, you are eating away at the
foundations of the capitalist system. Not only do you give
your workers far more than a minimum subsistence wage,
but you give them a purchasing power to use as they please,
you give them citizens' rights on the market, you invest them
with the status of customer and consumer, whereas, before
you came along, they were in the market only as another
form of merchandise—to be disposed of, but not to dispose
of itself.

"I now come to my summation. Let me recapitulate:

"One: You systematically reduce the selling price of your
product and raise the wages of your workers at the same time.

"Two: You take your product out of the luxury class and make it a basic necessity available to all.

"Three: You take the worker and his labor out of the category of merchandise on the market, and make him a customer and consumer.

"Four: The net effect of what you have done is to make Messrs. Smith and Ricardo look like fools, and furthermore to cut the ground from under Mr. Marx, whose whole revolutionary theory rests on the fact that in the capitalist system the worker can never, never raise himself above subsistence level and attain the status of customer.

"I must ask you not to smile, Mr. Ford; you ought to be ashamed. You are a heretic, indeed the worst of heretics. Not only do you deny the teachings, the capitalist teachings according to the Gospel of Adam Smith and Ricardo, but you expose them to ridicule, since despite this, as I am forced to admit, you keep on getting richer and richer, which is the supreme goal of the capitalist; you keep on getting richer and richer without, apparently, even trying to do so and almost casually, which is the dream of every capitalist; you keep on getting richer and richer, although you ought to be on the road to ruin. Were we not living in an enlightened age which has banished all superstition, I might be asking myself if there were not some witchcraft at work, and if you were not such a rich man, Mr. Ford, how I would relish sending you to prison!

"Once and for all, let me make it clear that, according to the orthodox capitalism for which I speak in this court and in the name of which I have condemned you, your fortune, though enormous, has been dubiously made since you made it by enriching the poor instead of further impoverishing them, and your use of this fortune is illegitimate since you aim to have it profit everyone instead of carefully preserving it for yourself. Your fortune cannot be considered legitimate, since you are flouting the rules by which wealth is acquired. And now, I leave with you the irrefutable rejoinder of the Austrian generals to Napoleon, after he had beaten them: 'All your victories are as naught, for they were won against military regulations.' "

Political economy is so bleak a subject that the reader will forgive me for having lingered over the comic aspects of this situation. Like the situations in Molière's plays, this one is comic only because it both conceals and reveals an enormous fraud. As established by Adam Smith, Ricardo, and Karl Marx, political economy seems no less a fable and a myth than medieval alchemy. The trial at which Ford faced the Dodge brothers is unique in that it unmasked this fraud. That is why it kept teetering on the edge of comedy. It should be as celebrated in political economy as the trial of Socrates in philosophy or that of Galileo in astronomy.

The reader will perhaps forgive me if, before leaving the subject of that extraordinary trial of orthodoxy, I give rein to my imagination once again. Let us suppose, then, that Henry Ford's lawyer had kept a diary. Here is the entry he might have made on the night of February 7, 1919:

"Today I lost a case. The most important case in my whole career. Some tens of millions of dollars and the control of one of the largest companies in this country were at stake. I was defending Mr. Henry Ford of Detroit. The Judge found against us. Needless to say, I dislike losing a case, especially when such vast interests are involved. And yet my feelings tonight are strangely mixed. I cannot say that I feel in any sense sad, and I certainly have none of the bitterness that comes with defeat. My client himself was overjoyed. I should add that throughout the trial he did everything he possibly could to set the Judge against us. It is certainly his fault that we lost. But my client could scarcely have been happier, had we won. I remember a saying of Montaigne's: 'There are some defeats more triumphant than victories.'

What happened today could not be more briefly or better described.

"If someday historians turn their attention to this trial, they may well decide that it was the most extraordinary trial of the century. Strange as it may seem, I honestly believe that it is more important than the Versailles Treaty which is to be signed this year, and more ideologically significant, more concretely revolutionary, than the 1917 Ocotober Revolution in Russia. The case was against Ford, but it was actually society that was the accused and was defending itself. Ford was found guilty, but I have no doubt whatever that in the end it was society that lost the case, and we who won it. In other words, from today on, we Americans will have to recognize that the traditional capitalist economic system is not only obsolete but absurd, and unsuited to America.

"For some time now I have been aware of this evolution, or more properly, revolution. I have read our great economist, Henry Charles Carey, and it seems to me that it was Carey's ideas that Ford presented before the court, just as it is Carey's ideas that he has applied in industry. I made every effort—vainly, I must confess—to remind the Judge that America is no longer a British colony and to explain that it would be as much to our advantage today to rid ourselves of English ideas of economics as it was for our forebears to throw overboard the divine right of the King of England and the tyranny of Parliament. Now that the Marxist version of the English school of economic thought has triumphed in Russia, it seems to me that it is time we recognized that the consequences of capitalism are fatal and that America has been more than fortunate in having invented a political economy of its own which has nothing to do with, and owes nothing to, either capitalism or Marxism. But to this the Judge's mind was closed.

"The Judge was particularly incensed by Mr. Ford's quite obvious contempt for money. It bit deep into his capitalist soul. But Ford's attitude toward money is no different from that of Henry Charles Carey, the Carey who wrote, 'Money is to society what fuel is to the locomotive and food to the man—the cause of motion, whence results power.' Money is no more than that. To me this remark of Carey's is both profound and very American. This is exactly Mr. Ford's idea of money, too. Of course, it is an essentially anti-capitalist idea, but why not, if it is sound? The judge kept reproaching Mr. Ford for making Adam Smith, Ricardo, and Karl Marx look like fools, and it did not seem to occur to him that in political economy perhaps that is just what they were, and that it is Mr. Ford and his master, Carey, who are right and who are the geniuses.

"It was perfectly clear to me that Mr. Ford, who is as thin as a rail, has the same contempt for capitalism as he has for people unfortunate enough to be fat. To accumulate money merely for the pleasure it brings seems to him as stupid as to hoard food merely for the pleasure of eating more and more. To everything there must be a limit. Doctors do not forbid food, but neither do they favor obesity. I find this a perfectly reasonable point of view. I remember having read in Boisguillebert, a seventeenth-century French economist, the injunction that "money must be driven back within its natural boundaries." That is what Carey urged, what Mr. Ford has actually done. For both men it is an axiom that money is simply a means, while public service is an end, of business. But people can no more forgive them this attitude than, when greed has made them obese, they can forgive those whose self-control has kept their bodies healthy, sound, and thin.

"In short, although we lost the case, I found it intellectually most exciting and memorable. It is really capitalism that America has put on trial, and the trial is not yet ended. America's method of trying the case is far more radical than that of Marx. America repudiates as false the supposedly scientific laws of capitalist economy, and it does much more than merely repudiate them, for it establishes positive proof, through existing fact and reality, that these laws are false. Needless to say, this scandalizes not only the Marxist who blindly accepts them, but also, and just as deeply, an orthodox capitalist such as our Judge, who reveres them.

"I shall sleep well tonight. What better fortune could befall a lawyer than to have the honor, for once in his life, of defending a client in a trial of orthodoxy in which the loser is certain in the end to win?"

20

Samuel Gompers and Lenin—
"More-and-More" and "All-or-Nothing"

In writing about Jefferson and Saint-Just, I tried to describe the spirit of the American political revolution, with its inherent sense of compromise which set itself limited and practicable objectives without ever retreating from them, as opposed to the essentially Utopian and totalitarian spirit of the Jacobins. An equally striking antithesis between two different spirits and methods of revolution can be seen in the American labor movement on the one hand and the socialist revolution on the other. Once again, rather than define abstract principles, I prefer to make use of two concrete figures who seem to me to exemplify these diametrically opposite points of view. Nikolai Lenin, better than anyone else, represents the spirit and methods of socialist revolution, while the American labor movement could hardly be more fittingly represented than by Samuel Gompers, whom George Meany has called "the leading figure of the industrial revolution in America." I myself would be inclined to qualify Meany's statement, for, as I have pointed out, it seems to me that the principles of the American type of social revolution were first laid down by Henry Charles Carey, and that a vital role was also played in the industrial revolution by Henry Ford. However, the fact remains that Samuel Gompers (1850-1924), founder of the American Federation of Labor, has been for more than a century a major source of inspiration to the American labor movement.

To turn first to Lenin, his father was a district supervisor in the Russian school administration. His mother was the daughter of a lawyer. When Lenin was seventeen his older brother, a university student who had joined a terrorist organization plotting to assassinate the Czar, was arrested, condemned to death, and executed. Execution usually entails dishonor; but execution for a political crime, or indeed any conviction for crimes of an ideological nature, is peculiar in that, far from dishonoring the condemned, it makes a martyr of him. The blood of martyrs has always brought a flowering of new faith. Putting people to death for ideological crimes fortifies and crystallizes the intellectual opposition and awakens a lasting sense of injustice. The martyrdom of early Christians multiplied Christian apostles. The execution of Lenin's brother made Lenin a revolutionary. He was convinced that his brother was the hero and that the society which had condemned him was a society of villains which deserved to be destroyed. There remained only the problem of how to bring about its destruction. That same year, 1887, Lenin in turn became a student at the University of Kazan and immediately distinguished himself by his subversive activities. From then on, his life was a ceaseless conflict with the government of the Czar, a conflict punctuated by imprisonment and banishment to Siberia, in the classic pattern of revolutionary careers in Russia before 1914.

The remarkable thing about this career is that it was the career of an intellectual, and moreover wholly, exclusively, and typically the career of an intellectual. In all Lenin's experience as a child and a young man there was absolutely nothing which could be said to have had any connection whatever with the common people, with workers and peasants, with the "proletariat." No doubt his brother's execution was a horrible thing for Lenin to face. But what, after all, did his brother's execution have to do with the conditions of labor and the peasantry? Strictly speaking, it had nothing to do with them. Yet it seems certain that this execution was a determining factor in Lenin's decision to be a political revolutionary. Blood calls for blood.

Lenin became a Marxist and very rapidly thereafter an authority on Marxism. But careful scrutiny of his writings shows that what concerned him most in Marxism was its revolutionary aspect. While Marx thought of himself as a "scientist," Lenin considered Marxism not so much a "science" as a *strategy of political revolution*. It was for this strategy that Lenin was to furnish the tactics. He himself explained why many Russian students became Marxists: "Of course," he wrote, "these students were not so much interested in Marxism as a theory; they were interested in it because it provided the answer to the question 'What is to be done?'; because it was a call to march against the enemy." To Lenin, Marxism was essentially a declaration of war and a call to arms. But to make war, it is not enough to recognize the enemy; there must be soldiers to march against him. Marxism was indeed a strategy, since it clearly indicated where the soldiers for the revolution could be found. The rank and file, the "cannon fodder" of the revolution, was to come from the proletariat, but only if, as Lenin made more than plain, it was provided with experienced leadership. "The spontaneous struggle of the proletariat," he wrote, "will not become a genuine 'class struggle' until it is led by a strong organization of revolutionists."

There is much the same difference between Marx and Lenin as between the Rousseau of *The Social Contract* and Napoleon. If Rousseau was a father of the French Revolution, Napoleon was its son. But Napoleon did not serve the principles of the French Revolution; *he made them serve him,* for it was with the soldiers of that Revolution that he won his imperialist wars. In the same sense, when Lenin spoke of the "class struggle" he was obviously far less concerned with the working class than with *the struggle itself.* By struggle, Lenin meant the socialist Revolution, and in his mind the working class existed for no other purpose than to provide the weapon for that struggle—the Grand Army of the socialist Revolution. When he spoke of the "dictatorship of the proletariat," the emphasis was less on "proletariat" than on "dictatorship" and on the seizure of power. For that struggle, workers would make ideal recruits. "The workers," Lenin said, "are prepared to fight even for demands which . . . do not promise palpable results." Workers are always ready to be mobilized for revolution, and that was the reason, and the only reason, that they mattered to Lenin, as the readiness of the French to be mobilized for war was the only reason that Napoleon "so loved" them. "Marxism," wrote Lenin, ". . . gives a gigantic impetus to the initiative and energy of the Social Democrats, opens up for them the widest perspectives and, if one may so express it, places at their disposal the mighty force of millions and millions of workers 'spontaneously' rising for the struggle." Again, as in Napoleon, one of the qualities most to be admired in Lenin is the clarity with which he expressed himself.

Revolution was to Lenin what war was to Napoleon: "a simple art which is all in the execution." Neither Napoleon nor Lenin was a monster. Absorbed in their "art," they saw only through a mist the individual tragedies that follow in the train of war and revolution. The dreadful saying that "you cannot make an omelette without breaking eggs" was their excuse. The essentially artistic nature of their great undertakings soon turned them into legend, and the Emperor found a Victor Hugo to celebrate him in verse. But even Victor Hugo had a sense of reality.

> . . . after all, in war,
> A man is no more than a shadow, and of little count.

Napoleon, who did France so much harm, is still the most popular figure in French history, as no doubt Lenin will remain popular in Russia, even if the day comes when the Russians are no longer Communist. Pilgrims flock to pay their respects to the tomb in the Invalides in Paris and the Mausoleum in the Red Square in Moscow where Napoleon and Lenin lie *among those peoples whom they so loved.*

And now to return to Samuel Gompers. He was born in London in 1850, the eldest of six children. His parents were Dutch Jews, and apparently very poor indeed. His father worked in a cigar factory. Young Samuel got his first education on the streets among the children of the neighborhood who were as poor as he. At the age of six he was sent to a Jewish school where he learned the rudiments of reading, writing, arithmetic, history, and geography, and also studied elementary Hebrew and began the Talmud. He was an excellent pupil, but at ten he had to leave school for good and go to work in the factory with his father to help balance the family budget. Years later, looking back with a certain bitterness upon the fact of having been taken out of school at so early an age, he remarked, "Mental hunger is just as painful as physical hunger." In 1860, in London, being a worker meant being hungry. Young Gompers, son of a worker and a worker himself, knew hunger, knew indeed both hungers— that of the body and that of the soul. Lenin, at the same age, knew neither.

Gompers' experience as a small boy was later to determine his vocation: the improving of the worker's lot. Here is how he himself described the climate of his youth in his autobiography, *Seventy Years of Life and Labor:**

> Many of our neighbors were descendants of French Huguenots who fled from France after the revocation of the Edict of Nantes . . . and in that new home plied their

* New York: Dutton, 1925.

wonderful skill in silk weaving that brought fame and wealth to Spitalfields. But the passing of time . . . had brought changes to the industry. One of my most vivid early recollections is the great trouble that came to the silk weavers when machinery was invented to replace their skill and take their jobs. No thought was given those men whose trade was gone. Misery and suspense filled the neighborhood with the depressing air of dread. The narrow street echoed with the tramp of men walking the street in groups with no work to do. Burned into my mind was the indescribable effect of the cry of these men, "God, I've no work to do. Lord strike me dead—and my wife, my kids want bread and I've no work to do." Child that I was, that cry taught me the world-wide feeling that has ever bound the oppressed together in a struggle against those who hold control over the lives and opportunities of those who work for wages. That feeling became a subconscious guiding impulse that in later years developed into the dominating influence in shaping my life.

In 1863, wearied of penury, Gompers' father, with wife and children, emigrated to America. Father and son went to work in a cigar factory in New York and joined the union for their trade. The New York cigar makers' union was to be young Gompers' springboard, and the nucleus of what later became the American Federation of Labor. In that year of 1863, the War of Secession was drawing to a close. This probably had some influence on the decision of the Gompers family to settle in the United States. Even more than a civil war, that war was a social war, and all over the world, workers were ardently hoping for the victory of the Union. To young Gompers the assassination of Abraham Lincoln had all the impact of a personal loss. "Like some cataclysm," Gompers later wrote, "came the report that an assassin had struck down the great Emancipator. It seemed to me that some great power for good had gone out of the world. A master mind had been taken at a time when most needed. I cried all that day. . . ." Nothing could be more moving than the tears of the fifteen-year-old boy. He too was to become a worker for social emancipation, but by that time he would long since have ceased to cry. It is not with tears that men win their battles.

Gompers made a profession of faith that recalls Clemenceau's famous dictum of 1917: "Foreign policy: I am fighting a war. Internal policy: I am fighting a war." This is what Gompers wrote: "In my religion, I am a workingman. In politics, I am a workingman, and in every nerve, in every fiber, in every aspiration I am on the side which will advance the interests of my fellow workingmen. I do not say this in the spirit of bravado or demagogism, but in all sincerity. Men of means have their political predilections but seldom allow their politics to interfere with their business interests. I take exactly the same position, except that I represent my side, the side of the toiling wage-earning masses, in my every act and in my every utterance."

The whole of Samuel Gompers' life went to prove that he meant what he said. He was certainly not against religion, but he did not belong to any church. He had profound respect for the religious convictions of other people. Most of his friends were Catholic, for the simple reason that at that time in America most workers were Catholic, and priests sided with their flocks and were natural allies of the labor movement. But Gompers insisted upon distinguishing between religion and trade unionism, which was doubtless just as desirable for religion as it was for trade unionism, since ambiguity is always an obstacle to progress. However, despite his many Catholic friends, Gompers entered a solemn protest against the execution in Spain of the atheist Francisco Ferrer because he believed him to have been unjustly condemned. He abhorred all ideological trials.

Gompers was completely indifferent to politics. He thought of the workers' problems in economic and social terms (the simple alternative of work and bread, or death), but absolutely never in political terms. In his opinion, trade unionism and labor conditions stood only to gain if the workers kept free of political allegiance and purely political ambition. He himself was sometimes nominated for political office but, like Carey, he always declined to be a candidate. He wanted American trade unionism to keep its independence of judgment intact, insisting that it must always be able to throw its support behind any candidate of any party, according to the circumstances of the moment, the personalities involved, and the local conditions, and with the single aim of advancing labor's position.

We now know enough about Lenin and Gompers to ask ourselves which of the two was the more likely from the start to understand the workers, to give them help where they truly needed it, and to create a philosophy of action that would lead to the emancipation of the working class. It can hardly be denied that it was Gompers. Lenin himself did not hesitate to admit that Marxism was begun by the bourgeoisie and spread by young bourgeois intellectuals, "carriers of the revolutionary bacillus." In his book *What Is to Be Done?* Lenin wrote:

> The theory of Socialism . . . grew out of the philosophic, historical, and economic theories that were elaborated by the educated representatives of the propertied classes, the intellectuals. The founders of modern scientific Socialism, Marx and Engels, themselves belonged to the bourgeois intelligentsia. Similarly, in Russia, the theoretical doctrine of Social Democracy arose *quite independently of the spontaneous growth of the labor movement;* it arose as a natural and inevitable outcome of the development of ideas among the revolutionary Socialist intelligentsia.

This admission certainly gives us the right to ask what possible connection there can be between socialism and the working classes. Perhaps the only connection is the execution of Lenin's brother. Socialism is an ideological movement, begun by members of the bourgeois class and spread by them. I have already shown that Marx no less frankly recognized his direct ideological descent from the bourgeois capitalism of Ricardo and Malthus. Socialism is a son in revolt against its father, but none the less the legitimate son of bourgeois capitalism. The Americans, on the contrary—Gompers as well as Ford and Carey—have nothing whatever in common with that family or with the quarrels that divide it.

A few pages farther on in the same book, Lenin declared that *"there can be no talk of an independent ideology being developed by the masses of the workers in the process of their movement."* Samuel Gompers gave the lie to this peremptory assertion. What Lenin had declared, without even bothering to prove it, was blatantly untrue. The whole factual history of the American labor movement goes to prove this. "The American trade-union movement," wrote Samuel Gompers, "had to work out *its own philosophy, technique, and language. What has been developed is different* from that of any other country. . . . I strove to make the American movement practical, deep-rooted in sympathy and sentiment. *I refused to concede one single inch of labor activity to any other movement.* I held that the trade union was capable of all manner of diverse services and that there was no need of creating separate organizations for different fields of interests—for such separation would only diffuse the power of labor."

Lenin further argued that "since there can be no talk of an independent ideology being developed by the masses of the workers in the process of their movement, then *the only choice* [Lenin's emphasis] is: Either bourgeois or Socialist ideology. *There is no middle course* (for humanity has not created a 'third' ideology, and, moreover, in a society torn by class antagonisms there can never be a non-class or above-class ideology). Hence, to belittle Socialist ideology *in any way, to deviate from it in the slightest degree* [Lenin's emphasis] means strengthening the bourgeois ideology." So here is still another Saint-Just, who sees no middle course; still another madman, as Danton would have called him; still another carefree and light-hearted venturer into the dialectic of all-or-nothing; still another voice to echo the words of the Lord Himself: "He that is not with me is against me." Since Saint-Just there has been no doubt as to where that road leads—straight to the reign of Terror. Marxists can accuse others of Utopianism as much as they please, but the worst Utopians are the Marxists themselves, because it is they who are totalitarian, it is they who never see a middle course, who cling obstinately to all-or-nothing, and who introduce the law of mysticism into politics with which it has no direct concern. But Lenin was in full flight of fancy, he had gone too far to stop, and besides, the Utopian never stops. "The spontaneous labor movement," he went on, "is able by itself to create (and inevitably will create) only trade-unionism, and working-class trade-union politics are precisely working-class bourgeois politics." To the question why trade-union policy can never be anything but a bourgeois policy, the only answer is that it is not a socialist policy —Q.E.D. And so poor Samuel Gompers, a worker, and the son of a worker, is irrevocably relegated by the bourgeois Lenin to the ranks of "bourgeois deviationists." Lenin was never afraid of being ridiculous.

At the heart of this farce is the fact that Marxists can see only two possible, and contradictory, relationships between capital and labor. Marx and Lenin believed that either capital enslaves labor and there is a bourgeois capitalist regime, or labor abolishes capital and there is a socialist regime. For them there was no third course.

But for America and Americans, *there is a third course,* a "third ideology," as Lenin would have called it, though I dislike using the word "ideology" in connection with America. That third course was clearly defined, after all, by Carey. It is natural and normal for the relationship between capital and labor to be a close association, to be what one might even call a marriage, *a marriage for the purpose of production.* Without labor, capital cannot produce. On the other hand, capital facilitates labor and makes it more and more productive. As Carey pointed out, Christopher Columbus's ship, the *Santa Maria,* was only ninety tons, yet to build it cost much more in time and labor and money than it cost four hundred years later to build the nineteenth-century steamers which rendered so many more services. And today, the cost of an Atlantic crossing is much lower, from every point of view, than it was in the time of Columbus. This reduction in price has been made possible only by the *accumulation* of the means of production, and Columbus's voyage is in itself a part of that common capital with which we build our transatlantic liners. Carey believed that production was something more important than either capital or labor. For in the last analysis, capital and labor have no meaning except when linked to production. But there can be no production without their association, though of course this association is perfectly compatible with a certain amount of antagonism.

To Carey and the Americans, Lenin's uncompromising attitude was rather like the proposition that all human beings are either men or women, and that everyone must be one or the other. This is self-evident; but the natural and normal condition of the two sexes is to be united in marriage for the purpose of producing children. Of course it is quite possible to talk at length about men and women entirely in terms of their mutual antagonisms. But a discourse on this subject might seem somewhat incomplete if it contained no reference at all to the possibility of their association, or to the

children who naturally result from it. Needless to say, not
every marriage is wholly serene; marriage does not eliminate
antagonism between man and woman. Also needless to say,
it is possible to conceive of a society in which women are completely enslaved by men, as in Islam. This is the case in capitalist society, where labor is completely enslaved by capital.
But the emancipation of the Moslem woman could hardly be
called successful if it were accomplished by abolishing not
only marriage, but men.

The position of a Samuel Gompers within the labor-capi-
tal relationship seems to me to be that of a high-minded but
headstrong wife who, however exacerbated by her husband,
would not only never dream of murdering him, but considers herself committed to the marriage, wants to stay married
for better or worse, and will not for a moment consider di-
vorce. Yet this does not mean that she loses her identity
as a woman. Samuel Gompers, who wanted the economic and
social emancipation of the workers fully as much as, and
probably far more than Lenin, would have laughed aloud
at being called a "bourgeois deviationist." Moreover, the
whole ideological edifice of Communism crumbles like a
house of cards the moment it becomes clear that between
Marxist socialism and bourgeois capitalism there can be a
middle course. There not only can be but there is a middle
course; it exists, it flourishes, and it owes nothing to either
capitalism or socialism. It is the American society.

Gompers was just as obviously anti-capitalist as Ford and
Carey. Indeed, he was undoubtedly more anti-capitalist even
than Lenin, since he himself had lived under the heavy yoke
of capitalism. In 1875, at a meeting of his own union, Gompers said, "All who are present today should be convinced
that our condition is growing worse every day and that the
future is threatened with danger. Who can deny that reduc-
tions are almost daily occurrences because the capitalists'

only ambition is profit?" And again, on another occasion, he said, "We recognize the solidarity of the whole working class to work harmoniously against their common enemy—the capitalists. We pledge ourselves to support the unemployed because hunger will force the best workmen to work for low wages. United we are a power to be respected; divided we are the slaves of the capitalists."

This was plainly a declaration of war, or rather a proclamation that a state of war already existed between workers and capitalists. It was a far cry from the social harmony that Carey had envisaged. In the first trade-union constitutions, as drawn up by Gompers, all the emphasis was on social struggle, and the enemy of the working class was unequivocally defined as capitalism. In that same period, Gompers and some of his friends published a manifesto that began as follows:

> Throughout the United States there exist numerous organized bodies of workingmen who declare that the present social and political systems are false and require to be changed from their very foundation so that the present degraded dependence of the workingman upon the capitalist for a means of livelihood is the cause of the greater part of the intellectual, moral, and economic degradation that afflicts society, that every political movement must be subordinate to the first great social end, viz., the economic emancipation of the working classes.

To recognize the need for radical change in society and to make the aim of that change the economic and social emancipation of the working class was hardly original, and I could go on quoting indefinitely statements of this nature by Gompers. But similar statements were issued by every contemporary labor movement not only in America but in Europe and Russia, and by every branch of the labor movement—anarchist, socialist, Communist, and so forth. They all recognized the same enemy; it was capitalism that held the workers enslaved. They were all fighting the same battle. What, then, was the difference between them?

What, for instance, was the difference between the American trade-unionist movement led by Samuel Gompers and Marxist socialism? Here, as so often, Gompers made his position plain. "I say to you, friends and delegates," said Gompers, in a convention debate, "that the man who would accuse me or charge me with being anti-Socialist says what he don't know anything about, he does not know Sam Gompers. I say here broadly and openly that there is not a noble hope that a Socialist may have that I do not hold as my ideal. There is not an inspiring and ennobling end that they are striving for that my heart does not beat in response to. *But our methods are different.* The Socialist Party and Trade Unions are different; inherently do they differ in their methods." At first sight, one might suppose that at least on this one point Lenin and Gompers were in agreement and that both believed that the difference between socialism and American trade unionism was simply one of method. Yet even on this point they did not agree. Their disagreement went much deeper, for they differed, if not in the aims they professed, then certainly in those they actually pursued. Lenin was quite right when he wrote, "The character of the organization of every institution is naturally and inevitably determined by the character of the activity that institution conducts."

Reading Lenin objectively and calmly, it is impossible not to recognize the fact that his real and ultimate aim was in no sense the achievement of the economic and social emancipation of the workers, for he looked upon emancipation only as a means, a propaganda means, to attract recruits to the Grand Army of the Revolution. His ultimate aim was nothing less than the overthrow of the Czarist autocracy, and political revolution. Lenin had the same mentality as the late

French monarchist Charles Maurras; both were political, always political, and nothing but political from beginning to end. Lenin was a mystic of political revolution; he spoke of it constantly as though speaking of a religious vocation. Unquestionably Lenin considered Gompers "a hopeless amateur." "A man," he wrote, "who resembles a trade-union secretary more than a people's tribune . . . who is inexperienced and clumsy in his own professional art—*the art of combating the political police*—such a man is not a revolutionist but a hopeless amateur! . . . *Give us an organization of revolutionists and we shall overturn the whole of Russia.*" This last sentence epitomizes Lenin. Having said which, however, it must be admitted that Lenin was the greatest revolutionary commander of all time; he was the Alexander, the Caesar, the Napoleon of political revolution. Compared to Lenin, Maurras was a mere chatterbox, an armchair strategist. No one has ever developed greater precision than Lenin in the techniques of revolution.

To describe Lenin's achievement even more exactly, he *industrialized* revolution. As Henry Ford defined and applied the methods of mass production, mass distribution, and the assembly line to machine manufacture, so Lenin defined and applied these same methods, precisely these same methods, to political revolution. He created the *technology of revolution.* He brought about *the industrial revolution of revolution itself. He carried political revolution from the empirical stage of manufacture by hand to the rationalized stage of manufacture by machine.* Who was it who said that "it is impossible to increase productivity to any extent by our primitive methods"? Was it Henry Ford, referring to horses? Not at all. It was Lenin, referring to the Russian political situation in 1902 and to the primitive state of Russian revolutionary methods.

Lenin manufactured his political revolution by rationalization. To the manufacture of revolution he applied Henry

Ford's seven principles: power, accuracy, economy, continuity, system, speed, and repetition. Passages can be found in Lenin to illustrate every one of these principles and to show how every one of them applies to revolution, which he thought of in terms of an industrial enterprise, in exactly the terms of an assembly line. There was, for instance, the occasion when he turned on an unfortunate revolutionary who had just published a lengthy tract of 132 pages. "What was the use," Lenin demanded, "of writing a pamphlet of 132 pages on 'Questions of Theory and Tactics'? Don't you think that it would have been more becoming for the 'eve of the revolution point of view' to have issued 132,000 leaflets containing the brief appeal: 'Kill them!'?"

Henry Ford envisaged production and distribution as a vast, continuously moving machine, and Lenin had the very same image of political revolution. In speaking of his plan to found a national newspaper, he wrote:

I continue to insist that we can start establishing real contacts only with the aid of a common newspaper, as a single, regular, All-Russian enterprise, which will summarize the results of all the diverse forms of activity and thereby stimulate our people to march forward untiringly along all the innumerable paths which lead to the revolution in the same way as all roads lead to Rome. If we do not want unity in name only, we must arrange for every local circle immediately to assign, say, a fourth of its forces to active work for the common cause, and the newspaper will immediately convey to them the general design, dimension, and character of this cause, will indicate to them precisely the most serious defects of All-Russian activity, where agitation is lacking and where contacts are weak, and point out *which small wheel in the great general mechanism could be repaired or replaced by a better one.* A circle that has not commenced to work yet, which is only just seeking work, could then start, *not like a*

*craftsman in a small separate workshop, unaware of the de-
velopment that has taken place in "industry," or of the general state of the given industry and the methods of production prevailing in it, but as a participant in an extensive
enterprise* that reflects the whole general revolutionary attack upon autocracy. *And the more perfect the finish of each
little wheel will be, the larger the number of detail workers
working for the common cause, the closer will our network
become* and the less consternation will inevitable police raids
call forth in the common ranks.

   In concluding this analogy between Lenin and Ford, I will
add one brief remark. I have already pointed out that
assembly-line methods know neither ideology, religion, nor
patriotism. Anyone can apply them anywhere, toward any
end. The same can be said of Lenin's revolutionary methods, for they are as abstract and perfect as mathematics. As
is well known, Hitler used them in Germany against Communism. Lenin himself had studied the manuals of the
Inquisition and the Jesuit constitutions. If the day ever
comes in Russia when a new generation decides to overthrow
the Communist regime, it could not do better than to read
Lenin, study him in detail, and apply his methods of "organization, discipline, and the technique of secrecy carried to the
highest stage of perfection." This in itself is proof enough
that what was most important in Lenin's doctrine was never
the emancipation of the working class, but something totally
different, namely, the *art of political revolution.* The art of
painting and the art of revolution are alike in their profound
indifference to both ideas and men: "a man is no more
than a shadow."

   Like the art of war, like all art, the art of revolution is
essentially aristocratic. It requires a real vocation, a special
initiation, an intensive training. No one insisted more than
Lenin on these requirements. It seems to me both obvious

and inevitable that he had to be an aristocrat. In revolution as in war, some must command and others obey. Henry Ford was also autocratic, but he at least admitted it, while Lenin always denied it. Lenin's answer to the charge of being anti-democratic was that, within the Party organization, anyone could rise to a position of command. True enough, but that does not change the fact that the structure of the Party is hierarchic. It comes down to saying, as was said of Napoleon's army, that every soldier has a marshal's baton in his knap-sack, but in his army, nevertheless, there were far fewer mar-shals than knapsacks. In the Catholic Church, too, a simple shepherd can become Pope, and this has quite often hap-pened, but once he is Pope, he is an absolute and infallible sovereign. When he speaks, all else is stilled.

A further reason why Marxist socialism is essentially aristo-cratic lies in its claim to be a science. In this context, Lenin began by quoting Engels: "Socialism, having become a sci-ence, demands the same treatment as every other science—it must be studied." Then he went on to say, "All those who talk about 'exaggerating the importance of ideology,' about exaggerating the role of the conscious elements, etc., imag-ine that the pure and simple labor movement *can work out an independent ideology for itself, if only the workers 'take their fate out of the hands of their leaders.' But in this they are profoundly mistaken*." So much for Gompers and the American trade unionists. And it was to prove how wrong they were that Lenin explained that there was no middle course between being a socialist and being a bourgeois capi-talist. And moreover, since socialism was a science, only a scientist could understand what it was all about. And further-more, since not everyone could be a scientist, there had to be a teaching faculty and a student body, by which of course he meant teachers with unquestioned authority and students who accept whatever they are told.

I have cast enough ridicule upon the pseudo-science of

Molière's physicians to have earned the right to concede to Marxist socialism its due. In its structure Marxism is indeed scientific. However, it is a science not of the experimental kind, but rather of the strictly theological kind. Having spent my whole life among theologians, I know how they reason; they reason exactly as Lenin reasoned—by deduction and from authority. In an extraordinary passage entitled, "Engels, on the Importance of the Theoretical Struggle," Lenin made a list of the accusations against him: "Dogmatism, doctrinairism, ossification of the Party, etc.," and then he commented, "We are very glad that this question has been brought up and we would propose only to add to it another question: Who are to be the judges?" His question seems to me of major importance, as well as extremely interesting and well put.

But what is the answer? If Marxist socialism were an experimental science, there could only be one possible answer: the judge, the supreme judge in experimental science, is the test of facts. However much one turns and twists this passage of Lenin's, there is still no getting round the fact that the only authority, the only judge he recognized, was Engels. And to argue from authority is characteristic of the theological method. In the opening pages of the *Summa Theologica,* where the theological method is defined, Saint Thomas wrote, "It is especially proper to this doctrine to argue from authority, inasmuch as its principles are obtained by revelation: and hence we must believe the authority of those to whom the revelation has been made." And here once more Claude Bernard is illuminating. The distinctions he draws between scholastic and experimental reasoning can well be applied to Lenin's intellectual processes, for they show that, essentially, Lenin was a scholastic. "The revolution which the experimental method has effected in the sciences," wrote Claude Bernard, "is this: it has put a scientific criterion in place of personal authority. The experimental method is characterized by being dependent only on itself, because it includes within itself its criterion—experience. *It recognizes no authority other than that of facts and is free from personal authority.*"

The fact that Marxist socialism is essentially scholastic and based upon authority explains, in my opinion, its success in nations long accustomed to theological debate. Its history closely resembles the history of the Church Councils. It is a question whether Catholic Europe, for so many centuries under Roman or Byzantine jurisdiction, has gained any advantage by exchanging the old theological jurisdiction for a new one. The authority of the Catholic Church would be an imposture if it did not emanate from the true God, as every schoolchild learns in the catechism. Catholic theologians, moreover, are at least willing to discuss their sources, whereas Marxist theologians are no more willing to discuss them than are the Mohammedans. Marx and Engels are the Koran. Lenin is their theologian. Faithful to his method of arguing from authority, Lenin cited Karl Kautsky: "Thus, Socialist consciousness is something *introduced* into the proletarian class struggle *from without,* and not something that arose *within it* spontaneously." Upon which Lenin, learned doctor of the Communist church, elaborated: ". . . there could not yet be Social-Democratic consciousness among the workers. This consciousness *could only be brought to them from without.*" Once again, Lenin was being no less theological than Saint Thomas, who wrote in the *Summa,* "It was necessary for the salvation of man that certain truths which exceed human values should be made known to him by divine revelation." Thus, Lenin's insistence that "class consciousness" can be brought to the proletariat only *from without* amounted to saying that the proletarian can do nothing about his own salvation, and that the truths he needs in order to be saved must be *revealed* to him from without. One of the reasons why it is not hard for an honest man to remain or become a Catholic is that Catholic theology has never concealed its method, or the fact that its method is based upon authority. Unfortunately, this cannot be said of the "theology" of Marxist socialism. The socialist intellectual has no right to speak until he has given unequivocal answers to the following questions: If socialism is a science, what is its criterion? Is it experience and fact, as in experimental science? Or is it the authority of revelation alone, as in theological science? And if it is the authority of revelation alone, how authentic is that revelation? Speaking for myself, I call theology a science, though I am aware that Claude Bernard would never have agreed with me—but that is another argument and one which would carry me too far away from my subject.

When it comes to Samuel Gompers, however, there is nothing equivocal about either his thinking or his methods. What strikes the reader on every page of his autobiography is his respect *for the facts, for nature, for the test of experience.* Like most Americans, Samuel Gompers has no trace of the theological temperament in his make-up, he has no use for argument from authority, he believes only in facts. He is *an experimentalist. "We must build our program upon facts,"* he wrote, "and not theories." Among all the enormous and incessant difficulties with which his trade-unionist struggle was beset, the most troublesome always came from people who persisted in "ignoring the facts of human nature." "My experience," he wrote, "had convinced me that legislation cannot accomplish that which is contrary to the general will and that far better results can be secured by reaching unanimous agreement after having made a survey of the facts in the case."

Here we reach the heart of America, and perhaps also the heart of America's dispute with Europe. For in the last, the very last analysis, we Europeans, all of us, rightists or leftists, Communists or reactionaries, Christians or anti-Christians, democrats or monarchists, are all, every last one of us, rooted

in aristocratic tradition and theological disciplines; we believe in authority in both the political and social realms.
America, on the other hand, believes only in political and
social facts. America believes that no one has the right to
force people to accept what they do not understand and do
not want. America is democratic, and it believes that laws
follow upon established custom rather than precede it.
Gompers was never satisfied by the mere fact that a thing
was good; he still felt the need to persuade others to want it
of their own accord. He always mistrusted abstract and in-
applicable laws, as he mistrusted conferences that lead only
to the concoction of laws of this kind. "Such a conference," he
explained, "would attempt to *'legislate' for industry,* whereas
really constructive changes and methods are *evolved out of
the experience of industry* by those handling its tools and in
control."

Let us keep this phrase well in mind: *the experience common to those who handle the tools of industry and to those
who are in control.* It was out of the common experience of
labor and management that the idea was born of a typically
American institution—the bargaining table. All that truly
mattered to Samuel Gompers was the economic and social
emancipation of the workers, and for that the bargaining
table served him as an ideal tool, a lever to raise the working
class out of its misery. The emancipation of American workers did not come about all at once; it did not come from
above, or from outside, or by legislation. Emancipation was
achieved little by little, day by day, through the constant,
grim, stubborn, unceasing claims—practical claims based on
the specific conditions of industry—that the workers presented to management, with continual reference to a common experience which furnished a solid, common ground, a
common criterion, for all discussions between workers and
management. And only when discussion broke down on the
discussion level at the bargaining table, then, and only then,

came the call to strike which is the final argument of workers, as war is the final argument of government: *ultima ratio regum.*

It is not *from outside and from above,* as Lenin claimed, that temporal salvation for the working class will come; it is *from within that class itself,* through its own spontaneous and unflagging efforts. "The past years," Gompers wrote, "have been a revealing test, sharply distinguishing the permanent from the ephemeral. They have demonstrated again the dependability of voluntary institutions·assuring individual initiative. They reveal that *genuine growth and progress do not come from above or the outside.* They do not come from formulas or declarations but from the educational self-imposed discipline of the life process and are manifest in *self-revealing work.*" Gompers was consumed with indignation at the mere idea that anyone should take it upon himself to tell the workers what they needed, or that they could not know their own needs unless these needs were *revealed* to them. The direct experience of misery and toil seemed to him to reveal infinitely more than any so-called "scientific" dissertation. *Super omnes docentes me, intellexi.* "I have more understanding than all my teachers" of my destiny and my salvation, Gompers might have said, recalling the words of the Psalm. Although at the start of his career he wrote Engels that he was not in the least against socialism, he ended by having an intense aversion for it. He could not endure the arrogance of vulgar pedants. "Perhaps there is no one," he once said, "who is so intolerant as the theorist who wants to do good."

Needless to say, Gompers' concept of leadership was the exact opposite of Lenin's. All Lenin's criticism of those whom he called "the Economists" and whom Marx called "the Possibilists" could also apply to Gompers, but he did not allow such criticism to weigh on him. He was not serving abstract political revolution; he was serving the workers, and them alone. The statement which I am about to quote could well have been Gompers' answer to Lenin. He wrote it in 1896, but when referring to it later in his autobiography he declared that it expressed "a lifetime principle." "You say," he wrote, "that if I value my position as a 'leader' of the common people, I should lead them now. This betrays what a poor conception you have of the fundamental principles of our labor movement. Your idea seems to be that an executive officer of an organization should be their 'leader.' You do not seem to understand that a leader implies followers, and that *where there are leaders, and followers, there are dupers and duped. You do not know that our movement is based upon the recognition of the sovereignty of the workers; that when they declare for a purpose, they're presumed to mean what they say, and to act in accordance with it; that they require their executive officer, not to lead them, but to execute their will.*" In flat contradiction to Gompers—and in case all that I have so far quoted from Lenin has not been enough—here is still another pronouncement: "A Social Democrat," wrote Lenin, "must concern himself first and foremost with an organization of revolutionists, *capable of guiding the whole proletarian struggle for emancipation.*"

And now here is how Gompers described the various tendencies in the labor movement in New York, in 1873, at the peak of economic crisis: "The group of radicals, so-called Communists, saw in the situation an opportunity for propaganda. Propaganda was for them the chief end of life. They were perfectly willing to use human necessity as propaganda material. Practical results meant nothing in their program. They were young heroes determined to play a great part, hence they were unwilling to do the unostentatious, quiet, orderly things that make for constructive progress. . . . They issued circulars that had artistic and literary merit. They made speeches that contained good headline stuff. They painted the skies with 'true' revolutionary plans and extravagant ideas. . . . Another group . . . urged that *relief for human beings was the real thing.*" In my opinion, words such as these fall upon Lenin, and the Communist and Communist-sympathizing intellectuals, like a rain of fire.

Gompers was to Lenin exactly what Jefferson was to Saint-Just: flesh-and-blood defending itself against Utopia. I am well aware that the Communists are always ready to accuse others of being Utopian. But the formulas of their learned doctors prove the essentially Utopian nature of their ideal. Theirs is the idea of all-or-nothing, of either political revolution and the dictatorship of the proletariat—or death. And when Lenin unloads his sarcasms upon the "Economists," taunting them with the Russian proverb about adding a kopek to a ruble, it is he who is the Utopian. Samuel Gompers clearly foresaw that the adding of a penny to a dollar every day would eventually bring about a radical change in the condition of the working class, by raising the worker from the degrading position of proletarian to the economic dignity of customer. But if the time were ever to come when there were no more "proletarians," then there would no longer be any recruits for the Grand Army of the Revolution, and this is what alarmed Lenin. Here Ford, the captain of industry, and Gompers, the trade unionist, saw eye to eye. Gompers' ideal was not all-or-nothing, but rather more-and-more.

In 1914 Gompers testified before a Congressional investigating committee.

QUESTION: Inform me on this: In its practical work in the labor movement, is the AFL guided by a general social philosophy, or is it not?

GOMPERS: It is guided by the history of the past, drawing its lessons from history. It knows the conditions by which the working people are surrounded. It works along the line of least resistance and endeavors to accomplish the best results in improving the condition of the working people, men, women, and children, today and tomorrow, and each day making it a better day than the one that had gone before. The guiding principle, philosophy, and the aim of the labor movement is to secure a better life for all.

QUESTION: Now, "the highest and best ideals of social justice," as applied to the distribution of wealth—wouldn't that be a system under which all the workers, manual, mental, directive, and executive, would together get the sum total of all the products of their toil?

GOMPERS: Really, a fish is caught by a tempting bait; a mouse or a rat is caught in a trap by a tempting bait. The intelligent, common-sense workmen prefer to deal with the problems of today, the problems with which they are bound to contend if they want to advance, rather than to deal with a picture and a dream which have never had, and I am sure never will have, any reality in the actual affairs of humanity, and which threaten, if they could be introduced, the worst system of circumscriptional effort and activity that has ever been invented by the human mind.

"A fish is caught by a tempting bait," and it could be said of Communism that it has made the largest miraculous draught of fishes in modern times.

When Lenin wrote, "Without a revolutionary theory there can be no revolutionary movement," what did he mean by the word "theory"? Clearly he meant socialism, and socialist theory is, alas, of a theological nature, and hence not subject to the test of facts. Carey would have called it an *invented theory,* deduced in its entirety by reasoning, rather than a *discovered theory,* determined by the facts. Claude Bernard wrote, "We must alter theory to adapt it to nature, but not nature to adapt it to theory." All the difference between Lenin and Gompers is to be found in these few words. Gompers was essentially an experimentalist. To Lenin, however, a theory was an idea, proclaimed as scientific, which was to govern everything, to control everything, and to be subject to no control, precisely because of its "scientific" dignity.

This is why, in the last analysis, Gompers was never able to come to any agreement with either the Russian, the European, or the American socialists. "The trade-union movement of the United States," he wrote, "is not without idealism but it recognizes it must function *in the world as it is* and that its development must be part of the evolutionary process in which many factors are involved. *There is nothing to be gained in taking an immovable stand for an impossible cause. . . .* I have no quarrel with radicalism that is based upon truths. On the contrary, the application of a truth is far more radical than ill-founded propaganda. I have no quarrel with Socialists, but I have no use for their proposals." At the time of the Russian Revolution, he sent a message of congratulation to the Russian workers, but he sounded the same note of moderation that Jefferson had sounded in advising Lafayette: "I warned them," said Gompers, ". . . that it was *impossible to achieve the ideal state immediately* and I pleaded with Russia's workers that they *maintain what they had already achieved* and seek to *solve practically and rationally the problems of today* and *safeguard the future* against reactionary forces." But the Russians heeded Gompers no more than the French had heeded Jefferson, and the Russian Revolution ended, as the French Revolution had ended, in slavery and dictatorship—at the opposite pole from what both revolutions had promised.

Gompers was ruthless in his analysis of the subjective reasons for becoming socialist. He characterized them as lack of simple courage, profound credulity, feminine emotionalism, and, above all, intellectual befuddlement. He agreed with Molière that "it's our disquiet, our impatience which upsets everything; and most men die of their remedies, and not of their ills." This is how Gompers put it. "According to my experience," he wrote, "professional Socialism accompanies instability of judgment or intellectual undependability caused by *inability to recognize facts.* The conspicuous Socialists have uniformly been men whose minds have been warped by a great failure or who found it absolutely impossible to understand fundamentals necessary to developing practical plans for industrial betterment. These were Socialists who were profoundly pessimistic about existing society."

In speaking of one of his old friends who had become a Socialist, Gompers wrote, "Then genial Gene Debs, with much avowed idealism, tried to fit the labor movement into a different shape from that into which it had naturally developed. It is hard for the reformer to realize that the labor movement is a living thing and that it must develop by passing through the normal stage of growth. It is not transformed by any dictum or overnight resolution, but it must grow into something different. When Debs began to *discount his judgment in favor of his emotions* he ceased to play a constructive part in the labor movement."

Others, however, took the opposite direction and came over from socialism to the practical and hard-working trade unionism of Gompers. "Many of those who helped to lay the foundations of the trade-union movement," he wrote, "were men who had been through the experience of Socialism and found their way to sounder policies. They were always men of vision, to whom the spiritual implications of fellowship made a strong appeal, but their *instincts for the practical* carried them safely beyond the emotional to principles based on a *better understanding of human nature.* . . . *Experiences* in Socialism served a constructive purpose if the individual was able to develop beyond the formulas of Socialism, for such carried to their practical duties a quickened insight and an understanding that tangible objectives are merely instrumentalities for reaching a higher spiritual goal."

Gompers was never vague; he was as precise in his thinking as Lenin. To the "class consciousness" so dear to Lenin, which was based on a quasi-theological "theory," Gompers opposed "class solidarity," based on concrete experience of labor conditions and a practical determination to better them. That was the point, the real point, at which their ways parted. It is perfectly possible to try to picture to oneself what the workers had to suffer in the London of a hundred years ago, just as one can try to imagine what it would be like to be in prison or ill. But no one who has not actually experienced imprisonment or illness can really know what they are. The only difference between imagined fact and fact itself is experience, but what a world of difference it makes. This was the fundamental difference between Lenin and Gompers.

Impatience and emotionalism are direct paths to violence. Add to them a systematic and completely Utopian mentality, as in Lenin, and the reign of Terror is bound to come. The use of Terror is above all a spiritual crime. Lenin wrote to Grigori Zinoviev, "One ought to encourage the vigor and wholesale character of the Terror against the counter-revolutionists." Terror is so integral a part of the Communist system that when Khrushchev denounced Stalin his accusation was that Stalin had made use of Terror against Communists themselves. It would never have occurred to Khrushchev to disavow violence as a system of government, nor would it have occurred to him to disavow the use of Terror against non-Communists. No one who does not adhere to the system is innocent. Whoever is not a Communist is damned.

Gompers, on the other hand, took a different stand. "Personally," he wrote, "I have an abhorrence of violence. . . . The labor movement, like all the institutions whose purpose is to promote a revolutionizing ideal, has had to resist tendencies to violence." Gompers considered violence mere childishness; he wanted the workers to be mature enough in mind and character to refrain from it. He knew that blood calls for blood, and that in the inevitable process whereby each brutality evokes a still greater brutality, men lose their judgment, fall prey to demagogues, and cease to be masters of their destiny. And yet, when the Chicago anarchists in the Haymarket Square riot were condemned to death, Gompers interceded for them, because their guilt had not been proved. There was also another reason for his interceding, as he explained to the governor of Illinois. "If these men are executed," Gompers said, "it would simply be an impetus to this so-called revolutionary movement which no other thing on earth can give. These men would, apart from any consideration of mercy or humanity, be looked upon as martyrs." Here again, what a difference there is between Gompers and the Communists. The Communists can never have too many martyrs. Nothing serves propaganda so well as martyrs, especially martyrs among the rank and file. Lenin and Stalin died in bed.

It was also Gompers' abhorrence of violence that determined his attitude toward strikes. He felt that the right to strike was like the right of self-defense. Only extreme necessity could excuse the spilling of blood. And any blood spilled is always a disaster. The political strike, the strike that is called for purposes other than those of direct benefit to the workers and only to the workers, seemed to Gompers monstrously wrong. The ideal was to win as much as possible for the workers and to win it without a strike. He was well aware that a halt in production ends by impoverishing everyone, including the workers. He envisaged, not the strike, but organization, federation, and self-imposed discipline as the principal means of social progress.

Anyone accustomed to the pronouncements of European trade unionists on the subject of strikes cannot fail to be extremely surprised by the way in which Gompers spoke of them. As early as 1887, he wrote:

The best way to defeat strikes and boycotts is to provide for them. There is no way of decreasing strikes so good as that of *making men experienced.* From a strong organization generous treatment follows and with fairness on the part of the employer there is no desire to strike or boycott on the part of the men. The best method to decrease strikes is to organize to defend men in case of strikes. *The stronger the union the fewer the strikes. We do not want strikes,* but if men are not organized they will have to strike. First, one employer will cut wages, then another, until the rate has fallen so low that the men must strike. *We are opposed to sympathetic and foolish strikes. Ignorance is not discipline.* It requires more discipline to pay an assessment of $1 a week to help those on strike than to strike in sympathy with them. The first thing a new union does is to want to strike. They over-estimate the power of the organization without re-sources. The old unions do not strike, their strength is known. They do not have to strike to resist encroachment.

Here, still recognizable, although Gompers has transposed them to the social realm, are those time-honored principles: "If you want peace, prepare for war"; "Show your strength and you won't have to use it"; "Speak softly and carry a big stick." Manifestly, this is not a social philosophy for weak-lings. To Gompers a strike was the equivalent of war. A war must sometimes be fought, but never desired. For it is a ter-rible blight upon innocent and guilty alike.

The last but by no means the least significant of Gompers' objections to socialism was the same as Molière's objection to the physicians of his time—verbosity and gibberish. "The loose use," Gompers wrote, "of such terms as socialization, Socialism, and the habit of oratorical exaggeration often gives European labor an illusion of 'radicalism' not verified by their operations. I have formed *the habit of precision in*

the use of words and my economic philosophy makes Socialist terminology destructive as a conveyance for my ideas."
Underlying Gompers' horror of vague and abstract words,
and especially of those economic and sociological terms end-
ing in "ism" or "ist," lurked the fear that he too might be
duped by them and thus drawn in spite of himself into a
betrayal, into a battle other than that of the workers. So far
as I know, he never used the world "proletariat." And if, in
the early years, he used the word "capitalists," it does not appear again in his later writings, for to him, as he said, there
were "really only two groups in society—the employed and
the employing." Gompers spoke as a man of science—a
Claude Bernard or a Pasteur—would speak, as a man speaks
who is used to submitting ideas to the test of experience and
to suspending judgment on everything not substantiated by
fact. He was forever exploding propaganda balloons. He always questioned the meaning of words and examined what
lay behind them.

An instance of this was his reaction at the Inter-Allied
Labor Conference held in London on September 17, 1918,
a highly significant date. "The afternoon of the third day
was devoted to Russia," he recalled, describing this session
in his autobiography, "first a Russian declaration and then a
long address by Kerenski. During the whole afternoon,
Socialism, the Socialist Revolution, and similar conventional
phrases completely eliminated such a robust word as 'labor.'
Just before the close of the session I remarked how strange it
was not to hear the word 'labor' used in such a conference
and as a representative of labor I submitted that wage earners should be called wage earners and not Socialists." Surely
that was too much, much too much, to ask.

Certain words are a call for general mobilization: the word
"socialism" is one of them. Certain words are like uniforms:
the word "socialist" is one of them. As soon as a man has an-
swered the call for general mobilization, as soon as he has

put on a uniform, he loses the right to determine his own destiny, he can only obey. In revolution, as in war, "the Guard dies, but does not surrender." Alas, however, men can die without knowing, even at the moment of their death, for what they are dying. But no matter, since there is always someone who knows it for them. In 1917, there were two people who knew the real meaning of the words "socialism" and "socialist revolution." They were Lenin and Gompers. Kerenski did not know it. That was why he was shelved, as an incompetent general is shelved. But Gompers had too sound an instinct to allow himself to be trapped into putting on a uniform. His objection to certain words was a conscientious objection. It would be an immense service to the whole world to promote this kind of conscientious objection. For the clash of slogans has exactly the same reverberation as the clash of arms.

Needless to say, conscientious objectors are unpopular in every camp. As in war, so in revolution, it is sometimes permissible to honor the enemy, but to despise whoever does not take sides is a command. By refusing to let himself be commandeered, by refusing to allow the American labor movement to fall into party politics, by refusing to put on a uniform and throw himself into a war of words which was neither his war nor the war of the workers, Gompers aroused a lasting mistrust in every ideological camp. At the International Conference held in Brussels in connection with the Versailles Treaty Conference, his position became more and more difficult. But he seized this opportunity to explain the difference between the American and European attitudes toward the workers' emancipation. Since this goes to the very heart of my subject, I shall quote the passage in which he described that occasion:

At once and continually, there was apparent the difference between the Old World and the New. Our political, social, and economic philosophy and methods are in sharp contrast as they have grown out of different environments and national characteristics. New World individualism and initiative have shaped our thinking and activity. The Old World was accustomed to dealing with labor problems through legislation and it was natural for Old World representatives to think of international legislation. They had in mind the development of a super-government that should develop standards for the workers everywhere.

In the New World, in addition to regarding labor problems as a part of the economic field in which methods are essentially different from those of the political field, we had the problem arising out of a written constitution and our federal form of government. It is very difficult for the average person of continental Europe to understand the spirit and the practical methods of America. The representatives from France and Italy were frankly in favor of a super-government and they could not understand that the objections Mr. Robinson and I advanced were based upon facts and concrete obstacles. They seemed to credit us with willful perverseness instead of an honest desire to indicate a real situation that had to be met.

Before this chapter is brought to a close, one question must be asked. In the battle which has now been going on for more than a hundred years to emancipate the workers of the Western world, who is the winner? Gompers or Lenin? Gompers, of course, believed that Lenin and socialism had failed. "Outside of other considerations," he wrote, "if there were anything required to demonstrate the absolute accuracy of my position, the Soviet regime in Russia has fully established it, for there are no bolder exemplars of Socialism in its fullest ramifications than are Lenin, Trotsky, and their associates. . . . Under their regime they put the philosophy of Socialism into practice with the resultant failure, brutality, and the introduction of compulsory labor. There after five years the Soviets have demonstrated beyond question that Socialism is economically unsound, socially wrong, and industrially impossible."

Since I myself have never set foot in Russia, I have no right whatever to speak of conditions there. But to judge from the book by Milovan Djilas, a man who does know the facts, it appears certain that the emancipation of the workers under the Communist regime is still a Utopian dream and that Simone Weil spoke the terrible truth when she said, "Who knows if the revolutionaries have not shed their blood as vainly as Homer's Greeks and Trojans who mistook a false semblance for reality and fought ten long years over Helen's phantom?"

No one will deny, in this year of 1958, that the economic and social emancipation of the workers in America has been largely achieved. When Gompers started the American Federation of Labor, he had a sum total of $350 and never ceased to worry as long as he lived about balancing the budget; this year, as I read in the newspapers, a single labor union spent $11,000,000 for a single strike. The American worker has kept his right to organize and his right to strike; the Soviet worker, on the other hand, has been stripped of both these rights. The American worker is no longer a "proletarian"; his work has given him the purchasing power that makes him a customer on the market and even a stockholder. He is still the free citizen of a free republic. He votes as he pleases, for whom he pleases; no one can dictate his politics, or tell him where he must send his children to school.

Above all, American workers have succeeded in persuading the entire nation to accept the wholly anti-capitalist concept that the labor of a human being is not a commodity. This was always the crux of Gompers' struggle. As early as 1891 he was saying, "You cannot weigh a human soul on the same scales on which you weigh a piece of pork. You cannot weigh the heart and soul of a child with the same scales on which you weigh any commodity." And later, referring to this remark of his, he added:

> That was one of my earliest attempts to declare publicly the principle that labor is not a commodity or article of commerce. I was at the time fighting theories of speculative economists, not only to protect labor from the quagmire to which their theories surely led, but to help to develop constructive economic principles that would serve as a guide in practical industrial problems.
>
> Labor power is a human attribute. Control lies in the will of each individual. This principle is essential in drafting legislation as well as in developing production methods. It is a principle we have taught employers, publicists, lawmakers, and some judges, but the slowest to learn have been judges. . . . When the courts put human labor and commodities in the same category, they laid the foundation for serious injustice.

He was right. Justice is slow; it is slow in every country. American judges failed to understand Gompers as they failed to understand Henry Ford, and for exactly the same reasons. Gompers, like Henry Ford, undermined, and possibly forever, the foundations of capitalist society in America.

Now that I have studied America and American society at first hand, I have come to realize that the great revolution of modern times, the only one that has essentially changed the forms of society, was carried out, not by Russia, but by America, without fanfare, quietly, patiently, and laboriously, as a field is plowed, furrow by furrow. I still consider 1914 a momentous year, but no longer because it evokes the tocsin and the war. Henceforward, for me, 1914 will always be the year in which Henry Ford, by establishing the eight-hour day, and more than doubling wages at one stroke, finally freed the worker from "proletarian" servitude and lifted him above the "minimum subsistence wage" in which capitalism had thought to imprison him. That was the year when Henry Ford made the worker a customer in the market. That was the year when he launched the first large-scale assembly line, thus paving the way for a new economic and social structure which was to be the American corporation. That was the year when he took the automobile out of the luxury class and made it a basic necessity. That was the year when the opening of the Panama Canal linked the two greatest oceans, and brought New York incomparably closer to China, and San Francisco to Europe. That was the year when for the first time it became possible to telephone from New York to San Francisco. That was the year when America passed the Clayton Antitrust Act which solemnly recognized the fact that the labor of a human being is not a commodity or article of commerce. This law crowned thirty years of bitter struggle on the part of the American workers against the capitalist position that man's work is a commodity to be bought and sold—to be disposed of, but not to dispose of itself.

The year 1917, on the other hand, no longer fills me with the slightest awe. I have long since ceased to believe that what we call "the Russian Revolution" should be dignified with so noble a word as revolution. I have long since ceased to believe that those famous ten days actually shook the world. In my opinion, the world would still be very much what it is had that Revolution not taken place. And anyway, I am profoundly convinced that no ten days could ever suffice to shake the world. If Milovan Djilas is right, as the verdict of history may well prove, 1917 stands for no more than a palace revolution in a country which has seen many others, a palace revolution which substituted a Red Czar for a White one. It was only a change of scenery in the same theater and for the same play.

But 1919 has kept its importance for me, not so much be-

cause of the Versailles Treaty—a play that had only a short
run and then "flopped"—as because of the Dodge brothers'
suit against Henry Ford. At the conclusion of the trial,
Henry Ford was condemned by a judge who represented a
capitalist system about to become obsolete. But the trial had
provided that same Henry Ford with the opportunity to declare, amid the applause of the whole country and in flat
contradiction to capitalist doctrine, that, in industry, public
service and the welfare of the workers must and can be placed
ahead of profits and dividends.

This revolution, which eliminated capitalism as the basis
of a society and substituted an entirely new social structure,
was first brought about in actual economic practice before
being legislated into the law. It took place without any dra-
matic element of surprise, with no *deus ex machina* bursting
upon the scene in the manner so favored by Lenin for political revolution. It came, on the contrary, as the time to reap
comes after the time for sowing; it was allowed to ripen
slowly, it was worked out painstakingly, it was experimentally tested and proved, and now at long last it is here. In
the economic and social realms, America has unquestionably
emerged from capitalism, without ever having had recourse
to witchcraft or magic, without having confused economics
with literary myth, the drama, or even politics. I have devoted considerable space in the second part of my book to
three men—Henry Charles Carey, Henry Ford, and Samuel
Gompers—because of what seemed to me their decisive roles
in this revolution. All three were typically American, as I believe no American could deny. None of the three was an intellectual, nor did any of them yield to the magic spell of words,
except possibly Carey, who yielded only rarely, and then out
of a certain clumsiness. What is so remarkable is that, different as they were from one another, all three were against socialism, and against it for the same reason—they considered
it too Utopian; and all three were also against capitalism, be-

cause to them it lacked grandeur and imagination. All three embodied the optimistic and essentially experimental American attitude. All three put their faith in facts and believed, to use Carey's terminology, in the value of discoveries born of observation and experience; all three refused to trust inventions nurtured exclusively within the theorizing mind. They were fully determined, not to reform the world, but to better it, which shows that, to begin with, they did not consider it wholly bad.

Europe is puritan in the economic and social realms as it is in politics, but America is not, though there are certain other realms in which America is also puritan. The ideological basis of puritanism is Manicheanism, and therefore America is not Manichean in the economic and social realms. But capitalism is Manichean, since it gives the devil much more than his due and claims that social evil is inevitable. Socialism is also Manichean, since the famous class struggle is merely a secularized version of Manicheanism, in which it is childishly believed that a political revolution will at last, like the Second Coming of Christ, set the sheep on the right hand and the goats on the left. The American is neither a reformer nor in Lenin's sense of the word a "revolutionary." The American is an experimentalist and a persistent meliorist. It is in this sense that the American is authentically revolutionary and that his revolutions, founded as they are upon a solid basis of facts, go farther than our revolutions in Europe. They are carried out slowly, but they are carried out to the end. The American economic and social revolution is the only revolution in modern times to have achieved its aim.

CONCLUSION

A Letter to Americans

Americans, I have come to love America. The Europeans who visit your country do so for a variety of reasons—sometimes out of curiosity, sometimes out of necessity, and sometimes merely in order to be able to say, "I know America, I have lived there." In my case, I arrived in your country in May 1950, just before the outbreak of war in Korea, and I stayed eight years. I have traveled from coast to coast, and in some ways I probably know the country better than most of you do yourselves. Like other foreigners, I too could write satirically about it, and earn the applause of all those in Europe and elsewhere who make a career of their contempt for America. Indeed, a book of that kind might even bring me a certain success in America itself. But my experience has not been conducive to satire. Now, after the eight years I have spent in your country, I can say that I feel about it what I feel about a friend, that it has brought new meaning to my life, that the mere knowledge of its existence makes me happy and proud to belong to the human race and to the same civilization. America has given me a hope for man's future that I did not have before.

This does not mean, of course, that I am unaware of your faults. If one were to love only the faultless one could love

no one but God; but quite apart from this fact, even your
faults do not lessen my respect for you, and in friendship
this is what counts. Indeed, most of your faults I rather like.
The greatest fault you have, as a matter of fact, seems to be
not so much a fault as the inability—an inability of which
you may even be proud—to make yourselves known for what
you are. Americans, you are not easy to understand, and perhaps for that very reason you are hard to love. But from the
moment one begins to understand you, one realizes with a
shock that the portrait of America and Americans accepted
throughout the rest of the world is not a likeness but a caricature.

You have a keen sense of privacy which, translated into
terms of international relations, means isolationism. You love
your country, you are always happiest when you are at home
and among compatriots, and this is quite natural. Your country is vast enough, rich enough, roomy enough to put you all
at your ease. You go on the principle that "God helps those
who stay at home," and you sincerely believe that this is the
key to peace. At the same time, you deploy your troops, your
planes, and your battleships all over the world, and now and
then you use them. You accept this as temporarily unavoidable and blame it on those tiresome Russians who refuse to
behave. Deep in your hearts, you look back with nostalgia
to the day when America had no world responsibilities. Since
you are not imperialists, having all you need at home, you
long for the return of a day which for you was so peaceful.
But you may as well make up your minds that that day will
never come again.

One evening in the summer of 1958, I was dining under
the trees on a Greek island. The revolution in Iraq had just
blown the Baghdad Pact and the Eisenhower Doctrine sky
high, and your Marines were landing in Lebanon. An American officer came to our table. Upon learning that I was
French, he asked me bitterly, "Why do we Americans have to

be in Lebanon? Why do we Americans have to intervene all
over the world? Why must it always be us—and never anyone
else?" With equal bitterness, I replied, "In nineteen-forty-six
you and the British forced the French out of Syria and
Lebanon. Had you left us alone, things might be better there
now; anyway, they could not be worse. And as for what you
did to us at the time of Suez—the less said the better." Without a word, the officer departed. It was probably the first time
he had heard the other side of the case.

But that was only a chance conversation. Today both his
position and mine have become obsolete. They belong to a
yesterday already gone forever, and now as remote as the
Stone Age. Moreover, nothing is more dangerous, nothing
more ridiculous than for us Westerners to reproach one another with our past mistakes; nothing is more dangerous,
nothing more ridiculous than for us to keep alive our quarrels, even the most legitimate of them. People under the
same roof do not quarrel when the house is on fire. If they
do, it is because they are deranged.

In a recent series of widely read articles, Walter Lippmann
attributes our principal errors of judgment to the fact that
we think of the world as one. Our errors, he writes, come
from "the fallacy of assuming that this is one world, and that
the social order to which one belongs must either perish or
become the universal order of mankind. But looking at the
history of the globe, the truth, as I see it, is that there has
never been one world, that there has never been a universal
state or a universal religion." This has been true in the past.
It may no longer be true tomorrow. In the year 2000, it may
be no more difficult to unify the planet Earth than it was,
two thousand years ago, for the Roman Empire to unify the
Mediterranean basin.

The foundations for unifying our planet have already been
laid. They are not of a political or religious nature. The most
solid of them is the technological progress that has already

changed part of the world and tomorrow will change the rest of it. The spirit in which modern industrial enterprise is undertaken may vary from country to country, but its structure remains substantially the same in America as in Russia, in Western Europe as in China. Industrial enterprise separates ownership from responsibility for what is owned; it collectivizes not only capital but the means of production and labor itself; and it concentrates all authority in the hands of management. It profoundly alters and reshapes traditional social relationships within the community and the family, as it does those between nations. Modern industrial enterprise has raised the standard of living, multiplied the conveniences, and advanced social progress. Thanks to modern industrial enterprise, America has eliminated the proletariat. Western Europe is on the way to attaining the same goal; so too is Russia; and China, through mass production and mass distribution, will also no doubt attain it tomorrow.

Walter Lippmann makes clear the precise point at which Communist propaganda becomes identified with the hopes of the overpopulated and underprivileged nations. For these nations, the example of America and Western Europe carries no weight. They cannot see a future for themselves in a process as slow as the industrial growth of America and Western Europe has been. By contrast, the industrial growth of Russia and China is taking place with such lightning rapidity that every last nation, no matter how backward, no matter how overpopulated, now sees the possibility of conquering poverty in the span of a single generation.

The imposture of Communist propaganda lies in the fact that Marxism has had nothing whatever to do with technical and industrial progress. A hundred years ago, the Communist Manifesto foretold that the old system of production would be destroyed. And the old system of production is indeed in the process of being liquidated all over the world. But it is not Marxism that has brought this about. It is not because of Marxism that Russia and China are increasing their industrial power so rapidly and raising their standard of living; it is because they have adopted the industrial methods invented and perfected in the West. Their present pace of industrialization is possible only because the West explored a virgin territory and blazed the trail. In 1912, at the time Henry Ford was launching his assembly line and demonstrating the phenomenal efficiency of his industrial methods, America and America alone embodied, for the poor on every continent, the hitherto inconceivable hope of throwing off the harsh yoke of poverty and achieving a decent standard of living, dignity for the individual, and political independence all at the same time. Today, that hope is divided. Although the underprivileged peoples still want their independence, they are now ready to sacrifice individual freedom to national or racial dignity, even when independence turns out to be illusory. But what they want first and foremost is to escape from the servitude of poverty and achieve a decent way of life. Through a tragic misunderstanding which in 1912 could not possibly have been foreseen, it is no longer the Americans who hold out that hope today; it is the Russians and the Chinese. You Americans neglected the noble role you could have played, and now you have been robbed of it. You alone had that opportunity at the start of the century; it is up to you to recapture it, not only for the security of the West, but for its honor.

Americans, you know how to defend yourselves in war. Why are you so inept in peace? You win wars, yet you lose revolutions. In this modern era, however, revolution conquers more surely than war. War can win territory. But revolution, when it wins territory, wins hearts as well. Russia has mastered the art of revolution. It has succeeded on the one hand in identifying Communism in the minds of the poor and underprivileged with an industrial progress available to the most backward peoples and with immediate victory over poverty, while on the other hand it has succeeded in identifying America with capitalism and all its past but unforgotten and heinous crimes, with war, with imperialism, with the systematic exploitation of the poor by the rich. The strength of this dialectic, which was the strength of Lenin's dialectic, lies in the fact that it does not give the backward peoples *a third choice*. If they want to shake off poverty and industrialize themselves rapidly, they must choose Communism and follow the Russian and Chinese example; if they want to remain in the camp of the West, they must resign themselves to endless poverty and exploitation.

You are right to resent the horrible caricature of America and Americans that Communist propaganda has drawn. But alas, resentment leads nowhere; it never solves a problem. To counter this caricature, as to counter every other phase of Communist propaganda, you will have to prove that the dilemma on the horns of which they have impaled you is a false dilemma; you will have to prove that there is a third choice, an "alternative," as Mr. Lippmann calls it, which completely changes the whole tenor of the problem.

Walter Lippmann is also quite right in saying that it is not enough to answer propaganda with propaganda, that there must be some grandiose, spectacular, and immediate action, and he suggests that America dedicate itself to making India a modern industrial power.

I wholly agree with Mr. Lippmann, but allow me to say that the situation also requires an effort of the intellect and a reappraisal of words. I hold it very much against you that you insist upon using the word "capitalism" to define your economic and industrial structure. You who are the greatest travelers in the world should ask yourselves what people outside America think of the word capitalism. To them, capitalism stands for imperialism, for the exploitation of the poor by the rich, for colonialism. It is a dishonored word, and one that breeds terror. You may well pay a visit to the moon, but you will never rehabilitate the word capitalism in the eyes of the world. Why then do you persist in clinging to a word which makes it so easy for Communist propaganda to impale you on the horns of that absurd dilemma: either capitalism and poverty, or socialism and the liberation of the poor? You will ask me why it should be you Americans who have to accept the definition that the rest of the world gives to the word capitalism, why it should not be the rest of the world which has to accept your definition of the word capitalism. But that is not the point. The real point is whether or not you want to win the world's confidence. Do not forget the last Czar of Russia. When, on January 11, 1917, the British ambassador pointed out to him that his position was deteriorating, Nicholas remarked, "Do you mean that *I* am to regain the confidence of the people, Ambassador, or that they are to regain *my* confidence?" We all know how such blind obstinacy ends.

There is, in my opinion, still another basis, besides that of technical and industrial progress, that could serve to unify the world. Paradoxical as it may seem at first glance, I believe that East and West are on the way to reaching a common ideological ground. For the last four centuries, Christian missionaries have been trying to convert the Chinese, with negligible results. But it has taken only a few brief years for the Chinese to be converted to Marxism. Where the Christian missionaries failed so lamentably, the Marxist missionaries have had an overwhelming success. Yet Marxist expansion in China resembles the Crusades and Rome's Congregation for the Propagation of the Faith, and both the Crusades and the missionary spirit are characteristically Western.

Unpleasant as it may be to admit it, Marxist Communism is in no sense an Eastern doctrine. Marx, in whose veins coursed the apocalyptic tradition of the Jews, was a German intellectual, nurtured in the schools of Hegel and of English capitalism. It is only within the tradition of the West that Marxist Communism is comprehensible. It is a Western heresy; it is even a secularization of Christianity. It holds that the Kingdom of God is on this earth; that the Second Coming of Christ, the coming of the Kingdom of Heaven, is none other than the Communist Revolution which once and for all sets the sheep on the right hand of the Judge, but the goats on the left. In only ten years, China was converted to this Western heresy, to this secularization of Christianity. Whatever the errors in Marxist doctrine, whatever crimes are perpetrated in the name of Revolution, heresy is closer to orthodoxy than is generally supposed. Both, after all, have the same root. The heretic and the orthodox Christian are not strangers, but brothers at each other's throats. Thus the conflict between East and West assumes the character of a religious war. But the West is accustomed to wars of this kind; it knows how to discover the vaccines for its maladies. Terrible as were the wars between Catholics and Protestants in sixteenth-century Europe, today their differences seem pale indeed by comparison with what they have in common.

The West launched Marxist Communism upon the world, as it also introduced industrial enterprise with all its fabulous efficiency. If the West were one day to rediscover a spiritual unity, that unity might encompass the world as swiftly as has the heresy. After all, the first centuries of Christianity were filled with heresies long since forgotten. There was a time, for instance, when Arianism swept over the East, yet afterward the Christian world rebuilt its unity. But to wipe out a heresy, to recreate a unity, more than authority, more than force is needed; there must be an immense intellectual effort. Perhaps what the Western world most lacks today is a clear and wholly comprehensible doctrine of man's earthly salvation, a doctrine not opposed to Christianity but inspired by it, a practical doctrine which can be put into practice through some such project as the one Walter Lippmann proposed with respect to India. It is, I believe, because Marxism presents itself as a doctrine of man's earthly salvation that it exerts such a powerful attraction.

For man, who has always had to face the question of his salvation in eternity and his personal immortality, must also face the question of salvation here on earth. This question has become more pressing than ever now that mankind is aware of the threat to its survival—the twofold threat of the atom and of hunger. I say that mankind has become collectively and pressingly aware of this twofold threat. What I mean is that mankind has become afraid and will perhaps before long become panic-stricken. But panic is no counselor. Panic-stricken peoples are capable, from one moment to the next, not only of the greatest errors, but of the greatest crimes.

Americans, it is your misfortune as it is the misfortune of the entire West, that you were the first, and until now the only, nation to drop the atom bomb on open cities. It is an added misfortune for you and for the West that you used the atom bomb against a colored race. It does no good to tell us that you were compelled to drop it, and that this terrible act, by shortening the war, saved more lives than it destroyed. The rest of the world remains unconvinced that you were compelled to drop the bomb. But the entire world is absolutely convinced that, even if you were compelled to drop it, you should have gone about it differently. The entire world is absolutely convinced that you should have given some warning, a limited demonstration, and that this act of destruction, the most frightening act ever to have been decided upon in the history of man, was decided in too great haste.

I will concede that not all its results were disastrous. It may well be that the memory of Hiroshima restrained the Russians at a time when, with your armies demobilized and Western Europe defenseless, there was nothing to keep them from advancing to the Atlantic coast. But even if true, this still proves that the use of the atom bomb served only the interests of the West. It only confirms the underdeveloped peoples in the belief, implanted in their minds by the Communists, that the West is prepared to go to any murderous extreme to preserve its material supremacy.

Americans, I do not touch upon this sensitive point—a point, by the way, to which you yourselves seldom refer—merely for the pleasure of setting your teeth on edge. I am deeply convinced that you will never be able to overcome and defeat Communist propaganda unless you fully understand its roots. If you choose to ignore the world's grievances against you, your country is indeed imperiled, and with your country the whole of the West.

Americans, when one loves America, when one is certain beyond the shadow of a doubt that it embodies the best hope on earth for the West and indeed for mankind, and when one sees how stubbornly you refuse to face the realities of your situation, one is seized with despair. For I am deeply convinced that if America does not do what it is up to America to do, and do it quickly, the world is very close to being lost. By the world, I mean this world, man's world with his individual and concrete liberties, his life on earth, a human life worthy of being lived.

It is not yet clear how to solve the problem of disarmament and still preserve our security, but there can be no doubt that this is the problem at the heart of man's anxiety.

Another aspect of the world situation, an aspect which would be less dangerous for the West if the unification of the world were not taking place so rapidly, is the imbalance between the relatively prosperous peoples of North America and Western Europe and the underfed millions of Asia and Africa who spend their lives on the verge of famine. The industrialized nations, primarily the Western nations, which comprise only fourteen per cent of the world's population, enjoy fifty-five per cent of the world's income. This disparity is constantly becoming greater, as a result of the prodigious increase in population in the underdeveloped countries.

It is only too easy to believe, and most people in the West do believe, that this situation can go on forever, with the comparatively sparsely populated nations enjoying ever-increasing material prosperity while the starving and over-populated nations—separated from the others by oceans and continents—have no other recourse than to resign themselves to poverty. But this is totally unrealistic, now that continents and oceans no longer separate and distance is abolished. China and India are now our next-door neighbors. The world today is exactly like the sixteenth-century society the Indians in Montaigne were describing when they first saw our civilization and said that "they had noticed that there were among us men full and gorged with all sorts of good things, and that their other halves were beggars at their doors, emaciated with hunger and poverty; and they thought it strange that these needy halves could endure such injustice, and did not take the others by the throat, or set fire to their houses."

Nothing can halt the industrialization of the world. First Russia, and now China have shown us that the most backward peoples can achieve it rapidly, very rapidly indeed. This means that all those other nations that still hunger today have only to make the effort and they too will become powerful. Does anyone imagine that, once powerful, they will remain hungry and resigned? This planet of ours is like a nightmare ocean liner. In the first class, a few well-fed passengers live luxuriously in spacious quarters, while on the decks and in the holds all the rest of the passengers are herded together in hunger and misery. Who can fail to see the dynamite in this situation? The ocean liner is one world, but a unified world does not necessarily mean a world at peace. It is only too obvious that the people on the decks and in the holds could mutiny, and by weight of numbers could easily overwhelm and enslave the first-class passengers. Our world is that ocean liner, headed toward an unknown destiny, but a destiny common to all on board. And now, it may be useful to abandon the metaphor and get down to concrete, stubborn, and irreducible fact.

For thousands of years, the world has been underpopulated. Soon it will be overpopulated. Medicine has made such progress that people everywhere now live longer. The world birth rate is constantly rising. Whereas in 1900 the global population was one and a half billion, by the year 2000 it will be almost certainly more than six billion. At the present rate of increase, within a century and a half it will probably exceed thirty billion.

This phenomenal increase works in favor, if one may so put it, of the colored peoples and the underdeveloped regions of the world. It also works in favor of the languages and cultures of the East; of non-Christian, indeed anti-Christian religions or ideologies. As a result the white peoples, the Christian religion, the languages of the West, in a word the West itself—already a minority—will become still more of a minority. Nowhere does the optimism of official statistics come closer to deceiving, more nearly border upon imposture. We are living by assumptions and equations now completely obsolete.

The Catholic Church, for example, with its half-billion members, is considered one of the largest religious bodies in the world. That was true in the sixteenth century before the Protestant rift, for, although there were less than a hundred million Catholics, there were not more than half a billion people in the entire world, and moreover the world was then still divided into almost hermetically sealed compartments. Official statistics show that membership in the Catholic Church is increasing every year. But what is the proportion of Catholics to the world population? In the sixteenth century, one-fifth of the world was Catholic; but in another hundred and fifty years, when the world population reaches thirty billions, will even one-thirtieth of that population be Catholic? The plain truth is that Catholicism faces the threat, more serious every year, of a less and less significant membership in terms of population.

Up to now the white race has maintained supremacy by industrial progress. But it is about to lose the advantage of this monopoly. Western Europe and America took two centuries to reach their present stage of industrial development. Russia has taken only forty years to reach approximately the same stage. China will need still less time. Other nations will follow suit, and those that fail to take part in the vast industrial expansion will not survive, at least not as nations. Industrial power combined with unlimited manpower will enable a nation like China to maneuver more freely than any nation in the West. Even without a war, China will be able to take risks and use methods of blackmail which no Western nation can ever permit itself. Twenty years from now, Western Europe and America would still not be in a position to risk the loss of two hundred million people, while for China so tremendous a loss of life would not be catastrophic.

Under these circumstances, nothing could be worse than for the West to be driven, through its own improvidence and folly, into a position where, within one or two generations, it would have to defend itself against the majority of mankind. Yet it is not at all unrealistic, now that distances no longer count, to picture this very majority, a coalition of the colored races, mostly non-Christian, mostly poor, and in any case infinitely poorer than the Western nations, yet commanding all the resources of modern technology and hence a fearful and boundless power.

The West would thus be placed, on a global scale, in the

political and social position of the white minority in the Union of South Africa today, but with one all-important difference: the South Africans see to it that the Negroes have neither power nor arms. But who is to prevent China from arming? The comparative poverty of Asia and Africa on one side and the comparative wealth of America and Europe on the other, and the consequent envy and hatred this contrast is bound to arouse, together constitute all the elements needed to precipitate a class war between the continents. And because of the difference in color, class hatred would turn into race hatred. More isolated than ever in a hostile, increasingly powerful and threatening world, the West and the white race would either be forced to submit to invasion and suffer the most oppressive colonization in recorded history—this time the enslavement of the white race by the colored races—or they would be forced to undertake the systematic, pitiless, and horrible extermination of all the underprivileged and colored peoples. Who will deny that for the West to commit such an act would be to betray not only itself but its faith in the Gospel and the Declaration of Independence? In either case, all that the West holds most dear would be irretrievably lost. Let me repeat that what I have pictured here is no fantasy. What is fantastic is to reason in the twentieth century as people reasoned in the sixteenth.

The West is close to having solved the social problem. To all intents and purposes, you Americans have solved it. You no longer have that bitter, obdurate antagonism between rich and poor which for so long has characterized it. It still exists, however, but now it is on a world scale, and this makes it all the more serious and urgent. If we are to save the world, and specifically the West, the antagonism between poor and relatively rich nations must at all costs be prevented from becoming more virulent; the gap that separates them must at all costs be closed. It is in this light that Walter Lippmann's proposal with regard to India assumes its true significance. Nor is it any less important, any less urgent, to prevent this world-wide social problem from being further envenomed by racial hatred. That is why I believe it to be of burning import for America to reach an honorable solution of its racial problem and for France to succeed in its effort to construct a European-African community.

I have made little mention in this book of the Negro question in America. There is a limit to what can go into one book, and I would have had too much to say. I am aware that, by tradition as well as by temperament, you Americans like to take your time, advance prudently, make sure at each step that you are on solid ground. But time is running out. With the very real possibility that within ten years the industrialization of China could bring us to the brink of a war that would set the colored races and the backward nations against the white race and the West, there is not a moment to be lost. If we want to save not only the West but the world, a world in which we are at least free to breathe, we can no longer tolerate anything whatever that might tend to create an irreconcilable rift between the proletarian and the capitalist nations, between the colored races and the white. We must move at once, and with immense determination, toward true solidarity and brotherhood between race and race, between rich and poor nations. We cannot be saved except collectively. Never in history have men so depended upon one another for their temporal salvation; it is all mankind that will be lost or saved. Ours is indeed one world.

Remember, Americans, the time has now run out. Those delays, those cautious measures, those formulas for compromise at which your politicians so excel, are not only contemptible but dangerous and grotesque. It is a disgrace that a negligible white minority should be able to prevent the full implementation of your Declaration of Independence and deprive your Negro citizens of their right to frank and fraternal acceptance in the community, and it is just as much of a disgrace that the great majority of your people, believing as they do in integration, should nevertheless continue to allow, year after year, a handful of racists to nullify the law of your republic.

Two nations now stand at the outposts of civilization: America and France. Should you Americans succeed in integrating your two races in the spirit of unreserved confidence and joy that always accompanies great achievement; should France in turn succeed in forming a European-African community through a wholehearted renewal of the French tradition of liberty and fraternity—the threat that hangs over the West would be averted. For that would be the proof that the rich by being rich can help the poor, and that to ensure all men equal rights and opportunity is also the best way to keep the world at peace.

Americans, Americans, return to the first seed you sowed, to that glorious Declaration of Independence in which, for the first time, the rights of man—I mean the rights of every man, rich or poor, white, yellow, or black—were explicitly defined and defended on the field of battle. I have made plain the fact, the unarguable fact, that the Communist Manifesto, too, is an essentially Western document. What ill luck, how great a misfortune it is for us all, that it should be the ideology of the Communist Manifesto, and not that of your Declaration of Independence, which is now conquering so large a part of the world and firing the imagination of the colored races. Americans, for this you may well be to blame, just as undoubtedly all Christians are to blame for the fact that today the name of Lenin is held in greater veneration in the world than the name of Jesus. We Christians have failed in missionary spirit. And you, Americans, have been too ready to look upon the Declaration of Independence as a document designed for yourselves alone and not for other nations. How fatal an error. . . .

Americans, it is time to admit that you have erred; it is

time to recognize that the Declaration of Independence is not yours alone. That solemn Declaration was made not just for you, but for everyone; not just for the men of one time, the eighteenth century, and one place, America—but for the whole world and for all the generations of mankind. You have done your best to make it work, or if not your best, you have at least gone a long way toward implementing it, and that is how you succeeded in solving your social problem, and why you are advancing, though advancing rather slowly, toward the solution of your racial problem. But now, Americans, your task is to extend the Declaration of Independence to the whole world, to all nations and all races. If you are to remain worthy of your heritage, you must now help solve the social problem between proletarian and capitalist nations, and the racial problem between white and colored peoples. The West would be doomed, and you eternally shamed, if today you proved incapable not only of fulfilling the splendid hope of the Declaration of Independence in your own country but also of bringing that hope to the rest of the world. It will mean your everlasting glory and salvation for mankind if, as I believe and hope, you can find it in you to proclaim and defend once again the right of all men to life, liberty, and the pursuit of happiness, and determine to consecrate your utmost strength, labor, and generosity to the task of making it possible for all men, in America and throughout the world, to enjoy these rights to the full.